WICKED VILE KING

JORDAN GRANT

PRETTY WORDS

Jordan Grant

BROKEN HEARTS

AUTHOR'S NOTE

If you're new to the Godless Heathens universe, please review the content warning provided on the next page. This book contains graphic descriptions of various mental illnesses including, but not limited to, **anorexia, bulimia, pyromania, and pyrophilia.**

Although you don't need to read the first installment in the Godless Heathens universe, Bloody Savage God, to enjoy this book (you won't find any cliffhangers here!), I do recommend it. You'll spot Gabe over there with our two other favorite lords of Chryseum Academy, Saint and Killian.

All right, that's enough red flags for now.

Put on your straitjacket and swallow your meds.

Welcome to the Asylum, darling reader.

- Jordan

CONTENT WARNING

Dear Reader:

This book is dark, graphic, and intended for those 18+. As with Bloody Savage God, **there are no anti-heroes here, only villains**.

Gabe Soros is a psychopath. He likes fire and fucking and finds bloody, gore-filled fights to be hilarious. He cackles like a madman at the most inappropriate times and has a problem with boundaries, mainly respecting Avery's. Please read the content warning before proceeding, which may be found below.

As always, your mental health matters.

- J

Triggers: All are explicit unless noted.

Main Characters
- Anorexia
- Branding

- Blood play
- Bulimia
- Bullying
- Burning
- Catatonic States
- Child abuse (verbal, NOT CSA)
- Disassociation
- Dubcon/noncon
- Dyslexia
- Dysmorphia
- Fatphobia
- Fire play & Fire play kink
- Flash Cotton/Flash Paper
- Fringe mental illness treatment — forced eating & sensory deprivation
- Imprisonment
- Mental illness — Psychopathy; Anti-Social Personality Disorder; PTSD; Eating Disorders
- Profanity
- Pyromania
-Pyrophilia
- Sexual assault (limited)
- Sexual situations

Supporting Characters
- Death
- Death by Fire
- Mental illness — those listed above

ACKNOWLEDGMENTS

A special thank you to:

Alpha & Beta Readers: Edie, Ashlee, Lainey, Danielle G., Martha, Jessica, & Nichole
Copyeditor: Owl Eyes Proofs & Edits
Proofreader: Owl Eyes Proofs & Edits
Cover Designer: Lori Jackson
Photographer: Ren Saliba

For those who reach for the flames, feel the heat, and step closer.

GABE

The halls reek of disinfectant and desperation as students scatter like locusts come to deliver the plague. There's no apocalypse coming and no wrath of God to be served upon us, though. The Book of Revelations came long before any of us ever stepped foot in these hallowed halls.

We are already in hell—medicated, institutionalized *hell*.

We're here to pay for our so-called sins and to protect the neurotypicals from us, the outcasts.

I don't mind hell.

I would prefer, though, that it come without the stench of industrial cleaning solution and cramped sweaty bodies. The furnaces in the basement must be acting up today because it feels like it's a hundred degrees in here. It's not a dry summertime heat either. It's wet and nasty. It sticks to the stone walls and clings to your skin, making you feel unclean. I need a shower, and it's barely seven in the morning.

It reeks of sex without the fun, and I don't like it. If I'm going to get sweaty, I want it to be from fucking or fire making, and none of those things have brought joy to my dark world this morning. I could deal with the stench and the annoying as fuck students preening in front of each other, like we all aren't animals in a zoo run by the administration. We are caged, put away here at Chryseum Reformatory Academy until we can show our parents and the world that we are rehabilitated. That is unless you're one of the unlucky bastards who doesn't make it that far.

I plan on making it that far, though, if only to spite my bastard of a father. God only knows what he's doing right now, probably more business dealings that make more enemies than friends. Or maybe he's with my mother, sipping mimosas at the country club while they pretend I don't exist. Better yet, I bet he's with his girlfriend pretending both me and my mother don't exist.

Whatever. I don't give a fuck, not that I am in here and not that he is no doubt enjoying my captivity.

Today's gonna be a good fucking day, and not because our babysitters abruptly gave up and abandoned us students at the place we call the Asylum, leaving us to fend for ourselves. And definitely not because God willed it either, if you believe in that sort of thing.

No, it's going to be a good day because I'll make sure of it, right here, right now, today. I'm the closest thing most of the heathens around here will ever get to meeting a deity anyway.

Bow down and pray, fellow students, because your Lord and Savior Gabriel Soros has arrived and he proclaims that today's going to be fucking awesome.

Well, for me at least. I don't actually know about them.

Now I just have to find my target first.

I walk down the hall past a pair of new guards playing grab ass, and I mean that in every literal sense. They are smacking the asses of girls as they pass, catching a handful of plaid skirts and white tights in the process before they guffaw every time like a couple of morons. It's going to be fun when they choose the wrong one and take an uppercut to the jaw or get shanked in a kidney and piss blood for a week. All the old timers around here know better than to attempt this shit, especially out in the open and outnumbered, but you've got to actually have a brain cell to last around here. By the looks of it, these two don't have a single one between both of them.

I don't have the patience to sit around and wait for them to choose the wrong victim.

I need to find my target.

Now.

I continue down the hall, heading toward my first class. Enid Circe blows me a kiss as she stands guard outside the nurse's office, waiting for the lady to open the door. She's probably going to complain about her period or a phantom headache or something else to get her out of class this morning, but no way is she getting written off for the full day. Not unless she loses an appendage, and everyone can see she doesn't have the stomach for that.

See, Enid is stupid about it. She does this shit every single week, basically trying to stay locked up in her dorm room until graduation. I think even the softhearted nurse is tired of it. *I* am tired of it, and it doesn't affect me.

Enid's got cock-sucking lips and a rack made for motorboating, but those are about her only two redeeming qualities. She's got a gossip's mouth, a nasty temper, and ablutophobia, which means her hair is always greasy, her skin's two shades darker beneath all of the dirt, and she smells like she rolled around in a dumpster. Maybe if she showered every now and again, I'd let her near me, but as she currently stands, I have no desire to let her within ten feet of my dick.

Well . . . at least not from the front anyway.

Sex used to quiet the noise, but now it's even become a chore.

I've moved on, searching for the next thing, whatever that may be to ignite the fire in my veins and make my blood sizzle.

Sometimes, fucking will still do it, when they come all over my cock and make me feel all warm and fuzzy about myself. Lately, though, I only crave the burn. I want to feel the heat on my fingertips until they turn black from the ash as the flames lick my skin and burn away all of my transgressions.

When I was six years old, I drew my family going up in flames, and my father called me a freak.

When I was seven, my best friend at the time said he was scared of me after I set a spider on fire in his driveway.

When I was eight, my mother armchair diagnosed me as a sociopath after I set our house on fire.

That's not my official diagnosis, though. I'm a pyromaniac, my "condition" comorbid with antisocial personality disorder. My old therapist, the one I had before I was brought here, said I was a sadist, but she didn't understand. They never do, and I don't care to tell them. The docs only see what they want to see anyway.

I don't want to hurt anyone.

I want them to crave the pain with me.

It's fucking different.

Masochism doesn't do it for me, though a dash of old-fashioned sadism is nice with the right girl, when the flames make them yelp and cry. Still, I *want* them to want the burn.

Fear and excitement buzz in the air this morning, and it makes me feel like I'm walking on a thousand tiny bubbles, tasting a hint of the high with each *pop*.

Scully Montege, one of the fuckers who follows me around like a lost puppy dog, whistles at me and brings her pinched thumb and index finger to her lips, silently asking if I want to smoke or, at least, set some shit on fire. I shake my head. I accepted her offer once before and regretted it immediately. She didn't like it when I took the lighter to her skin. She sobbed and wailed like she was dying and ruined our perfect moment together.

The problem is that Scully is not a real pyromaniac, much less a pyrophiliac.

Most of the people who claim to be aren't, not around here at least, not anymore.

There's Xander and Bex who need the flame, but the rest of them—the true believers—they've died, graduated, or been sent upstate to the adult mental illness facilities. Everyone else here only claims the title for shits, giggles, and to get close to me. The guys think I'll make them look cool, and the girls think that they'll worm their way into my pants, which is true. I do make the guys look more badass, and I've fucked nearly all of the girls at the Asylum at one point or another.

My reputation precedes me.

Hell, I've screwed pretty much everyone in the student population at this point. Well, the females, at least. More power to you if guys are your preferred hole, but it ain't my kind of party. I tried it once and didn't like it very much. Seventy-thirty odds would not try again.

Sex with women isn't fun lately either. It's stopped quieting the noise. They still scream my name and come all over my cock, but all I want to do is to tell them to shut the fuck up or I'll find another hole. Sometimes, I'll roll the lighter across my knuckles while they ride me, flipping it back and forth back. I'll even roll the wheel, press the button, and start the flame. When they see it, nine times out of ten, the girls will go wild, bucking and moaning. Only then do I finally get some peace from all the noise in between my ears and come.

But it's so fucking loud lately. I'm only eighteen years old, yet there's so much noise, I don't know how to escape it anymore.

I can't set the school on fire, not unless I want to go to jail this time, but the truth is I like owning these people more than that. I like being worshiped and told I'm worth something. God knows my father wouldn't agree. I can still hear the fucker from a thousand miles away. Even when he's asleep and not giving a single fuck about me, he's all I think about.

You stupid, ignorant fuck! What kind of son are you?

I can still feel the slap across my cheek like it's imprinted there, scarred into my skin.

You dumb sonovabitch! followed by a swift smack to the back of the head, hard enough to rattle my brain.

I hear his words until they are all I can hear, until they jumble together and it's just waves upon waves of loud incessant noise.

Today, though, I plan to silence the world, so I can enjoy myself and have a good day. I'll do something that I know will give me just enough of a high to drown out the noise and keep the nasty dark urges at bay. The urges wriggle beneath my skin, snaking underneath my flesh and whispering in my ear, telling me to light the flame and watch the world burn.

No fire for me, not this morning at least, though it's about the only thing anymore that holds back the rising tide of noise, suffocating the worries that wonder what it would be like to be worthy of my father's love.

Not that I want his love anymore.

Not that I want anyone's love.

I remember it vaguely, that desperate pit in the center of me from when I was a child that ached for his admiration and attention, but that died long ago. At this point, I just want vengeance. I want to burn everything he has, everything he hopes for, every dream for every lifetime, and let the wind carry the ashes away.

But I can't, not yet, so right now I'll settle on making today a good fucking day.

I walk down the hall, my books tucked loosely under one arm. I don't know why I bother going to class anymore. I could cut, and none of the professors would care. Hell, it's easier for them when they don't have to deal with people like me.

Up ahead, Michael Mares is talking to Xavier Daveraux about who the fuck knows what. They are standing in front of a classroom across from each other and looking way too serious for a boring Tuesday morning.

Target fucking acquired.

I smirk to myself as I continue forward toward them and down the hall. It's time to have a little fun and make the noise disappear for just a minute.

Michael and Xavier are still balls deep in whatever conversation they're having when I shoulder-check Michael, sending him stumbling into Xavier, who's known for his short stature and even shorter fuse.

"What the fuck?!" Xavier yells before he takes the stack of books he's holding and clocks Michael in the face with it. Blood showers in the air like it's my own personal thunderstorm, and I laugh as it hits the tops of my hands and the side of my face, freckling them in a bright, beautiful red.

Punches are thrown, and a guard starts yelling.

"Get on the ground!" he shouts. "Get on the ground now, motherfucker!"

It's not like either Michael or Xavier listens, though. They are too busy trying to kill each other.

I fucking cackle as the blood and punches add to the noise until it's one steady buzz ringing inside my skull. It starts like it always does, a nervous reaction, inevitable and one that used to creep the fuck out of my parents and scare the other kids when I was little. A minute in, though, and I'm laughing for real because these two beating the shit out of each other on a random Tuesday is perfection.

I have to hold onto the wall to gather myself as my middle

hurts. The punches cease as both of the dumbasses are restrained with wrist hobbles and carted away to the hole.

Finally, when they are long gone, I stop guffawing and head to my first class.

It's math, and I fucking hate math. The numbers get all jumbled in my head, and I spend hours going down my pitted and potholed memory lane, reminiscing about my father yelling at me and telling me I'll never be good enough.

At the thought, my hand slips into the pocket of my black dress slacks, Academy issued and approved, to find the cool metal of the Zippo tucked inside. I open the cap and roll the wheel, pressing the lever as I've done so many times before. It lights on the first try. My girl always does, well except when I'm out of juice and have to steal some from the lighters in the employee locker rooms on the fourth floor.

I should catch my pants on fire, but I don't. I never do because I have my index finger wrapped tight around the nozzle. I feel the flame heat the underside of my finger momentarily, burning that spot on me once again. It snuffs out quickly due to the lack of oxygen, but I like when it burns. I've permanently disfigured the underside of my finger by now, but at least it burns away the memories.

I'm not listening to my father light into me.

I'm lighting myself on fire instead.

I do it again on my way to class, over and over, until even beneath the well-worn callous, my finger starts to sting.

I want it to stop.

I can't stop.

I turn right at the classroom at the end of the hall and head inside, taking the middle seat at the back like I always do. I place my books on my desk and don't open a single one. They are basically for fights nowadays or for when the rogue newbie decides to take a shiv to me in the hallway to try to earn his place at the top of the food chain.

They're fragile fucking things, designed to be safe for us crazies, and they are about to fall apart at this point, stained with blood and pitted from all the shit I've put them through. Sometimes I'll peek inside and see what's going on, but not today. It's too early for that shit, and I know what I'll find inside, all the numbers and letters jumbled up and reversed, becoming an entirely different alphabet.

Kill falls into a seat at my right, looking dead inside. He didn't bother to bring a single book, but I think they changed his meds or something because now he's sleepy all the time or angry, always looking for a jolt of something to wake himself up.

Students spill into the classroom one after another along with the professor until the bell rings and class begins. A minute later, a girl with strawberry blonde hair and blue eyes stumbles through the door, nearly falling to her hands and knees, probably because her student guide is an asshole and shoved her.

The sunlight coming in from the windows hits her hair just right, and it erupts into a thousand tiny strands of orange, red, and gold.

Like the sun.

Bonfires.

Burning *flames*.

Fuck me.

I go still as the moron at the front barks at her to take a seat. There's only one open, and it's beside me. She walks down the aisle with her head held high, and when her eyes, the color of the sea, scroll to mine and don't back down, I wonder what I'm going to have to do to see her dressed in flames.

I cock my head at her as she takes a seat at the desk beside me. I catch a whiff of her scent, sugared strawberries, and I nearly come undone.

"I think I love you," I tell her as she takes her place beside me.

She freezes and looks over at me as doped-up Kill manages, "Ha! What the fuck, Gabe?"

Up close, her blue eyes are endless clear tropical waters, enough to douse the flames of her hair.

"What did you say to me?" she asks, her mouth falling open.

I smile, and she flinches.

It makes me feel warm and tingly all over, and the noise in my head goes silent for a moment.

That's . . . new.

"I said," I repeat, flashing my teeth, "that I think I love you."

She blinks at me. "You're crazy."

"That's the consensus, baby girl," I reply with a wink.

I laugh when she recoils, shifting her desk away from me in disgust.

2

AVERY

I don't know why the creep at the desk beside me won't stop staring. He's been gawking at me for almost the entire class, and I just want him to stop and leave me alone. The creeper's stare is intense. It's like a demon climbed out of hell to sit beside me with brown irises so dark they nearly match his black pupils and messy, chocolate-colored hair that tickles his eyes. I don't think he's even blinked in the last five minutes, and I swear he lacks normal human reactions.

Is he breathing?

Also, who the hell says I love you to a person they just met?

Apparently, the guy next to me does, the weirdo.

I shouldn't even be at this place, except my father thinks this one might actually work this time.

Pfft, yeah right. I doubt it.

I've been to the best inpatient rehabilitation centers across the continental United States *and* abroad. I've been hospitalized three times with feeding tubes shoved down my throat and undergone intensive therapy since I was eleven years old.

I'm not stupid enough to think that my parents want me

cured, not anymore at least. I've become the daughter that doesn't exist, the one they don't talk about. My mother will never be proud of me, while my father will claim to be, but when push comes to shove, he will pussy out like he always does. They don't give a shit about me, despite what my father wants to believe. It took seven years for my mother to even admit that I might have an eating disorder because that would mean the esteemed Mrs. Bardot had to accept that she probably gave me one.

If that wasn't bad enough, my father doesn't see his wife for what she is and forgives her most awful transgressions, namely fucking me up. His brain knows what she's done to me, but I don't think his heart will allow him to see it. She does no wrong, while I am shuttered, locked away from the world in my crumbling tower.

I am so over trying to get better. I think I wanted to a few years back at least, but at some point, I just stopped caring about recovery and wanted control instead. I can't take it anymore, the doctors, the specialists, the rehabs, my parents, and most of all, the weird boy seated next to me who keeps playing with something in his pants pocket that I don't want to think about. He's looking at me like he's trying to bore a hole through my skull and pinpoint my thoughts. I make the mistake of making eye contact with him, and he still doesn't blink, the robot.

A moment later, the bell finally rings, and I leap into action, jumping up, gathering my shit, and beelining away from the creeper.

"Hey, Firefly," he calls to me, and I keep on walking. "Don't run away!"

"Go to hell," I murmur, and I don't care if he and his demon eyes hear it. I also definitely don't give one flying fuck that he looks like he walked off a fancy European runway and smiles like he knows exactly what emotion to emulate to get into a girl's pants.

I don't care about him at all.

Not one tiny bit.

Wait . . . where am I going?

I don't know where my next class is, but I also don't care. It doesn't matter. This stuff is all temporary. Just like always, my father will grow tired of all the money he's throwing at this place soon enough, and then I'll be called into a meeting with him and the headmistress—the uptight bitch who runs this place—while he pulls me from here and carts me off to somewhere else.

It's like counting to a hundred at this point. I can predict the pattern in my sleep.

He'll get unhappy with my lack of progress and want to bring me home.

My mother won't let me come home.

He'll send me somewhere new.

Rinse and repeat, just like he's done for the past six-odd years and sixteen private schools and wellness centers.

I continue down the hall, dipping between students walking to and from class and filling the hallway. I'm looking for a bathroom, but I have no idea where I am going. Guards mill about like they own the place, not that I care that they all look like they majored in how to give you a bad day. They carry the batons that leave welts for weeks after they hit, but still, they don't scare me. I've been here before, not here exactly of course, but at places like Chryseum Reformatory Academy.

At first, my father tried the posh private institutions on the West Coast that promised holistic treatments to cure all of my bad thoughts about myself. When those places didn't work and then the three after them also failed, he started putting me in other places that remind me of Chryseum. This one might take the shit cake before it's all said and done, though, given that the nicest thing so far is the building, a tall castle on top of a lonely mountain, beautiful, gothic, and downright sinister. From what I've seen in here already, the food sucks, the living quarters suck, and the company most definitely sucks. No one gives a shit about the students in here, me included. They're basically taking my father's money just to make sure I can't break out of this shit-box, not that I haven't thought about it.

I broke out of the last one, but then again, it wasn't in the middle of fucking nowhere surrounded by acres upon acres of forest and all the creepy crawly things that live there. So, I'll wait it out until my father gets fed up that this place hasn't cured me, and maybe I'll end up in the hospital again or six feet under this time, either one would probably be a relief to him at this point. Hell, maybe they'll even go full-blown ward of the state and institutionalize me.

I squeeze between a group of girls hurriedly talking about something and spot a placard on a tall wooden door to my left that designates the girl's bathroom. I swing the door open and step inside, the hideous shoes of my new uniform clacking on the ugly white tile. Three stalls line the wall to my right across from three porcelain sinks to my left, and the place smells like cleaning solution and lemons.

I beeline for the mirror against the exterior wall—well I guess I can call it a mirror, but it barely earns that designation. It's one of those unbreakable ones that sort of looks like a sheet of metal and makes your face resemble a disturbing funhouse version of yourself. It's bolted to the wall, but I managed to remove one from the last place my father sent me to, though it took three weeks and a lot of broken pencils. This one shouldn't be too hard if I need to come back to it later.

I examine myself in the shitty mirror and check my eyeliner, not that I can touch it up. All of my stuff, makeup included, is still with Headmistress Graves being searched for all things bad and banned. I spot a little smudge in the corner of my eye and turn on the sink to wet a finger and fix it as best I can.

When I'm done, I take a moment, step back, and look at myself. My mother used to call me Big Red when she was pissed off, but that was before she found the insult that cut deep and stuck beneath my skin.

Oink, oink, piggy!

A girl stares back at me with strawberry blonde hair and big blue eyes that the shitty mirror makes look gigantic, even more so with the puffy bags beneath them. She looks how I feel, miserable and pissed off.

A toilet flushes behind me, and a girl exits a stall a second later.

She's all things my mother would love.

Blonde, thin, and a teeny, tiny waist.

She walks up to the sink next to me and turns on the water to wash her hands. She finishes quickly and shakes them dry into the basin. Then she makes the duckiest of duck faces in the mirror. It takes everything in me to not chortle, but I've learned over the years to control my emotions, lest I end up getting shanked by a bitch.

Deep in my belly, my stomach pinches as I suppress my laugh. It's a feeling I know all too well. I've already consumed ninety calories today, half of an overly ripe banana and a black coffee with two packets of sugar. Caffeine with a shot of glucose helps to keep the hunger at bay. My mother would be proud of me and say it's a good way to boost my *slow metabolism* as well.

Today, I'll skip lunch like I always do. Sometimes, I skip dinner too, but it gets hard to sleep when my stomach is rumbling loud enough to wake my neighbors. When I sleep, though, I don't often dream, and it's a deep slumber that carries me through the worst of the stomach pains. If I dream, I dream about the numbers, and I fucking hate dreaming about the damned numbers.

I know all the calorie counts.

Fifty calories for a single mandarin orange.

Zero for a black coffee.

Fifteen for a packet of sugar.

Five hundred for a baked potato with butter and cheese, but that depends on the type of cheese. I better make it seven hundred if it's the American-processed crap.

One hundred sixty-five per 100 grams of chicken.

Eighty in a teaspoon of buttercream frosting.

Up to six hundred for a slice of pepperoni pizza, but it's only ten if I eat just one pepperoni.

As I said, I know all of the numbers.

It's a fine line between death and living, and I've gotten really good at toeing the line. Hell, my old psychiatrist would freak if he knew I could still recite the calorie counts of most foods, and if I can't, I just estimate on the high end. That doctor thought he had fixed me up and set me on the path to being cured. Little did he know that while he believed what he wanted to believe, I googled how many calories are in toothpaste—none if you don't swallow—and mouthwash—also zero if you don't swallow. If I chew gum and spit it out, that doesn't count, but if I accidentally swallow the piece, that's another twenty consumed for the day.

My stomach pinches again as the girl at the sink beside me leaves, and I stare at myself in the mirror. Like always, my mother's voice is the one I hear.

Oink, oink. Do you want another serving, piggy?

I bite the inside of my cheek to ensure my silence. It's second nature at this point, a habit from my rare visits back home. I learned it from dealing with my mother. If you fight her, it makes everything worse until she's screaming at you, spittle flying with her words and making everyone stare.

I was six years old and at a pageant competition when she pointed at the mirror, the kind with lightbulbs around the edges like I was a movie star, and said, "You're getting fat, piggy. Nobody likes the big girls in beauty pageants."

"But I'm hungry," I had whined before I could stop myself.

"What a pig!" my mother laughed, throwing her head back and cackling like a witch. "Should I get you a trough? Would you like some slop?"

She snorted, wrinkling her nose like a swine.

I hate that damned memory.

On instinct, like it always does, my fingers find my love handles—or where they would be if I still had them, I guess, and I pinch the skin tight. My fingers dig into my sides, and I may be staring at the girl in the mirror, but I'm not actually looking at her. Staring back at me is my mother from over a decade ago, her bleached-blonde hair drawn tight into a ponytail. She stares at me, pinching my sides with her manicured claws, and scrunching her nose up as the other girls with normal moms look over and whisper.

"Pig, pig, pig!" my mother practically shouts, squeezing me harder, and bringing fresh tears to my eyes. I would have promised anything to shut her up. I would have told her I wouldn't eat for a year, that I would run more laps in the back-yard, and not sneak snacks up to my room late at night. But she never gave me the chance.

Duckface girl opens the door to the bathroom and leaves. The scrape of the door against the floor as it closes pulls me back from my childhood hell, and I look up to find the creep standing against the wall.

Where did he come from?

I catch eyes with him in the mirror as he shifts positions, leaning against the wall with one shoulder lazily pressed against the subway tile, staring at me.

He is cute for a total freak.

But then again, I ain't about that freak life.

Who says I love you to someone they just met, even if they qualify it with *I think?*

I think I love you.

Whatever, weird boy.

I don't care that he's got a face pretty enough to model in Paris and a body that belongs on the big screen. He crosses his arms over his chest and stares at me, his biceps stretching the white fabric of his dress shirt. He's lost the tie, or maybe he never had one, I can't remember. If he did, he took it off, though I don't blame him. It's hot as hell in here, and it makes me a little dizzy as fresh beads of sweat pop up low on my back.

My stomach pinches again, and I wince a little, I can't help it. He cocks an eyebrow, appearing more interested than concerned, but he doesn't say anything. He just stands there and stares at me. It seems like a pattern with him.

"You going to say something?" I finally ask him, matching his raised eyebrow with one of my own. "Or are you going to just stand there and try to remember your words?"

He cracks a toothy grin that makes me tingle all over as the door opens and a girl walks into the bathroom. She's pretty in a Disney princess sort of way, looking like Snow White just escaped the seven dwarves, but she's wearing a leather collar with a ring at the front around her neck, and the whole vibe she's sending me gives me pause.

Like what the fuck? I didn't realize we had permission to accessorize, not that I have my shit back to accessorize with yet.

Halfway inside the bathroom, the girl freezes, turns around, and looks at the creep, her mouth dropping open. She stands there a moment, frozen. Then she looks at me and looks back at him. He gives her a sharp glare that threatens something I can't quite figure out. A second later, she leaves the way she came and backs out of the room. Or at least I think she backs out before the world wobbles a little and my stomach does a great impression of a knife-twisting-slash-stabbing thing.

I lurch forward and grab onto the sink for support as the world turns like a Ferris Wheel. In the mirror, I see my stalker still staring at me as my vision goes black at the edges. I take a deep breath, and the world refocuses, but he is still there.

And now he's looking more pissed off than interested.

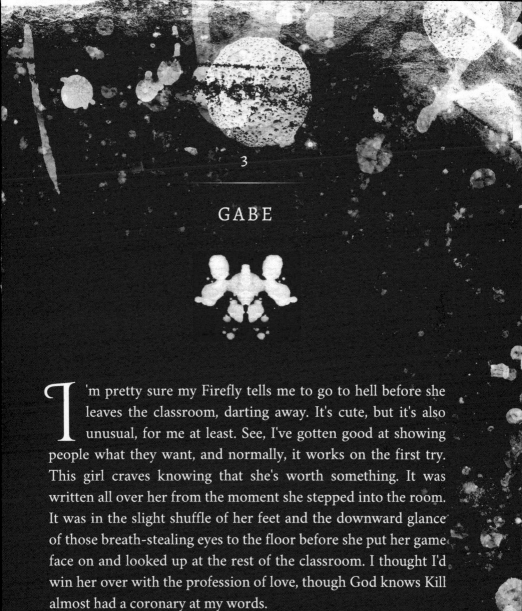

3

GABE

I'm pretty sure my Firefly tells me to go to hell before she leaves the classroom, darting away. It's cute, but it's also unusual, for me at least. See, I've gotten good at showing people what they want, and normally, it works on the first try. This girl craves knowing that she's worth something. It was written all over her from the moment she stepped into the room. It was in the slight shuffle of her feet and the downward glance of those breath-stealing eyes to the floor before she put her game face on and looked up at the rest of the classroom. I thought I'd win her over with the profession of love, though God knows Kill almost had a coronary at my words.

Bastard knows better than anyone that our kind doesn't love, not me, not Saint, and especially not him. Sure, we feel anger, hate, fear, and anxiety like the rest of the world, but love is something for other animals, not for us. Psychopaths aren't out there whispering loving words and doting on others. Well, not unless it benefits us. I came on too strong. I see that now because even the ones that crave attention don't tend to appreciate weird behavior.

Fuck.

I should have said *hello* first or *you're beautiful* or even *wanna fuck?* I think any of those options would have done better than my profession of love. Goddamn, maybe I am a moron like my father likes to say.

I've got to fix this. I need to catch my Firefly. I have no idea what I'm going to do with her when I do, but I haven't been this excited since I set the dorm rooms on fire freshman year. Luckily, a guard just happened to be nearby and had a fire extinguisher handy, or we would've all been toast, me included. What can I say? Sometimes the burn is too hard to resist.

I should have tried to be normal, but God, when was the last time I had to try to be anything I'm not? Sure, I show people what they want to see, but that's easy. People tend to see what they want to see regardless of what I do or don't do, and there's an unspoken law. A pretty face must correlate to a nice person, or at least a nice personality, but that's not the case with me. If anything, I should come with a warning label.

Attention: Contents are extremely asshole-ish and deceptive. Also, they like to set shit on fire.

Luckily for me, that's not required, but the girl didn't seem at all affected by the look I'd been giving her for most of class. I know for a fact that look offers to take her into the nearest supply and bury my head between her legs until she squirts all over my face.

Her reaction was different, but I'm not easily deterred, so I grab my stuff and follow my Firefly. I jump over a desk, skipping the line to do it. I don't know exactly where she's going, but I catch sight of her darting down the hall, her red-and-gold hair disappearing and reappearing between the bodies.

She's moving in an odd zigzag pattern like I'm a freaking alligator and she's trying to lose me, which is stupid. One, because that doesn't actually work for alligators, and two, because I am me and she should be sprinting away, screaming as fast as she can.

But she's not doing either. If anything, she looks lost or like her vertigo is acting up, hitting one side of the hallway and then the other. Why not just tell the other students to move instead of going around them? She veers off course suddenly and disappears behind a tall wooden door.

It's damn laughable. I know where she went, straight into the girl's bathroom. Either she thinks I won't follow her in there, which is fucking crazy, or she truly believes she's lost me. Both options significantly underestimate me, and like a frog drawn to a firefly, I follow her. I take my time. After all, the hunt is one of the best parts of the chase, and I slip between oblivious bodies that don't automatically get out of my way. Normally, such behavior would have earned them a shove to the shoulder or an order to fucking move, but I'm enjoying the torment at the moment, drawing out the inevitable win.

I open the door to the girl's bathroom and slip inside, cutting off one of the new transfers as I do. The girl looks at me, all wide-eyed and tosses a coquettish grin in my direction that I don't return. Instead, I glare at her, and it's enough to make her recoil and ensure that my Firefly and I won't be disturbed. The girl acts like she wasn't going into the bathroom anyway and does a ridiculous-looking about-face in the hallway and heads in the other direction, nearly colliding with three people on her mission to get away from me.

I'm silent as I walk inside, sticking to the shadows near the wall as I walk into the bathroom, my hand catching the wooden door and shutting it quietly behind me. I find my Firefly in front of the mirror looking at her eyeliner or what's left of it, at least. It's messy and kind of smudged. It looks like she's been crying, and she fixes it as a girl flushes a toilet and exits the stall. I continue watching them from the shadows, and I swear the girl must be a caricature of a person in the way she makes duckface to herself in the mirror. I almost laugh when I catch my Firefly trying not to lose it herself. The girl abruptly heads toward the exit, sees me, and walks a little faster.

It's an unspoken rule around here.

You don't interrupt me. Well, not unless you want to end up sizzling on the floor.

I have the patience of a man on his deathbed, and I do not like to explain myself. It makes for an unpleasant combination.

Finally, after the girl is gone, my Firefly looks up and freezes when she finally sees me. I lean against the wall and wait for her to talk first.

"You going to say something?" she asks after a long moment, giving me a cute raised eyebrow. "Or are you going to just stand there and try to remember your words?"

Fuck, I like her sharp tongue enough that I might just have to save it before I burn the rest of her. Will her hair turn fire-engine red when it blazes or crumble instantly to ash? My fingers twitch with the urge to grab the lighter and regain control. She's not the one in charge here. I am.

Saint's pet walks in a second later and looks between us. Back and forth and back and forth again, like she's trying to figure it out, though, I know she already has. She's being nosy, and I'll make sure Saint gives her something extra later to pay for it.

She leaves, and I push off the wall as my Firefly almost turns to face me, but stops herself. She might say something else, but I don't know. I haven't really been paying attention. I've been too busy imagining all the ways her skin will blister when it burns. A pyromaniac turned pyrophiliac, how lucky am I?

She grips the sink like she's going to fall over if she doesn't, which by the looks of it, she might anyway. She's currently the color of clouds and whipped cream and when she says, "Uh oh," I'm not even sure it's a voluntary utterance.

Her sharp glare finally locks on me again, and I have no doubt that if she could, she'd shoot a torpedo at me and sink me with her eyes.

"What are you doing?" she asks me, sounding utterly annoyed by the fact that she has to ask.

The question makes me smile because she really seems to have no idea of what's coming, but I'm quick, much quicker than she is given that she doesn't even react before she is against the decrepit tile wall, one of my hands around her throat and the other at her waist.

Her eyes go wide, probably because I'm pushing on her windpipe hard enough to test how hard I need to press before it crushes beneath the pressure.

"What are you doing?" she croaks at me, and she can't be this gullible. She's my Firefly. I won't accept it.

I cock my head and silently dare her. *Study hard, baby girl, and figure it out.*

"Let go," she says, swallowing—or trying to, at least—against my palm. By some miracle, she turns even more pale, so void of color that I can see the veins spiderwebbing at her temple and snaking down toward her ear. Even the freckles that bridge her cheeks and scatter across her nose like ashes in the wind are a shade lighter. I relax on her windpipe a little, but I'm enjoying it too much to let go completely.

"I don't appreciate being ignored," I tell her, keeping my head cocked at her like I'm confused and not pissed. I *am* pissed, but it is confusing too. I don't normally have to give chase, but this is different, and it's nice and it reminds me of . . .

Don't think of her.

Never think of her, Gabriel.

She's the girl who almost proved I have a heart, even if it is black, ugly, and charred to a crisp.

She brings her hands up between us, shoving at me hard, but

it's not hard enough. I barely tip back on my heels, and her gaze widens even further.

That's it, I think, maybe you're getting it now, Firefly.

At that moment, ever-annoying Oliver something, I don't remember his last name—we just call him the peepster—barrels into the bathroom. God knows what they have him on this time because he hits the door so hard that it slams into the wall and sticks, catching in the hole worn into the tile by many, many people who have done the same.

"Lucy," he calls to the room, "I'm home!!"

He fucks up the line, but that's also not surprising given his pupils look like saucers and he's sweating even more than I am in this heat. Thick beads dot his forehead and stain his white dress shirt as he goes to the first stall, completely oblivious to us, and kicks it in with the heel of his boot. It's empty, all of them are, but he hasn't figured it out yet as he goes to the next stall, kicks that one in too, but this time grumbles something.

The final stall is, as I predicted, as empty as the other two, and he curses loudly, spitting some version between fuck and shit that sounds like *fickit*. He whirls around, unsteady on his feet, and nearly face-plants. Hell, maybe he got into the illegal stuff this time or broke into the dispensary and got his clubby fingers on something strong. Neither one would surprise me at this point.

Many have tried to break into the dispensary over the years, me included, but that's nearly impossible because it's the one place in this building that is locked up tighter than Fort Knox. It's a challenge, and a fun challenge at that, with all sorts of goodies that you get if you win.

As he steadies his lumbering feet, he locks eyes with my Firefly, and it's like I'm not even there, like his brain has already decided that I must be a figment of his imagination or something.

I've known about his proclivity for assaulting unsuspecting girls, but it's a weird thing to see in person. It's a good thing Saint's girl skedaddled when she saw me because if he was looking at Willow the way he's looking at my Firefly right now, they'd have to bring a shovel to scrape him off the floor after Saint got finished with him. I have a bit more self-control . . . a *tiny*, thread-like bit that he is currently whittling down to nothing.

Of course, it fucking snaps when he takes a step forward and says, "Mine."

Then two things happen very fast. He lurches forward, and I let go of my Firefly and snatch my lighter from my pocket. He's a big motherfucker, and it takes a lot of force, but he is not expecting the figment of his imagination to start acting up as I shove him against the wall, flicking the roll on the lighter, and hold the beautiful flame up to his face.

Look at it, Gabe.

Look. At. It.

NO!

"Get the fuck out of here, Oliver," I tell him, "unless you want to see what happens when I burn your dick off."

Maybe it's the smoke tickling his nostrils or the heat so close to blistering his skin, but he actually goes still for a moment while he stares at the flame. I get it. It's hard not to stare, but I still don't think he sees me, so I yank him by his lapels and throw him the fuck out of the bathroom sending him skidding across the tile and into the hallway. He nearly hits a guard on his exit, who rolls his eyes, takes one look at his sweaty disgusting self, and tells him he's going to the hole.

I shut the door behind him, and my Firefly blinks at me, one hand still planted on the subway tile as she pales to a delicious color of death. Her eyes pinch, and her nose scrunches in pain.

Interesting.

"Thanks, I guess," she murmurs with a swallow before blinking rapidly, "but you can go back to Hell now, Satan."

"What's your name?" I ask her.

I'd really like to pin her to the wall and wrench it out of her, but she wraps one hand around her middle and winces again.

The fuck? Was she stabbed or something before I got here?

I'm pretty sure that right now the wall behind her is the only reason she isn't on the floor yet. She doesn't answer me. Hell, I'm not even sure she hears me as I step forward, closer to her.

Her breath shakes along with the rest of her.

"Five grams, seventy . . . seventy . . ."

What is she talking about?

"Ten grams, one hundred fifty . . . no, one hundred forty . . ."

Her gaze shutters a moment before her eyes pop back open. I watch them roll inside her head.

What?

"Uh oh," she says with a swallow. She closes her eyes and takes a slow, shaky breath.

What the fuck?

Her eyes pop open, and they roll again before they find me once more.

"Hey, creeper," she tells me, her voice wavering on what she probably thinks is an insult.

I take it as a compliment.

"Yeah?"

"Fuck off." Then her eyes meet the back of her skull a third time, and she slides down the wall. She hits the floor like a dead weight. I could catch her, but instead, I just watch. When she finally lands, slumping over like she's dead, I start to laugh, the sound echoing off the walls.

4

AVERY

Cloves.
         Cigarettes.
         Char.

The singe of smoke swims through my dreams of nothingness and tickles my nostrils. I want to sneeze, but I can't. The smoke latches around my ankles and tugs me out of the blackness and toward the light. It plasters itself to the back of my throat and makes me want to cough. I try to cough, but I can't figure out how to get my mouth to work. Everything is sluggish and delayed as the smoke tugs me out of the darkness and my sleepless slumber.

My body is slow to respond.

My brain is slow to wake.

And my eyes are slow to open, but I finally manage to crack one eyelid and then the other. My vision reels on choppy waters and then steadies like a calm sea. I am laying on something hard and cold, and it takes me a moment to figure it out. It's the bathroom floor. There's a crack cutting through the white tile in front of me and a pair of men's black loafers behind it that connect to ironed black slacks. My gaze continues upward over crouched knees and across a starched white dress shirt and up to a beautiful face.

A chiseled jawline.

Full lips.

Cheekbones sharp enough to cut diamonds.

A straight Romanesque nose.

And eyes so dark that it's like looking into the pit of Hell itself.

The creep.

Oh no.

I want to scramble to my feet and demand to know what's going on, what exactly he has done to me, but my body still isn't working as it should. I remember leaving class and going to the bathroom. I remember seeing the girl play duckface in the mirror, and I remember looking behind me to find the weirdo from class already there.

Oh double no.

He continues to kneel beside me, his head cocked as he examines me. On any other guy, his expression might be cute. It might remind me of a confused puppy, but it's not cute on him. If anything, that cock of his head is a challenge, and one I don't remotely want to be a part of. He lazily takes a drag of a cigarette. By the looks of it, the cancer stick has been lit for a while. Then he blows smoke out of his mouth directly into my face.

Cloves, char, and cigarettes hit me all over again.

Oh God.

Has he been doing that the entire time I've been passed out?

What the fuck!

My brain chooses this exact moment to notice that we are too close—weirdly close, even—and I scramble away from him, plastering myself to the tile wall behind me and coughing out the dose of secondhand smoke.

My scramble down the wall lands hard, and I'm dizzy again, way too dizzy. The world somersaults for a minute before it rights itself, and the strange guy is there again, his head still cocked to the side as he studies me. The fucker has no manners as he continues to stare. He brings the cigarette back to his lips, taking a long drag and blowing the smoke out. This time he has the courtesy to at least blow it away from me.

I can still taste the shit on my tongue, though, and smell it in my nose. Seriously, how long has he been blowing smoke in my freaking face? Doesn't he know that's bad for you? It cannot be good to do that to a person who has fainted.

Questions pitter-patter inside my brain, running wild.

Was he trying to wake me up, or did he just not care?

Did he stare at me the entire time I was out, or did he at least check my pulse?

Did he do a single thing a normal person would do? He certainly didn't call for help by the looks of it, but why not?

What exactly was his plan if I didn't wake up?

And most fucking importantly, did he do something to me?

I feel like I'm still me, and I'm pretty sure that I awoke exactly where I landed, so I don't think he did anything to me. I'm not sure I want to know the answers to all of my other questions, though. Most of all, I don't think I want to know what his plan was if I didn't wake up.

Though waking up is not the correct phrase because I wasn't sleeping. I would call whatever that was the opposite of sleeping. It's something that pretends to be sleeping but in reality, is just pitch-black nothingness. If anything, I'm more tired than I was before, and with every second, it weighs heavier on me as I sit cowered against the wall, watching my new stalker take another drag from his cigarette as he stares at me.

I don't like that look.

I don't like that look at all.

It makes goosebumps break out across my skin and all of me shiver.

It feels like he can see me, the real me, all of my insecurities, each of my fears, every last nasty bit of it, and I don't show that shit to anyone, worst of all to a stranger.

"What have you been doing?" I ask him when he violates all of society's norms and still doesn't say a word.

"I've been watching over you," he answers.

"Watching over me?" I ask. "Watching over me and watching me are not the same thing. You know that right?"

I'm truly not sure he does, but he ignores the dig with a frown that warns of unspeakable things. Would he set me on fire too, just like he threatened the student earlier?

Okay, I'm starting to get concerned about what the fuck he was going to do to me if I didn't wake up.

"I get it now," he murmurs, smoke sifting through his teeth on the exhale. It's a dark and dangerous sight, and something in my stomach coils not for fear but for an entirely different reason. "You're one of them, aren't you? One of the eating disorders, right?" He *tsks*. "You sure got lovely bones, baby girl."

What the fuck does that mean?

I went to deny him lumping me in with the eating disorder kids. I start to, at least.

"No," I say. "What are . . ."

He cuts me off with another *tsk* and a shake of his head. "Nah, we ain't playing that game, Firefly. Denial isn't a good look on you."

Why does he keep calling me that? And more importantly, why do I like that he's calling me that?

He stands slowly, climbing to his feet. He looks like a giant from this angle, tall, dark, and handsome like the angel of death come to collect me.

"You'll sit with me at all meals," he says.

Uh, excuse me? Who does this guy think he is?

I answer to no one, and especially not some torch-freak playing king of the castle.

"No," I shake my head, and it sends the world wobbling again. I squeeze my eyes shut and try to calm the wobble. The creeper drops his cigarette to the tile floor a few inches in front of me and stomps it out, leaving it there like a colossal asshole.

"It wasn't a question," he tells me. His tone says the matter is already decided. It absolutely is not.

"You're an asshole," I tell him, tipping my chin at the crushed cigarette butt. "You litter all the time or just on special kidnapping occasions?"

He raises a dark eyebrow. "My littering bothers you, Firefly?"

"Yes."

"You sure it doesn't bother the person you think you should be?"

I scoff. "Don't do that psychological bullshit with me, you stalker. It bothers me because your littering is gross."

"Why?" he crosses his arms over his chest. "This place is a shithole. That cigarette makes the floor look better; don't you think? The staff doesn't give a shit about this place. Why should I?"

I know I'm goading him, but this is starting to piss me off.

I'm not going anywhere with him, and I'm not going to let him win this argument.

"It should bother you," I quip, "because this is not the staff's world that they have to live in. It's yours, and your argument is weak anyway. In your world, no one would ever do anything decent because other people don't care like they should."

"And yet you care about that?" he asks, his gaze narrowing on me. It feels like he's picking apart my brain. "You care about people doing the right thing?"

He has to stop psychoanalyzing me. I'm too tired of this push-and-pull bullshit with him. He offers his hand to help me stand, but I push it away, still a little woozy. I'm trying to calculate how many calories I need to consume to wake the fuck up, but the numbers keep jumbling into nonsense. He apparently grows tired of my refusing his help and hooks a large hand beneath my elbow and yanks me up to stand. The world sways, and I'd fall again if not for him.

He curses under his breath.

"You'll sit with me," he says like the matter is decided . . . *again*. "Now come on."

"No," I protest, trying to wriggle free of his grasp. "I'm not going with you."

I raise my hand to shove him away, but I must miss him entirely. My hand falls to my side and never meets its target.

God, I'm so woozy. I should have eaten the full fucking banana.

"Yes you are," he snaps. "Now come on. Let me help you to the dining hall."

"No!" I argue again, pushing him away this time, and somewhere in the distance, far away from where I stand, something in me screams that this is a bad idea.

Going with him is bad.

Staying with him is worse.

I need to end this now, but I don't get a chance to before he hooks his index finger beneath my chin and forces my head up to look at him.

"Baby girl, you will come with me," he says. "The only question is if I get to smell the scent of your flesh burning before you do."

What the hell does that mean?

It takes a solid ten seconds before I realize that I've said it aloud.

"It means," he says, cocking his head at me as he removes a black Zippo from his pocket and flicks the lid, igniting it, "either you let me take you to the dining hall, or I will burn compliance into you."

Holy fuck.

Okay, this weirdo is officially scary, and I can't remember why eating is such a bad idea right now. I need something to drink at least, so I don't hit the floor again, and him burning me sounds so much less appealing than going with him. If there's anything I hate more than listening to my own internal monologue berate me while I eat, it's the idea of my flesh sizzling.

Fire's scared me for nearly as long as I can remember, ever since my mother, angry after one of my pageant losses, took a turn too sharply on the ride home. The car rolled across the asphalt, and when we finally stopped tumbling and came to a screeching stop, the seatbelt across my car seat trapped me as the engine block went up in flames. Old scars split open inside my brain as I stare at the lighter's tiny dancing flame.

The stench of tires burning.

The crackle of popping glass.

Me screaming for help, begging my mother to wake up.

The only thing scarier than gaining weight is right in front of my face, warming me.

So when the freak brings the lighter even closer and threatens to burn me, my decision is made.

My stomach pinches violently, and I wince a little as he shuts the lighter and my arms go around my middle.

He takes my silence as acquiescence, pockets his lighter, and walks me over to the bathroom door. He opens the door, steers me through it, and helps me out into the hallway with one arm around my middle to keep me upright.

Why does he smell like campfires?

And why doesn't it scare me as long as the scent is coming from him?

Why does it make me want to be even closer to him?

Fuck, I might be losing it this time.

"You look like death," he remarks, as we head down the hall.

"At least I don't look like you," I tell him, and it's a piss-poor insult, but it's all I can come up with at the moment.

Whoa. The world wobbles again.

He steers me down the hall and to the stairs. I manage them with one hand on the exterior wall and my other hand on him. He is solid and steady beneath my palm.

Faces blur.

Walls blur.

The entire damn world blurs.

Yet we keep moving forward until we walk through a pair of tall double doors and enter a dining hall. The place smells like too many calories, and he points me toward a table in the middle of the room. Everything's too white in here, too bright. With both hands on my shoulders, he directs me to sit at the table and gestures for someone. A moment later, a cup of clear liquid is deposited in front of me.

"Drink," he orders.

"What is it?" I ask.

"Water," he says, but when it hits my tongue, I know it's a lie. It's too sweet and too carbonated to be water. I choke on it, wanting to spit it out, my mind drowning in the calorie count, but I don't know what it is, not exactly, or how much is in the cup or what's sloshed over the sides already and hit the table. The creep sneers before he grabs me by the jawline, forces my mouth open, and tilts my head back.

Then he snatches the cup from the table and brings it to my lips.

"Drink it," he commands before he starts to pour it into my mouth, and I choke on the liquid as it hits the back of my throat. I sputter and spit, trying to breathe, but his grip is ironclad. He won't let me move my head. I claw at his arms, but it's like he doesn't even feel it. He keeps pouring, and I can't get away.

"Drink. It," he repeats, and it's either swallow or choke to death. Liquid pools at the corners of my mouth and trickles down my chin. He doesn't stop, though. He just keeps pouring, and I have to swallow or else I'll suffocate.

I swallow once, then twice, until I'm drinking the entire cup. My mind races, trying to remember the calories in a can of Sprite, but I'm still dizzy and I don't exactly know what it is or how much he's given me. I can't keep up.

Fuck!

Finally, when my lungs burn and the ache stretches, sending stinging tentacles across my entire chest, he pulls away. I am coughing and wheezing as he grips me by the chin and forces me to look at him.

My blue eyes meet his black soulless gaze as he hisses, "You're going to eat everything I give you, Firefly, and if you try to fucking purge it, I'll make you drink it out the goddamned toilet myself."

Surely, he wouldn't.

I don't want to believe him.

But as he stares down at me, his expression thoroughly blank, I find that I do.

Disgust, rage, fear, it all weaves together inside of me, solidifying until I feel sick. I can't throw up, though, not right now at least, and that scares me more than anything.

I don't know how I can live with myself if I do and he makes me lick it off the nasty, dirty floor.

5

AVERY

I nibble on a green bean that tastes like butter and metal had a gross, overly cooked baby. The stalker sits next to me, and he's too close, sucking up my air, his knee brushing against mine every so often as he watches what I do.

What the hell is wrong with him? He's staring at me with those unholy black eyes of his, his head cocked, his expression brutally cold. He looks like he could be modeling or planning my murder, and it's even odds on both.

How does he do that, turn off his blinking?

Don't his eyes sting?

Lord help me, but I think I misjudged him. He's not a demon with a soulless stare. He's a flesh-covered robot, and somebody forgot to program his manners.

I can't take it anymore, him staring at me, *assessing me.* I'm not sure I'm up to passing whatever test this is. I look away from him and down at the table. I go through everything remaining on the white plastic tray in front of me.

One piece of plain bread, eighty calories.

A disturbing version of Salisbury steak, which appears to

have previously been canned, three hundred calories, with a hefty helping of a gelatinous gravy, that adds at least another hundred calories.

A red Jell-O-looking substance in a plastic cup, seventy calories.

The remaining overly cooked green beans, forty calories, but there's a yellow, buttery liquid leaking from them, so I better add another fifty for good measure.

An applesauce-looking substance that probably—most definitely—does not contain any actual apples, seventy calories.

I could do this in my sleep.

When you spend most of your childhood and all of your awkward tween years consumed by thoughts about how fat you are, you either slit your wrists or develop a world-class eating disorder. I'm too chicken for the first option, so anorexia it was.

Yay me.

Calorie counting is easy. It gets hard when you have to figure out how many more miles you can run and still walk the next morning. If I didn't feel like such a steaming pile of crap right now, I'd probably take the silicone knife thing that came with the stupid tray and attempt to stab the King of All Creeps beside me, but I'm still a level eight out of ten on the wooziness scale. If I even managed to do it without falling out of my chair, I don't think I'd manage a decent slash.

It doesn't help that he is *still,* many minutes later, all up in my space, sitting next to me, crowding me, and breathing my air. He has one hand on my thigh, just above my knee, hot and heavy over the itchy tights that come with the girls' uniform. His grip isn't tight enough to hurt, but it stays there, unmoving without so much as a single finger twitching. I know what it is. It lets me know he's there, always paying attention and putting me back in line.

He watches me, *studying* me like I'm something to figure out, and I really wish the robot would learn a new trick and fucking blink.

Across the table, a blond Norse god with the face of a homecoming king cuts his icy blue eyes from his friend, looks at me, and says, "Why'd you have to bring a stray into our space, Gabe?"

The creep—Gabe, I guess—shrugs, and finally looks away from me to the Norse god.

"Saint gets his pet," my stalker murmurs, "and I get my Firefly. It's only fair."

I wish he would stop calling me that. I don't want to be his Firefly. I don't want to be *anything* to him and especially nothing to do with fire. The blond one scrunches his nose and curls his upper lip in disgust.

"Ugh, fine, but I can smell the death on her." He leans against the table, his elbows hitting either side of his tray as he stares at me. I swear that if there was a person who looked as though God accidentally forgot to give them a soul, it would be this guy. Well, he and the guy next to me and probably also the one farther down the table who looks about two seconds away from going completely unhinged and committing mass murder as he strokes the hair of the girl beside him. I can only deal with one psychopath at a time, though, and I meet the blond one's stare and don't blink either.

There's absolutely nothing in his blue eyes, no spark, no compassion, no anything, except arctic, deadly cold. He looks like he could murder me and not even remotely care. It makes me shiver.

He says his words to the weirdo beside me, but he continues to stare at me.

"I know you can smell it too," he says finally. "The death."

I'm losing patience with the fuckwad telling me I smell like a damn crypt, and I really want to lob my tray at his face. The only thing stopping me is the knowledge that if I do, there's an almost certain chance that the weirdo beside me will make me lick the contents of the tray off of the blond guy and the floor. I'm not a germaphobe by any means, but if I have to lick wannabe Thor or clean up the literal floor with my tongue, I might actually prefer being set on fire.

The emo-looking one at the end of the table hooks an index finger around the ring of a girl's collar and reels her in, kissing her fast and hard. I don't even think she was done chewing, and it's kind of gross.

Ew, nasty.

How many calories are in spit anyway?

My stalker shifts in his seat beside me, drawing even closer to me, and his scent tickles my nose. I don't want to like it, but maybe the low blood sugar caused brain damage because I swear if cigarettes and bonfires had a baby, they would smell like this guy. He tips forward a little and sniffs me, and I lean away from him, but I'm still woozy. I almost slide off my seat as he reaches onto my plate, grabs a green bean, and shoves it into my mouth, fingers and all.

"I can smell it on her too," he says with a grin to his blond friend as I start to chew. "And I fucking love it."

Then he moans loudly, so loud that it makes the people at the nearby tables turn and look at us, and I feel a burning blush scald my cheeks.

I chew the green bean and swallow, feeling a little better. Every bite is a challenge. It always is, but especially so when my father uproots my life and moves me across the country again. Considering I'm pretty sure the guy next to me will light me on fire if I don't eat, though, I continue to force my food down, one bite after another and then another.

When the green beans are gone, I move on to the next lowest caloric option, the applesauce, and begin to slowly spoon it into my mouth.

I feel like I've been deposited into an upside-down world as my dictator shoulder-bumps me.

"Eat every bite, Firefly," he murmurs, "or you won't be excused from the table."

I look down at the tray. I expected it, a requirement to eat something. I did not expect, however, for him to demand that I eat the entire thing.

"I'm going to throw up if I have to eat all of this," I tell him.

I mean it too, and I'm not only talking about the quality of food either. I also mean the amount because the tray holds a lot of food, and what's left on my plate is about as healthy as a damn mud pie.

A smirk plays at the corners of the freak's full lips as he tips his chin at me. He doesn't even whisper his next words. He just lets them slither between his straight, pretty teeth. They strike when they land.

"We're going to get to know each other really well, Firefly. Now eat up, or you're going to smell like a barbeque before this day is over and that'll ruin all of my fun."

Okay, well, that freakish comment confirms it.

There is definitely something that can drown out even my mother's shrill, berating voice, and it's the creep who just uttered the creepiest of all things. I'm actually afraid of what this weirdo will do to me if I don't eat at this point, and by the looks of it, he wants me to defy him, if only a little, so he can unleash the lighter in his pocket and go full-fledged fire fetish.

I dig a hole and bury the shudder working its way up my spine. I scoop a spoonful of applesauce with my silicone fork and shovel it down my throat.

My body reacts involuntarily with a shudder that I can't hide this time, but I continue to eat as fast as I can before my brain can process what's happening and give the calorie counts of every teaspoonful. My stomach rolls, and I think I might be sick, but I tell myself it doesn't matter anyway, that I'll just throw it up later when this guy isn't there to stop me or stop her voice from coming to visit.

Fat, disgusting pig! I hear my mother shout.

Oink, oink, lard ass.

I choke on a swallow.

Don't think about her. Don't go there, Avery. Just fucking eat!

"Don't get in a hurry, Firefly," he tells me, looking up at the ancient clock hanging on the wall. "We'll be here for a while, or at least a couple of hours after they stop serving food. If you still somehow manage to purge after that, I will find you, and I will make you drink it out of the fucking toilet."

He's smarter than he looks, dammit.

"Nasty," the blond one remarks, and oh, look at that, we finally fucking agree on something.

"Stop calling me Firefly," I tell my stalker. "My name is Avery."

His hand tightens on my knee, and I take another spoonful off my plate, opting for applesauce again. The untoasted bread looks like it crunches when you bite it, and the steak resembles and probably tastes like a shoe.

I finish the applesauce and then start on the Jell-O, but I have to slow down. I feel nauseous as the calorie counts come back.

Seven calories per spoonful, ten if it's a big one.

I eat, taking one bite after another as they talk at the table. I'm barely listening to their conversations, though. I'm not dizzy anymore, but my stomach hurts, and there's a good chance I'm going to throw up.

"I'm going to be sick," I tell the despot at my side, Gabe, as the emo-one and his Disney princess, Saint and Willow I've learned, leave the table.

"As much as I'd like to stick around and watch you break this one," the blond one—Kill, I think—says with a scoff, "watching this *thing* attempt to eat is boring and sad."

He, too, leaves without another word, and I can't say that I miss his company.

Good riddance as far as I am concerned.

We sit there a long time, the weirdo and me, long after my food goes cold and a storm rolls in, dropping snow and turning the world outside the tall windows to a blinding white. Then we continue to sit there, his hand still atop my knee, me slowly forcing one bite after another down until the entire dining hall clears, the guards leave, and the doors to the kitchen shutter.

Finally, I finish my plate, but then the tyrant makes me sit there, feeling it digest. I'm gross and bloated, and somewhere in the creases of my brain is my mother oinking at me.

As we sit there, my stalker takes a lighter, a solid black metal Zippo, and rolls it across his knuckles, back and forth. He makes it look easy, like he's flipping a quarter and not the bulky metal box. He looks content as he watches it, but I spot the undercurrent there. I'm feeling a lot less lightheaded since I ate, and I can see it now.

It's not contentment that's plastered on his face as he watches the lighter.

It's a lid, his complete and utter control over boiling rage.

How angry is he exactly? And why do I get the feeling I never want to be on the receiving end of that anger?

I'm getting really tired of sitting here, but I also have zero doubt the freak will use the lighter on me if he deems it necessary. That's the first rule in a new boarding school: do not escalate. Now normally I only abide by it about fifty percent of the time, but then again, this place is disturbing as fuck and so is my late-afternoon lunch companion, so I'm not inclined to put it to the test.

Although I'd love to take my tray and slam it upside his face, I've never been stupid about fights, which is thanks to growing up in private schools, I guess. Once you get your ass beat enough times, you learn to be smart about who you pick a fight with.

And this guy is what?

Six-foot-one? Six-foot-two? With at least forty or fifty pounds of muscle on me?

I'd have to be an actual moron to take those odds.

So I sit there, and he sits beside me, rolling the lighter back and forth across his knuckles until he abruptly stops, flips the lid, rolls the wheel, and ignites the flame. Everything in him goes abruptly still, and it's crazy to watch as his fucking pyromania takes over. He's dived in, captivated by the pretty colors, the tiniest bit of heat, and the tiny orange and yellow flame flickering in front of him.

Slowly, it may be minutes later, he tears his eyes away from the flame and brings the lighter between us.

"Don't attempt to purge," he tells me, "or I'll watch you burn, baby girl."

I swallow hard.

"Why do you care?" I ask him.

He chuckles wryly, and I get the feeling that he doesn't actually want to give a fuck about me. Instead of the truth, whatever that may be, he says simply, "Because you're my Firefly."

Then he snuffs the flame out with his thumb, shuts the lighter, grabs the back of my head, reels me close to him, and says, "See you tomorrow, baby girl."

A moment later, he stands and walks away. My scalp still tingles from his touch as I tread the empty halls up to my dorm until I shut myself inside my room. Once I'm in there, I go straight into my bathroom, where the creep can't see me, and I shove my fingers down my throat.

As I stare at the bottom of the porcelain bowl, not a damned thing comes up.

6

GABE

I lay in my bed, annoyingly awake and wondering what my little Firefly is doing. The radiator clicks and pops beneath the windowsill as snow falls outside. It's been falling for hours, ever since I made my Firefly sit with me at lunch. It's got to be up to a couple of feet by now, maybe more.

New Year's Day will be here in a few short weeks, and families who pretend to care will all come to visit the good boys and girls of Chryseum for the holiday. It'll be an all-day affair, and Headmistress Graves will pull out the big-ticket items to impress them.

She'll instruct the kitchen staff to serve fresh meat with every meal and handmade desserts, so she can pretend like it's an everyday occurrence.

She'll have the school banners hung in the halls, showcasing the alternating colors of dark green and black, and she'll make sure the guards don't allow anyone to rip them down and choke themselves or someone else with the fabric.

Most importantly, she'll instruct all staff members—guards,

teachers, and all medical personnel—to be on their best behavior. They won't be allowed to fuck off when we ask for help, especially if we do it in front of our parents.

A senior last year asked Headmistress to help him apply to college. Let me tell you, her face was priceless. Of course, she agreed, and from what I heard, she actually helped him too, but I guarantee she hated every minute of it. That's the thing about putting all the crazies together. By the time one of us comes here, our parents have heard everything, and they either don't believe us or don't care when we ask for help. If a mentally unwell person claims they are mistreated, are they actually mistreated, or is their mind tricking them into thinking they are? Worse yet, are they lying to fool you into doing what they want?

I wish no one came to visit for the holiday because all that shit does is give the poor souls here false hope that their conditions will improve. I certainly hope my family doesn't come. It was bad enough to see my father at Thanksgiving. I'd rather not have the prick ruin the start of an entire new year as well. Plus, I need to devote my time to my Firefly.

Speaking of time, what time is it now anyway?

Is it early morning or still late at night?

How many more hours do I have to endure before roll call?

Maybe if it snows enough over the next two weeks, it'll keep my father at home and away from me. I hope so at least. I'll pray to whatever bastard I can that a blizzard comes and traps us all inside the Asylum. Snow keeps the outsiders away. Plus, you have to admit fire looks even brighter when it burns against bright white snow.

Tompkins is asleep on his bed across from me. My lucky roommate could sleep through anything. In fact, I don't think I've ever seen him out of bed after 8:00 p.m. or awake before roll call each morning. The fucking alarms could be blaring, and a convoy of police cars, fire trucks, and ambulances pulling up outside, and I guarantee he wouldn't so much as mutter in his sleep and roll over. I know that for a fact because I've literally seen it happen . . . *multiple* times.

I, however, am not as fortunate as Tompkins, but then again, at least I can fucking talk. See, Tompkins is a mute, and from what I remember when he still somewhat communicated with me through the pen and paper he always keeps at his desk, it's something to do with a heavy dose of teenage trauma. I don't remember what, though. Maybe he wrote it down, I don't recall. It might be fucked up, but also, I don't care. It's not like Tompkins is regaling me or anyone else, for that matter, about his past anytime soon.

Thank God for his continued silence in times like these because I don't think I could deal with him interrupting my thoughts about my Firefly. I do that plenty enough myself, my mind skipping from one topic to another like it's playing jump rope with itself.

Everyone in the building is silent now except for the animals locked up in the hole, who fucking howl at the moon and try to turn into werewolves. When the wind curls around the turrets just right, you can even hear it carry outside the padded walls.

I remain in my bed, unmoving, and blink up at my ceiling. Moonlight enters in through the window in the stone wall behind me, scattering a thousand fireflies across my bed and onto the floor. It reminds me of her, not that I appreciate the extra kick to the balls right now, knocking me back to thoughts of her.

Always her.

Is she asleep?

Is she dreaming about me?

Is she wishing I was there?

I roll the lighter back and forth across my knuckles, going faster and faster and probably setting a damn world record. I continue that way until it's not enough and it hurts.

I stop abruptly, and my thumb flips the lid, and I start hitting the wheel, igniting the flame, and then shutting it off.

Off. On. Off again.

I'm playing a dangerous game, especially when I can feel the exhaustion starting to wear me down, weaving through the gray matter between my ears and telling me to give in to the pull. One little flame is all it would take to burn half this school down, and I have that in the palm of my hand. On a good day, I don't need an excuse to set shit on fire just to watch it crumble to ash, but during times like these, when I'm tired and obsessing over something I shouldn't be, the urge is multiplied. It refracts like slivers of light entering through a kaleidoscope until it's all I can see and everything I can think about.

I need to burn something.

A flock of fireflies plays across the floor too, reminding me of her.

Fuck.

I need to repress.

I need to stop this before it's too late.

Who am I kidding? It's already too late.

I smell her like she's right in front of me, sugar-coated strawberries cutting through the singe of the smoke from my lighter.

The game began the moment she sat down next to me, and I couldn't help myself. I needed a reaction, so I opened my mouth, professed my love, and started whatever this is.

My old psychiatrist used to tell me to put an end to it before it began, to stop obsessing as soon as I recognized what I was doing. That's how the cycle always begins.

Obsession.

Compulsion.

Repression.

Repeat.

The shit has been banged into my head for the last three damn years by the medical staff that has graced these hallowed halls. Dr. Cross loved to preach those words to me every two weeks before Saint and his pet murdered the fucker in his office and exposed all of the doctor's naughty secrets in the process. The fucker's secrets were dark too, involving his proclivity for drugging and assaulting female students.

I shouldn't say Saint killed him. I think he did, but I'm not entirely sure. It's not like we're comparing body counts up in here, though no one commits a good bloodbath like Saint, except for maybe Kill, and I know for a fact Kill didn't do it. He was with me, watching the necrophiliacs be all weird at the campus cemetery while the good doctor was murdered.

At the risk of repeating myself, I'd have to say I'm like ninety-five percent sure Saint fucking did it. It had his mark all over it.

Blood, pain, and perfect violence.

If he did, I wouldn't blame him.

If Saint went to those lengths and did it publicly, then I know Dr. Cross deserved it. My friend may lack the ability to empathize, but he's not a sadist. Most of us psychopaths aren't, and if you are, you won't last long around here.

Kill, Saint, and I we coexist because we don't fuck up each other's carefully constructed worlds. Saint is allowed his pets. I'm allowed my fire fetish. And Kill is allowed to desecrate all things religious, especially those things of the female virgin variety.

We respect each other's boundaries because we understand each of us suffers from the same tendencies as the next. There's no room for a sadist in our world because a sadist doesn't respect anything. There are no rules with sadists, except to inflict as much pain as possible on as many people as possible, regardless of the consequences.

Saint won't tolerate anyone fucking with his pets. I won't tolerate anyone jeopardizing the flames. And Killian would kill anyone for messing up his unholy plans.

I'm still laying in bed when I reach over and dig my pack of cigarettes out of my pants discarded on the floor. I tap the pack against the palm of my opposite hand, still holding the lighter, and choose one carefully before I light up. I take a long drag, but the nicotine does nothing to calm my nerves.

I'm still thinking about my Firefly—obsessing about the strong-willed girl with a penchant for smartass remarks and hair the color of spun gold. If I was a good man, I would put an end to it now before I go too far down this rabbit hole and we both end up in Wonderland. But I don't like pretending to be something I'm not.

Thinking of her, I blow smoke rings up to the ceiling, cutting through the fireflies and blowing one through the other, making smoke puppets that only the ghosts and I will see. It's unfortunate too because I set a new personal best—four rings within each other, all evenly spaced—before they hit the stone ceiling above me and dissipate.

Even when I'm not thinking about her, I'm indirectly thinking of her. One of my fellow seniors and a self-proclaimed pyromaniac tried to give me a blow job earlier today. She's pretty too, Sila Shelley, with big tits and blonde hair that she likes to wear in pigtails, one reign for each hand when I fuck her from behind.

I expect she thought that the offer for a blowjob would lead to another sexscapade in one of the empty classrooms, but it didn't. At first, I couldn't even get it up, which is totally unlike me, but she wouldn't stop talking, and every time she screeched, the more I remembered that she wasn't my Firefly. She played with a limp noodle for a solid five minutes before I finally told her to please shut the fuck up, closed my eyes and thought of her, my Firefly. Then I screwed Shelley's mouth like a deranged animal.

She cried around my dick, snot and tears wetting her cheeks.

She turned red when she couldn't breathe and then pale when I continued ramming into her anyway.

But she was a good girl. She didn't even bite me when I said my Firefly's name and came in her mouth.

My Firefly.

I like the sound of it.

With the cigarette still hanging from my lips, I grab the book on the bed beside me and hold it up to read beneath the moonlight. There's enough light on a rare cloudless night like tonight, but still, even with the light, I can't manage it. It's bad today.

Pieces of the letters are missing, turned around, and reversed. Words become something else entirely on the page, melding into hieroglyphics. I try to focus, narrowing my eyes on the page, finding the first word and moving on to the second, but the numbers blend again, blurring and changing, and I wave goodbye to the last of my patience. I throw the book across the room, and it hits the door in my frustration, knocking against it hard—not that it disturbs Tompkins—and falls to the floor.

Somewhere thousands of miles away from here, I just know my father sits at his expensive desk and laughs at me. This is why I always watch the movie version of the book.

You stupid, ignorant fuck, he would say. *Does the wittle baby boy not know his wetters?*

I hope he chokes on whatever he's drinking—probably whiskey at this hour. I shut the lighter at my side unceremoniously, keeping the lit cigarette dangling between my lips, and climb out of bed, my bare feet hitting the cold stone floor. I walk over to the door to my room, pick up the book, and walk back across the room to my desk, where I snatch the ruler from the top right-hand corner where I always keep it. It may be Academy-approved, but even silicone is up for this task as I align the ruler with the first line on the first page.

Chapter 1, I read.

The words come into focus.

Slowly, methodically I read like that, line-by-line, and it's the first time in a long time that I've actually somewhat enjoyed a book. This one's a horror, written by someone who died ages ago, but it's actually not bad. The process with the ruler is tedious, though, as I go line by line like a fucking child.

Eleven pages in, I give up.

Again, this is why I always watch the movie version. Far away from here, my father mutters that he told me so.

If I asked them to, my wannabe pyromaniacs would read every word aloud to me, all of them always so eager to please, but that shit gets old fast. At first, when I arrived at Chryseum on the cusp of my thirteenth birthday, friendless, and hating my entire miserable existence, it felt powerful, but not anymore. Now having them follow me around feels like an obligation.

At least my Firefly isn't so eager to please. I don't think she even likes me, but then again, it's nice to not be liked. Saint, the fucker, always says that we crave the same things, Kill, him, and me. I asked him what that was one time, and he said *an end to the boredom*. Only I'm not bored, though, not most days, but I am always searching for something that will quiet the noise and give me the same high that the fire does every time I light up. I want it to make me feel like I'm glowing from the inside out. I think my Firefly might do just that.

I leave the book and the ruler on my desk and walk to the bathroom. I shut the door and spin the knob on the shower, turning it on. I normally need to think of flames and fire to get going, but as I step in the water and begin to stroke my dick, I think of her, my little Firefly. With my cigarette still dangling from my lips, I imagine her kneeling before me, naked, bound, her skin freshly sizzled, and I come, shooting jets onto the wall, one after the other.

I hope on the other side of campus, my Firefly is doing the same.

7

AVERY

Bang, bang, bang! sounds before the light comes on, bright and blinding me. A second later, my thin itchy blanket is yanked off of me, and I'm jerked out of bed by a guard, landing on the hard floor like a baby giraffe trying to find its footing. At least the man keeps me upright as I try to figure out what's happening. I blink rapidly, trying to make my eyes adjust to the bright light, as he looks me up and down. His gaze lingers a second too long on my bare thighs and white panties, exposed beneath the hem of my Academy sweatshirt. I don't like that look. It reminds me too much of other looks by older men at other schools. If he tries anything, I'm going for his eyes first.

The guard's upper lip curls, exposing yellowing teeth, before his cruel gaze raises to mine again.

"Get dressed!" he barks at me, his fingers squeezing my elbow tightly. Despite his words, he hasn't let me go yet, and his fingers dig deep into my flesh, certain to leave a bruise. "The headmistress wants to see you."

At this hour? I want to say, but I don't.

I know better than that.

It's the number one rule, after all, or mine at least.

Do. Not. Escalate.

Well, don't escalate with a slimy guy who could overpower you in three seconds flat while the two of you are together in your bedroom.

I've been here before with other private schools. All the reformatory academies do the shit they don't want anyone to know about in the dark hours, when no one's awake to hear you cry and yell for help. It's not even time for roll call yet when the guard finally lets me go. He doesn't leave my room, though, as I walk over to the closet, grab my clothes, and start to change. I close one of the closet doors as best I can, shielding myself from the guard. I dress quickly before shoving my feet into my Mary Janes. Then I walk out into the hallway, and the guard follows me.

The doors to the other rooms are still closed, and my shoes click on the hard stone floor as we walk down the hall to take the spiral steps down the tower to the first floor. Another guard joins us once we exit the stairs, and now there are two of them, which seems like overkill. I'm not exactly known for my violent tendencies, well, unless being harmful to myself counts. I haven't even gotten into a fight at Chryseum yet, which has to be a new personal record.

I learned my lesson the last time after the queen bee at my old school called me a bitch, and I gave her a knockout punch that hurt my knuckles for weeks after. I'm pretty sure the bone is still bruised or something because I swear it still hurts every time it rains.

I'm not looking for a fight this morning, but the two guards together on either side of me make me nervous, especially after *the incident*, as my father calls it, a year before. *The incident* involves the one and only time my father actually removed me from a school for issues not related to my eating disorder. To no one's surprise, even allegedly devout men believe in sexual assault every now and again, and it was hard to dispute my allegation when they found my teeth marks on his dick.

So, as we walk down the hall, I'm making plans and thinking of ways to get away from these fuckers should it all go sideways. We walk through the maze of interconnected hallways, but my mind is running through scenarios and deciding what organ I need to hit first if they try something. My psychiatrist would call it a trauma-induced coping mechanism. My father would be horrified. And my mother, despite all the evidence, would refuse to believe me and say it's a ploy to come home because fat girls don't get assaulted.

A question whittles at my temple as we continue into the heart of the building. It drills in deep and causes a hole I want to ignore, but can't. That question asks why I haven't been making escape plans to get away from the creep.

I could've tried harder at lunch. I could have snatched the lighter and threatened him with it instead. I could have clawed at his eyeballs and gone feral and tried to rip out his tongue. I could have bit him, just like I did the man who assaulted me before. But I didn't.

Why?

I'd blame it on the fact that he already had the chance to assault me and didn't do anything, well, except smoke a cigarette in my face. A little voice on my shoulder, though, whispers that maybe that's not the truth. Maybe it's because, despite his demon eyes, force-feeding fetish, and threats to set me on fire, I feel wanted when I'm with him.

Feeling wanted is scary, though. Because what does it destroy inside of you when you aren't wanted anymore? Gabe makes me feel worthy, like I'm more than my muscle-to-fat ratio and how many ribs I can count when I look at myself in the mirror. And that's terrifying.

There's a difference, I think, between want and desire. The man who assaulted me desired physical pleasure from using my body. Gabe wants me, though. He asked my name. He saved me from the asshole kicking down the bathroom stalls. He fed me, I think, in a fucked-up attempt to help me. He wants me, all of me.

Maybe this place is getting to me, though, because I'm starting to sound like the psychiatrists and therapists I can't stand. And why do I care if the creep wants me? I don't want him.

Right?

Outside the building, wintry wind whispers, curling around the tall turrets and parapets. I can feel it, cold leaking inside through the ancient windows that we pass, cutting through the glass and decorative iron. The Academy is scary on a bright sunny day, but right now when nightfall still lays on the horizon and dusk has yet to wake, it is downright disturbing. Shadows cling to the walls and climb to the wooden ribs arched across the ceiling. Whispers sound in the quiet halls, and I don't know if it's ghosts of those who are long gone or those still here, locked in the place the students all seem to fear.

Isolation, the hole, solitary confinement, the place Head-mistress warned me about time and time again, where they will do whatever it takes to produce results.

All the students are afraid of it. All except Gabe, that is. The freak doesn't seem to fear anything, and that might be the most disturbing thing about him. If he were afraid, he'd stay in line and mind his own business. He wouldn't follow me to the bath-room, try to force-feed me, or threaten to light me on fire.

We follow countless turns, one after another, as we continue down the halls in silence, and I'm still thinking about how I'm going to have to incapacitate one of these assholes before we follow a line of dimly lit wall sconces tucked along the crown molding. We veer abruptly to the right into an office when the fat guard throws open the tall wooden door.

I recognize this place now. It's where the driver took me after I first arrived, and just like then, I'm assaulted by the stench of mothballs and yellowing books as I enter the room. There's no one behind the front desk today, though, no old ladies with blue hair waiting for me.

"Come on," one of the guards orders as he heads through the swinging door built into the long desk that stretches across the room. We continue down another long hall before we reach the end. The guard knocks on a door hard and fast, three loud pounds.

The sound reverberates like knocks against a coffin.

"Come in," a woman eventually answers from the other side, and a moment later, the tall guard with his belly lapped over his belt throws open the door and shoves me inside. Headmistress's office hasn't changed since I was here a few days ago. There's still the giant stained-glass window behind her desk, and she still has a too-large desk for the too-large room. It's an office built for a giant, but she's the only one in here except for me. Despite all the little knickknacks on the built-in bookcases—sculptures and Russian nesting dolls next to books and photographs of land-scapes—it still feels vacant. There's no personality to it. It's like she attempted to emulate what a home decor magazine would suggest for a large study, but it feels plain and underwhelming.

Headmistress waves a hand, gesturing for me to come closer, as the guards shut the door behind me. The latch on the door sounds like a death knoll to my dying hope of getting out of this place anytime soon.

"Step on the scale," Headmistress orders, and I follow her gaze to an old scale in the far corner of the room, near the window. It's the kind with the lever at the top that the nurses have to move back and forth when you go to the doctor's office, and I wonder if they dragged it out of a nurse's office on campus just for me.

I walk over to it and step on it. The headmistress rises from her desk, her chair screeching noisily, and comes over to me. She fiddles with the lever until she's satisfied it's measuring properly. Then a moment later, she announces my weight and writes it down.

I feel sick.

I wish she hadn't told me that.

Mother always said I had to weigh under one hundred and five pounds if I wanted to be pretty.

I'm not pretty.

Oink, oink, little piggy!

"Your father asked that I personally see to your success in the program," she explains to me, looking down the line of her nose at her notes.

I wonder if she ever sleeps, then again she might be a vampire given I only see her in the early morning. Then again, I'm betting my father is paying her enough to buy a small island and requires her to follow his west-coast schedule.

That sounds about right for him.

"I tried to convince your father that Dr. Boucher would be more than sufficient," Headmistress continues. "He has helped many of our students who suffer from eating disorders, just like you, but alas, we are stuck together, you and me. Now take a seat, Ms. Bardot."

My stomach still rolls, and bile nips at the back of my teeth as I drop to one of the black leather chairs in front of her desk. She walks around to the opposite side and sits.

"We have a maintenance plan designed for you," she tells me, cutting straight to the point. "Going forward, your trays will be weighed every day, starting today, to ensure that you are at minimum eating your maintenance calories. In addition, you will be weighed every morning, rain or shine. Absent death, I expect you to show up for your morning weigh-ins. Is that understood?"

I've done this long enough that I know what answers people like her expect.

"Yes ma'am," I say, and she gives a small nod, her hair in a tight bun on her head barely twitching with the movement.

"Good," she replies, "because I won't have you undermining the program. God knows your kind likes to go off the deep end every chance they get and purge."

What the fuck did this bitch just say?

"My kind?" I ask, the words slipping between my clenched teeth. If possible, I think I hate this place even more than I did before.

I know I'm pushing it, but it doesn't count if you just sort of lay your finger on the button, right? I mean I'm not *pressing* it.

Headmistress sends a nasty glare in my direction, and I'm pretty sure if my father wasn't paying her so much money, she'd already be shouting at the guards to drag me to the hole for my comment.

"I don't appreciate the attitude, Ms. Bardot," she snaps. "Your father has promised a substantial donation to my institution if we cure you of this affliction, so I will be seeing to your rehabilitation personally going forward, in conjunction with help from Dr. Boucher and our other medical personnel, of course. You will leave this place reformed. You will gain and maintain a normal weight. I will not accept anything else. Do I make myself clear?"

I nod. "Yes, ma'am."

"Good." She clasps her hands atop the monstrosity of a desk in front of her and tips forward, her flat chest brushing the top of the desk. "I want you to understand, Ms. Bardot, that I will do whatever is necessary to see that you are successfully rehabilitated. I will not allow you to starve yourself to death in my school. If I have to, I will shove the food down your throat myself. Understand?"

"Yes," I answer, my tone clipped before I add a terse, "ma'am."

That's new. Literally, no place has ever done that, not the place in California, not the retreat in Washington state, not the new age bullshit one in France three years prior. If I got bad, they hospitalized me, but no one ever threatened to do it themselves.

"Chryseum is not like your former institutions," she continues.

No shit.

"You've been through cognitive-behavioral therapy. You've attended group therapy as well and completed standard rehabilitation protocols including nutrition counseling and, when necessary, inpatient hospitalizations. Those methods have not worked. You will find that we deal in much more extreme measures. I have no tolerance for weak individuals, Ms. Bardot, so learn to swallow your food or I will have it pumped into you."

Holy hell.

There are unspoken words in between the lines that say she only cares because of how much cash my father's promised to cough up if they cure me.

"Now," she looks down at her notes on her desk, "I see that you've lost some weight between your registered weight at your last institution and today so," she opens the drawer next to her and one by one plucks out six sugar cubes, or at least they look like sugar cubes. She stacks them in a neat pyramid on a porcelain tea plate and scoots the plate over the desk to me.

"These are nutritional cubes," she tells me with a disgusted sneer in my direction. "Designed in-house by Dr. Boucher, our head psychiatrist, himself. They are for those who suffer from your same . . . *ailment.*"

"Uh," I begin, trying to count the caloric content, but I have no idea what's in them. Surely, they can't be more than fifty calories per cube.

"Eat them," she tells me.

Slowly, I grab one off the plate and look at it. It looks like sugar but feels heavier. Is it really just sugar, or is it something more? Why do I feel like she's already playing mind games with me?

"Eat them, Ms. Bardot."

I barely hear her words. I'm staring at the cubes, trying to figure out if she's bullshitting me.

"Eat them!" she spits, practically shouting this time.

Is this some sort of test? It feels like a test, and I've never been a good pop quiz taker.

I'm estimating fifty calories per sugar cube, so she's got at least three hundred right there. Despite what she calls them, I doubt they have much nutritional value. I'm sure they'll lead to a glucose spike, which my mother would say leads to fat storage. Still, as she watches me, I fight every instinct inside of me and bring one of them to my lips.

As the headmistress stares at me, my mother's thoughts come back to haunt me.

Oink, oink, piggy!

I nearly vomit when I open my mouth, put the cube in my mouth, and the artificial sweetness hits my tongue.

It tastes like sugar as my mother's voice rises to a shout inside my skull.

No one will love you when you're fat!

No one will want you when you're fat!

Shut up, shut up, SHUT UP!

Headmistress stands abruptly at her desk and walks around to me. As she arrives, her fist hits the desk in front of me, once and hard.

"Swallow them," she hisses, "or I will make you swallow them, Ms. Bardot."

I reach for another, but I'm not fast enough. She grabs all six and shoves them inside my mouth. Then she seals one hand over my mouth and nose and one at the bottom of my chin, forcing my head up and keeping my mouth shut. I can't breathe, and I start to struggle before she lifts a finger away, and I suck in air through my nostrils.

"Swallow," she commands and I start to chew. I stare at her as I do, my fists clenched at my sides. I want to hit her or run or scream, but if I do, they'll shove a tube down my throat and put me in the hole, where I won't have any choice about what goes into my body.

I just have to wait it out until my father decides this place isn't working and maybe he gives up for good this time and finally lets me go.

I could run away.

I've done it before, but I know there's nowhere my father won't find me and drag me back down to the depths of hell. He's threatened me with institutionalization and worse. He might actually do it if I kill this bitch.

"Do I need to call the guards?" Headmistress demands, and I shake my head a little and swallow one bite after another, the chewy, chalky substance sticking inside my throat.

In my head, my mother oinks, her nose scrunching and her upper lip curling over her teeth.

That's it, piggy, she taunts. *Gobble it up.*

God, I feel like I'm going to be sick.

I swallow again, and it catches in my throat and makes me cough, but Headmistress hasn't removed her hands, so it never leaves my mouth. Finally, I choke it all down with one more swallow.

"Good," she says, finally removing her damn hands. "Starting tomorrow, check in at the nurse's station for morning weigh-ins. On days you meet with me, you may weigh yourself in here. I'll see you again next week, same day, same time. Skip a session with me, Ms. Bardot, or make me wait on you, and I'll lock you up where we keep the really bad ones. Do you understand?"

I nod, trying not to be sick, as she opens the door, shoves me at the pair of waiting guards, and says, "Get this one away from me."

8

AVERY

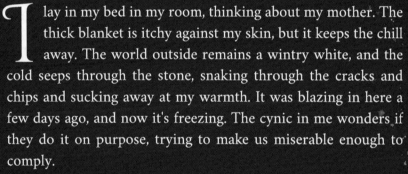

I lay in my bed in my room, thinking about my mother. The thick blanket is itchy against my skin, but it keeps the chill away. The world outside remains a wintry white, and the cold seeps through the stone, snaking through the cracks and chips and sucking away at my warmth. It was blazing in here a few days ago, and now it's freezing. The cynic in me wonders if they do it on purpose, trying to make us miserable enough to comply.

My mother would be proud of their mind games, and fuck, now I'm thinking about her again. She has to be my least favorite thing to think about too. It's the weekend, and I should be happy because at least that means I don't have to see the creep—well, in class, at least.

I don't have to feel his black-eyed stare boring into the side of my temple, scattering starbursts across my skin until I'm burning up while I try to pay attention.

Or sit next to him while his large hand lays heavy on my knee as his beautiful mouth tells me all the scary things I need to hear to make me eat.

Or stare back at him, my gaze lingering too long, when he looks right back at me and doesn't even blink.

I should be happy.

I *am* happy, dammit, though right now I don't want to be alone with my thoughts. Between lunch with the creep and my thoughts, I might actually choose the creep at this point. I don't know if that means he isn't so bad or if my thoughts are downright murderous. Probably a little of both, though I'd never admit it, not to Gabe, at least.

I shouldn't call him that.

He should be the creep, my stalker, the weirdo, or the freak. Calling him by his name makes him human, forging a connection.

Stop it, Avery! Shut. It. Down.

Today was a bad day. I had another weigh-in this morning with Headmistress Graves, and after it, I had to eat another plate of the things she calls nutritional cubes. This time, she made me eat ten of them, and I barely managed to keep them down for twenty minutes before I snuck into the bathroom during a fight in the hallway. With my hands on either side of the disgusting toilet bowl and the cold tile hard against my knees, I purged every single last one. They weren't sweet coming up, and it made me retch even harder until my jaw hurt and my throat burned.

Then to top it all off, I had to play another day of keep away with the pyromaniac. He tries to make me do what he wants, and I try to stay away, not that it does much good. If I refuse, he takes out his lighter and threatens to set me on fire, giving me an impossible choice.

At lunch, he didn't make me eat the whole tray today. I think he actually felt bad for me, given that the blond one, his friend Kill, told him to cut me a break since I didn't just smell like death today. I looked like it too. That was a fantastic way to commemorate receiving three text messages from my mother this morning.

The first was a message that sounded straight from her psychic-turned-spirit-guide, probably trying to kill off any remaining dregs of motherly instinct.

MOM

Remember that time we went to visit La Leaumonte? That was fun.

For the record, no, it wasn't. It was fun for her. She got to introduce me to her spin instructor at the upscale gym. Then she pointed out which parts of me she wanted him to focus on fixing for the next hour.

I didn't reply to her text, so as is her pattern, she continued to harass me.

Next, she sent me a photograph I didn't even know she had taken that day of me sweaty, disgustingly out of breath, and as red-faced as a politician surprised by his own sex scandal.

I didn't reply to that one either. Years ago, I learned to not interact when she gets in one of her moods. If I show a reaction, she'll keep going for the entire day. It's like being in two high schools at once with two sets of bullies. God knows she never grew out of being the mean girl. I guess it makes her feel powerful, picking on me.

I wasn't the daughter she hoped for. As a child, I didn't care about ballet or beauty pageants. I tried to, for her, but it wasn't good enough. I wanted to play in the mud and climb trees in the backyard. I didn't fit her preconceived notion of what I should be. She wanted me to become her mini-me, but I wanted to be me instead.

Not even thirty minutes after the picture, she sent my third punishment for being born.

MOM

Fine, ignore me. I was just trying to cheer you up. You've always been an ungrateful bitch.

God knows when she actually sent the texts. Service is spotty around this place. She got her reaction, though, even if I won't give her the satisfaction of letting her know it. In my bed, I pinch low on my sides at my love handles, if you could call them that. I can feel the upper curve of my hipbones when I do it, and the harder I pinch and the more I try to silence her voice, the louder it becomes.

You're not thin enough.

You're not pretty enough.

You're a fat, fat, fat piggy.

It's too much. I pinch harder, sending pins needling through my sides. I can still hear her, though.

No one will ever love you if you're fat.

Don't you want to be loved?

I stand, scrambling out of my bed, desperate to get some relief from whatever hell is playing out inside of my brain. I go to the bathroom, and as I stare at myself in the mirror attached to the wall, I see my mother's face looking back at me, telling me that I'm the reason my father hates coming home. I know it's not true. It's because as hard as he tries, he can never make her happy, but the memory hurts just the same.

I look down at my body and the ugly white panties and plain bra they make us wear until we get our shit back after it's been searched for contraband. I look at myself, and I think I see it for a minute, the real me with wobbly knees, indents between my ribs, and a gap between my thighs. It's there for a second and gone in the blink of an eye. The dysmorphia takes over, like it always does when I look at myself for too long.

I've had it since I was six years old, when Mom wanted me to compete in pageants and always win the big trophy, like my self-worth was tied to hers. I competed for years until she finally lost it when I didn't make it to the local semi-finals. She said I was too fat, too big to compete, and that all the other little girls and their parents were making fun of me.

I broke down and cried, ruining my mascara. I believed her, but now I understand the truth. She was the only one making fun of me as the other moms looked on, horrified. The damage has already been done, though, and as much as I tell myself that all of her mean, nasty words over the years were lies and that I am worthy of love and respect, I still can't see it. She's scarred me where you can't spot the marks, carved deep into the very center of me.

I don't think the doctors realize that no amount of therapy is going to undo that for me. I needed a mother, and I got a fucking bully instead.

I remember my last pageant before she pulled the plug completely, announcing I was too big and ugly to participate. I was eight years old, and I was so thirsty. I just wanted a sip of juice. My mouth felt like I'd been chewing on cotton balls after the bright stage lights that morning. There was a table for the contestants filled with juices, water bottles, prepackaged snacks, and bite-size cookies. I snatched a juice box off the top of it. I didn't think she was watching. She was so engrossed in talking to another mom about her pageant days, but then she was right beside me, snatching it out of my hand.

"Don't drink that," she snapped. "The sugar will make you even fatter."

She threw it in the trash and handed me a bottle of water.

I unscrewed the lid and started to drink. I thought she might let me have something to eat off the table. She was in a good mood that day after all. She even let me have a biscuit at breakfast, and she never let me have morning carbs.

"Mom," I had said, greedily gulping the water before taking a deep breath. "I'm hungry. Can I have something off the table?"

She looked at the table, her gaze scrolling across the assortment of crackers, cookies, Goldfish, and Rice Krispie treats.

"Pigs are always hungry," she told me, "and you're a pig, aren't you? You want to eat that crap?" She cackled. "I might as well buy you a bucket of slop."

I started to cry, and my father frowned as he looked over at me. He murmured something about embarrassing ourselves in public and how my mother needed to calm down. It was just a snack after all. Too bad for me, it was the only time he ever used his backbone. He's always been enamored with her, my fucking mother.

She was everything he ever wanted, captain of the cheerleading team that went to state finals, a model on the weekends, and the epitome of a pretty wife for a pretty life. Then there was her money too, inherited by her parents and theirs before them, and the social connections that come with loads of cash, like being invited by the governor to his personal dinner parties on occasion. She was everything he ever wanted, and he got it all, at my expense. Now he ships me across the continental United States because he can't deal with his failures and seeing what he let her do to me.

The fucking coward.

Oink, oink, oink.

It's harder when the dysmorphia takes over because then I can't really see where my mother is wrong. Instead, it all blurs together, and I see the fat at my sides, the bit of a belly on my abdomen, and the cellulite sprinkled across the backs of my thighs.

I zero in.

I find every flaw.

Until it's all I can see, and I am the sum of the worst parts of myself.

I look in the mirror attached to the wall, but it's too short and small. Even when I stand on my toes to try to get a better look at my body, I can't see much more than my top half.

Piggy, pig, pig.

I pinch harder, shutting my eyes, and trying to silence the incessant noises. I pinch so hard it takes my breath away and drills the pins and needles deeper. I start to cry from the pain, but I know she's still there, waiting for the perfect moment to fuck me up some more and strike. Tears stream in tiny rivulets down my pale cheeks, and I'm not sure how long I stand there, pinching myself, trying to see the real me.

I don't know exactly how long I'm there, but I know it's until I don't have any tears left, and it feels like I have cried myself into dehydration.

I'm back in my bedroom on my bed, staring up at the ceiling, when a female guard lets herself inside my room. She didn't even knock, but I'm still in my bra and underwear. I find that I don't care, though. Maybe I should. It's an invasion of the little privacy I have, but I don't. My mother probably killed off what's left of my feelings this morning.

"Headmistress asked that we escort you to dinner," she tells me, her gaze lingering on the dark bruises on my sides, black and blue from my fingers. "Get dressed."

Oh great.

I guess my father isn't happy with my lack of progress. He could just pull me out of here and send me somewhere new, but apparently, he's going to make me work for it this time.

I stand, walk over to my closet, and get dressed, half-ass tucking in my white button-down shirt and not bothering to brush my hair.

The guard waits for me before she escorts me down the hall

to join other female students in line, and I guess my father paid good money for this place, but not quite well enough, not enough to earn me another personal escort at least.

I assess the situation. I recognize the other girls. I've caught at least one of them purging five minutes after dinner like a fucking moron who wants to get caught. I've seen another flat-out refuse to eat and be sent to the hole.

They're making all the anorexics and bulimics eat together now.

Lucky me.

We exit the girl's dormitory, take the stairs to the first floor, and walk to the dining hall. I don't mind being put into this new fucked-up club, though. When I get to the cafeteria and she steers us to all sit at one long table, I catch eyes with the pyromaniac. He looks up from his table, his confusion switching quickly to annoyed and then escalating to pissed off. It feels like a win in this game we've been playing. He tries to save me, to *control* me, and I try to let the rest of me wither and die like the grass beneath the snow outside.

I tell myself I don't want to be saved.

Not by him. Not by anyone.

He may be king of the castle but even the king reports to God. I guess Headmistress is who we all kneel before here.

We sit at a long white table, all of the students with eating disorders. We stare at each other, the table, the guards, at anything before food is delivered. A tray is dropped on the table in front of me, and I assess it.

Mashed potatoes, peas, a chicken-looking thing that looks like they triple fried it in peanut oil, and a chocolate shake that I know just from looking at it tastes like it's been mixed with sand. The other girls and guys at the table poke at their food, and I haven't even touched mine yet because I am listing off the calorie counts in my head.

One hundred calories for the hefty helping of peas.

Two hundred fifty for the mashed potatoes with butter.

Five hundred at least for the extra crispy fried chicken.

And I bet the shake's another three hundred at a minimum since it appears to be one of those nutrient-dense, not-really-chocolate-flavored ones that is capable of making you hate your life even more.

I stab a singular pea with my fork and force it into my mouth.

I eat one after another and then another until I've eaten them all.

The guy across the table from me takes some of his food, coughs, definitely spits it into his hand, the amateur, and drops it below the table. Three seconds later, he's brought to standing by a guard who hisses, "Think you can fool me, you little prick?"

The guard shoves the guy away from him and at another guard, who already has the wrist restraints ready.

"Take him to the hole," the first guard says, and the guy starts to cry, thick tears running down his hollow face. Across the dining hall, the king of the asylum stares at me, his hair the color of coffee beans and eyes as black as night and starts to laugh.

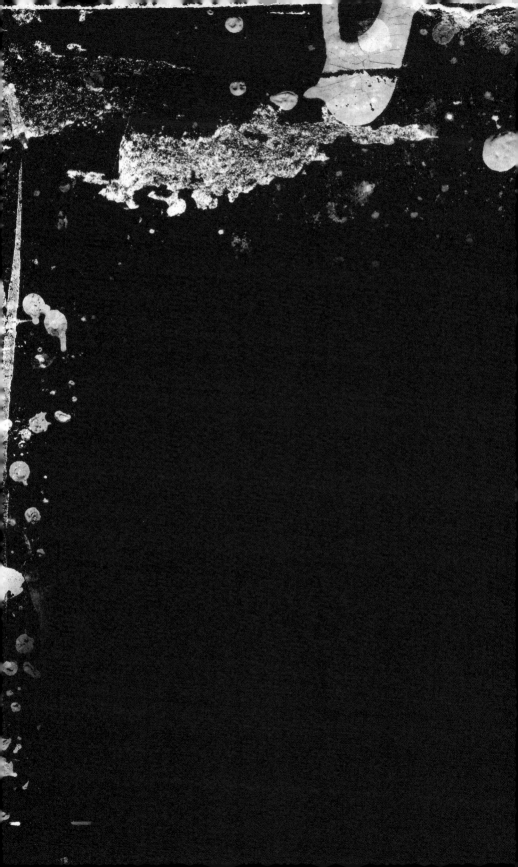

9

GABE

I'm on my way to the cafeteria, playing with my lighter in my pocket. I roll the wheel and hit the button in one fluid motion, keeping the nozzle for the flame pressed against the underside of my finger. It's barely audible, but I hear the click, over and over again, as the flame starts, only to be immediately suffocated by my flesh. I've done this thousands of times, yet it still starts to hurt as the metal heats and burns the bottom of my finger.

Roll and click, then on.

Roll and click. On.

Roll and click. On.

Roll and click. On.

Over and over again.

It's the only thing keeping me sane at the moment. The letters are bad today, worse than normal. I couldn't even get through the first paragraph of a book I'm trying to read. It makes me feel inadequate, stupid, and worthless. I pulled out all the tricks. Going line-by-line with a ruler, reading aloud, sounding out each letter after the next, and none of them worked.

My father would laugh and ask why I even bothered to try. No one can fuck you up as well as your parents.

I'm hungry, and I'm feeling antsy because I haven't seen my Firefly in a few days. Well, I've seen her, but I haven't been able to get her alone. There are no classes on weekends, and the headmistress has her in the new and improved special nutrition program for the students with eating disorders. Now from what I've seen and heard in the hallways, all of the food fighters and rexies take their meds together and share their meals together.

At least today, I'll see her again in class.

She can't avoid me there, and it doesn't matter if she screams bloody murder because they won't let her go back to her room and I know it. Not unless she's literally going to bleed to death if she doesn't, and I doubt she has the stomach for that kind of gore.

On and off, on and off, I roll the wheel and press the button, igniting the lighter again and again. It calms my nerves a little and quiets the noise, all of the voices from the students in the hall, the cackling of a guard as he shares a joke with his buddy, and most of all, my father's fucking words from this morning.

He was a prick. He's always a prick, but he cut deeper than normal today. Talking to him on a good day pisses me off, but on days like today, when I spent much of the early morning disgusted with myself as everything blended together on the paper, talking to him makes me boil.

He started off by asking me if I'd learned to read yet.

I kept my mouth shut and pretended like his barb didn't sting when it landed.

What else was I supposed to do?

I hate feeling fucking powerless, but I am, compared to him, at least. When you're powerless, you're forced to be patient if you want revenge. Otherwise, the owner of the magnifying glass fries your tiny ant ass before you can come up with a plan, so I'm patient, even when it feels like being patient is going to make me explode.

If he wanted to, my father could send me to one of the other mental institutions, the ones for the sickos who like children a little too much or who think that God told them to drown their babies. He could lock me up in one of those vile pits and throw away the key. He'd probably go after conservatorship too and tie me to him and whatever hellhole he put me in for life. At least once I get out of this slice of hell, I can disappear. I *will* disappear, and he won't be able to control me anymore.

I've been told my entire life that I am unworthy.

By my father, my mother, my doctors, and my teachers.

I'm dyslexic and, as if that wasn't bad enough, I had a speech impediment that took years to break.

I'm stupid according to my father and a troubled man according to mother.

The fires help control negative thoughts and keep them at bay. They help me grin and bear it, just like I did with the new psychiatrist this past Friday, a middle-aged bald fuck with the personality of a shoe. After the last one, Dr. Cross, got shanked to death in his office, I doubt the position was very popular, but you would think that they would at least try to hire someone who can actually talk to people. I can't honestly remember if he said an entire word during our hour-long session together. He just sort of stared and nodded occasionally. On second thought, I'm pretty sure he had headphones in, tuning me out.

Whatever, I think I fooled him at least, so there will be no more talk about going back to weekly sessions like the old doctor used to require before he choked to death on his own blood. Well, that's how I hear he went out at least.

I told the new brain doc that I think of calm thoughts and happy places—the beach at sunrise, clouds in the sky, all that pretty shit they like to hear—to control the urges. I told him I haven't been obsessed over anyone or anything in a long while, though that's a blatant lie. But if there's no obsession, then there's no compulsion and no necessary repression.

I wish I could fool my father as easily as I fool these people. They don't have to believe that I'm totally cured. They just have to believe that I'm not going to light the place on fire with them inside of it. I think I've managed to convince the new doctor of that, at least. Maybe not the head honcho—Dr. Boucher aka the Butcher—but I only have to see his ass if I get carted off the hole. I don't plan on going to the hole, not with my Firely to entertain me.

Now I've worked up an appetite, thinking about my Firefly.

Sure, maybe I'm swapping one bad habit for another, but I'll take it if it means igniting something inside of her instead.

Kill's always said I have a thing for lost causes, which is laughable because that fucker is the king of lost lambs. He's all about the religious crackpots. I don't mean the ones that just believe in a higher power. I mean the girls who come here completely broken, fucked up, and discarded but still manage to have faith, probably because faith is the only thing holding their popsicle-stick minds together. They are the ones that sink to their knees in front of the doors and beg for mercy. They talk in tongues and bow their heads before every meal. They go to the chapel and pray on their knees until they pass out. Then they self-flagellate in their rooms, whipping and cutting themselves to atone for their sins. Personally, I find it laughable. I don't know if there is a God, but I know he must be one sick bastard if they go through all of that, and he still won't save them from Killian.

He's especially fond of the virgins. They aren't my thing, but more power to him, I guess. I've got no idea what his thought process is there—maybe it's the blood that gets his dick hard—but his exploits are talked about for days. Not because he brags.

He doesn't give a shit what any of the people around here think of him, but because normally, it turns ugly and public very fast. The last time he took a v-card—well, the last I know of, at least— he asked the girl after if she thought she'd still get into heaven. Then he left and walked to the dining room like he didn't just upend her entire existence. She came into the dining room, screaming about it, ranting, raving, and still naked from the waist down. She called him a demon. Then she tried to stab him with a crucifix like he was a vampire.

She got tackled before she got too close, though Kill would've probably enjoyed the struggle. Then she was carted off to the hole and transferred by her ultra-devout parents a week after. If that ain't some fucked-up religious shit right there, I don't know what is.

Kill would probably be the leader of his own cult if he hadn't ended up here, but he's as fucked up as the rest of us. I don't know the whole story. He shares bits and pieces with Saint and me when he drinks too much homemade booze or is feeling especially sentimental, but I know enough.

He watched his daddy cut up his mommy into tiny little bits while his daddy talked to the heavens, waving his arms, and saying God demanded a sacrifice. Childhood Kill would have probably been next if not for his father fucking up, slipping in the blood, and eating his own machete. I thought Saint had been through the wringer after I learned he was kidnapped as a child by some bastard trying to force his father into a business deal, but Kill's father killing his mother is about the nicest part of his childhood. And that's saying something.

It all stems from our parents, I guess, at least for the three of us. That's always the question, isn't it? Nature versus nurture and all that bullshit, but I know I wasn't born this way, at least I don't think so. Sure, my brain was fucked up. It's not like I sponta- neously developed a learning disorder because my dad's a prick.

But my father definitely contributed into who I am, and Saint's father definitely fucked him up, and Kill's, well, he takes the first prize at the Academy fair for screwing up his son's childhood.

Kill, Saint, and I are a psychiatrist's nightmare too because we aren't about to share any of that shit with anyone, not unless we trust them. And I don't trust anybody in this world other than Saint and Kill. Last I heard, Saint still pretends in his mandatory group therapy sessions that his parents are divorced, and that's the root of his problems. Kill won't say a single word to the Butcher, not even *fuck you* and *goodbye*. And me, I just like to screw with the docs. Maybe if they wanted to cure us, it would be different, but what's the point in sharing when they have already written us off? We know what we are, cash cows and pots of money for this place to suck dry like we're feeding a dollar-guzzling succubus.

I have to disagree with Kill, though.

He may say that I have a thing for lost causes, but I don't think my bright Firefly is lost. There's hope in her yet. She is different, though, which is nice. She's not so agreeable. She doesn't praise me or try to get my attention by preening like a peacock strutting her feathers for me.

Maybe if I fix her, I can help myself because at the end of the day, there's no one I hate more than me.

The fires feel like a drop of dopamine every time I start the flame. They burn away all the negative shit and all the noise that makes me feel less than and unworthy.

Roll and click, on.

Roll and click, on.

Roll and click.

My father's words replay in my head, repeating like a radio station I can't turn off.

Have you learned to read yet?

Have you learned to read . . . yet.

The fucking prick.

I turn down the hallway, heading to the dining hall. One of the pyromaniac posers, a pretty girl with an ass like a Kardashian, spontaneously appears at my side, or at least it feels that way. She's like a damn ghost, materializing out of thin air just to haunt me.

"Gabe," Shelby purrs at me, smiling widely and putting her claw on my shoulder, "where have you been? I've missed you, baby."

She should know better than to call me that. It reeks of desperation. The only babies between the two of us are the ones I shot down her throat eight weeks ago.

She digs her talons in a little deeper, and I shrug her off of me. Maybe I could have forgiven her for faking her love of the flame, but right now I need her to go so I can find Avery.

"Bye, Shelby," I tell her, jogging ahead of her. That's about as polite as she's going to get from me right now.

I narrowly avoid a pair of guards who eat up nearly the entire space when my Firefly almost collides with me. She's crying, and to my surprise, I find that I don't like it. Now I don't exactly *not* like it either, but I don't understand why.

I haven't given her anything to cry about, not lately at least, so what is she doing?

"Avery," I call, following her. "Wait up!"

To the surprise of no one, she keeps going, sprinting away from me, and doesn't turn back.

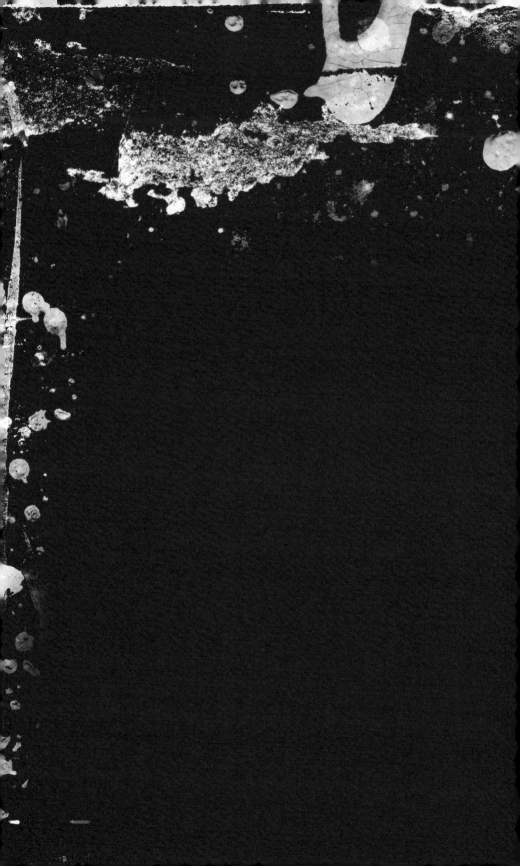

10

GABE

I follow after my Firefly, but she doesn't slow down. She's practically bolting through the halls, one foot barely hitting the floor before she's pushing forward and onto the next step. Students and guards mill about, headed to the dining hall or class. No one cares what the blue-eyed girl with hair the color of gold and fire is doing.

I will admit that someone sobbing in the hallway is practically a daily occurrence around here. Hell, it would be weird if someone wasn't crying in a corner somewhere. Still, I need to know why. I'm pretty sure it's not because of me. I think I would remember ruining her day. We haven't been to class yet.

One of her eating disorder friends sees her, stops walking, and turns like he wants to ask her what's wrong. Now I do care about this guy trying to come in like he's Prince Charming to save her from the bad dragon. I have a news flash for him, though. Princes aren't welcome around here, only dragons. She's my treasure, and I will light him up brighter than the George Washington Bridge on New Year's Eve if he gets in my fucking way.

The moron doesn't even belong at the Academy. He came here after what had to be one of the worst suicide attempts in the history of freaking planet Earth. And I don't mean that it was an especially bloody or violent attempt. No, the freak swallowed three bottles of gummy vitamins, and I guess his overprotective mommy freaked. After three failed rehabilitation attempts, she sent him here to put him on the path to salvation.

But I mean . . . come on. Get the fuck out of here, *literally.*

I have so many unanswered questions.

One, why'd he take the vitamins?

Two, why were they gummies?

Three, did they taste good?

And four, were they the child or adult variety?

Wait, also, did he purge them after?

I mean, really, what exactly was his thought process?

Still, he's pretty popular with the thinspo folks around here, though it probably helps that he looks like if a young Brad Pitt had a skinny clone made of himself. Still, I don't particularly like it when he looks at my Firefly, especially like that.

She's mine, fucker.

All mine.

I catch eyes with the blond Lothario and give him a look that makes his eyes nearly pop out of his head as he hurries to walk a little faster.

I have set thousands of things on fire.

Books.

Buildings.

Schools.

Students.

He knows it. They all do around here, learning eventually one way or the other, and the look I throw him confirms that I will most definitely set him on fire too.

Hell, it might actually be nice to throw a guy in the mix.

That would be new.

I wonder if they smell the same.

I watch as my Firefly darts around a guard, who's on his radio and calling for backup. I don't know why he's calling for backup. Surprisingly, I don't find that I don't care why either. Normally, I'd love the opportunity to drown out the noise, but whatever shitstorm is brewing can wait.

I need to know why she's crying, and then I want to hurt whoever hurt her.

Also . . . new.

I do care about my sudden inclination to protect her.

I don't protect anyone.

I smoke. I fuck. I ignite things and people.

I don't protect. Not ever.

So, what the hell is happening to me? What is she *doing* to me?

A minute later, I watch as best friends and occasional lovers —I think their names are Dean and Zane—throw down in the hall. They are big bodybuilder types who move like they skipped about a hundred too many leg days. Dean must be pissed Zane made him be the bottom last night because he shoves Zane with both hands. It's a brutal shove, downright violent and so hard the dude's head must feel like his brains just got scrambled.

The guard nearby radios for backup again and calls for them to break it up. He doesn't actually offer to break it up himself, though, but in fairness, he would be dumb to intervene between these two. Dean and Zane get into some sort of altercation once a week at minimum, and their little spats almost never devolve into anything more than dumb and dumber hitting each other.

No one around here cares about another fight between the two of them. They fight over everything and anything, class, other students, food, and probably the weather. I can see it in my head.

Zane asks if it's hot outside.

Dean responds that it's not.

Zane throws down when he opens the door, and it's eighty degrees Fahrenheit.

Everyone is bored with their bullshit, or at least I am.

The two morons should really just go to couples' counseling at this point and get it over with.

Dean shouts something at Zane, spit flying everywhere, and Zane turns the color of a fire truck before he barrels for his bro dude and tackles him to the floor. In the process, his head or elbow or something connects with Dean's mouth, and blood and at least one tooth go flying. It splatters, hitting Kill's pants and shoes, who's minding his own business and on the way to class. I see the beautiful moment when my friend stops walking and looks down at whatever shit has fucked up his kicks. Then he looks over and spots the bomb to his morning plans.

Zane's wailing on Dean, more blood shooting everywhere, and I start to laugh because there's too much energy inside of me again, too much noise. I can feel it tickling my brain now, making me laugh even when society says it shouldn't be funny. Granted, I do actually find this to be hilarious, though, and even more so when Kill looks up from his splattered shoes, raises an eyebrow, locks eyes with me, and shrugs a shoulder.

Oh shit. I was wrong.

Dean and Zane might not be smart enough to incite a riot on most days, but now they've gone and done it. They've annoyed Killian, and everybody knows my boy only likes blood play when he's fucking, and he definitely doesn't like it from the male gender.

He's about to fuck some shit up, and it makes me laugh even harder.

Kill's stare slices across the hall, and he finds, like I do, that Dean and Zane are grunting and rolling on the floor, their noses busted and their eyes swelling shut. We both know he isn't going to get the satisfaction of an actual fight from one of them. They both look ten seconds away from being down for the count.

He watches as an overmedicated sophomore walks by, oblivious to the commotion. The dude's pupils are so dilated that he looks like an alien, and he probably doesn't even know what planet he's on, but he's a big motherfucker, and I bet Kill thinks he'll give it back as good as he takes it.

Kill takes three steps toward him and slams the guy into the wall. With one fist clenched around the dude's lapel, Kill lands an uppercut that I think I can hear even over the shouting. I'm still laughing as I slip by them, and fuck, it hurts.

My chest and my middle ache from my laughter.

It's so funny though, and I can't stop. I can't even breathe.

The overmedicated moron doesn't really even snap out of it until Kill's knuckles connect with his nose this time. Then the dude wails like he's been shot.

Fuck, it's hilarious.

Oh my God. I can't breathe. I can't see him. I'm crying and laughing, and I'm desperately trying not to do both, but the noise is so loud.

It's so fucking funny.

My Firefly doesn't even turn around and look at the disaster unfolding behind her. The guard on the radio backs away to the wall and watches for a moment, slipping his baton from his belt. He doesn't try to break up Dean and Zane or Kill and the oblivious kid either. He's afraid someone's going to come at him, and it's a smart instinct.

Distracted and with his back turned, someone definitely would.

Maybe me.

Maybe Saint.

Probably Kill since he's in a bloodletting mood at the moment.

We're not allowed to have lockers, or the medicated kid's skull would've made a nice clang against the metal. Three newbies show their faces, and I get it. I've been there too. They want to be badass and solidify their spots as the next three kings. They all come up behind Kill, and I should intervene. I will if he can't handle it, but fuck, I grab onto the wall, bleary-eyed and sucking in air as I cackle. I wipe my tears away and watch.

I guess they think that if they gang up on my friend, it'll be easy, but they underestimate him.

When the first punch lands to the back of his blond hair, Kill doesn't even stagger with the hit. He just lets the guy on the wall go, and the kid slides down, melting into a human-shaped puddle at his feet. Then Kill turns around and knockout punches the biggest asshole in the face. His short ass falls backward, hitting the floor like a dead weight, and oh my God, this is perfect.

I can't stop laughing.

My lungs hurt.

My stomach hurts.

My cheeks hurt.

I'm cackling like a maniac, and there's not a damn thing I can do about it, but I have to keep moving. My Firefly needs me. I dart between bodies as I try to regain control of myself. I catch up to her at the end of the hall, and I grab her by the shoulder and force her to stop.

"Firefly," I manage between laughs, trying to kill the noise, to stop laughing. "What happened?"

She looks at me while I choke on air, trying not to laugh. Her upper lip retracts over her teeth with her sneer, and it makes me feel . . . inferior. I don't like it.

"Fuck off," she snaps with an eye-roll.

It takes everything in me to stop laughing, to suck it back in and hold the laughter inside me. The twitch in my fingertips and the tickle in my brain long to grab the lighter and ignite the flame.

I need to calm down.

I need to get out of here.

This is too much, too much noise, too much stimulation, too much everything when my brain struggles to process letters on most days.

If I can't laugh my ass off or light the flame to silence all the shit in the world, I need another way instead.

There's too much damned *noise* right now, and it makes all of me prickle.

Quiet!

"Come with me," I blurt.

"Go away, creep," she says.

Someone gets tackled to the floor and more blood splatters across the stone. Guards are showing up now, tearing students off of each other and putting them in restraints. She grimaces, her cheeks flushed the color of burning embers, her eyes wide and wet, and her mouth sticky with thick saliva.

"Why are you crying, Firefly?" I ask her.

She doesn't answer.

"Who made you cry?" I demand.

She shakes her head and closes her eyes, trying to drown me out too, I guess.

I get it, but it pisses me off.

"Your mom?" I push. "Your dad? A boyfriend back home?"

She doesn't have a boyfriend, though. The ones that do always bring it up like it's a badge of honor, like it will save them from me. It doesn't. If anything, I take it as a challenge.

"Did you gain weight? Is that what's bothering you?"

I hope she did.

Doesn't she understand? Maybe not, I barely do, but I know we're tied together, her and me. I need her alive and well, my little Firefly, to keep the noise at bay and control all the bad thoughts, the memories and urges that come back and threaten to bring me under. And she needs me to save her from herself.

"Get away from me!" she snaps finally. "What is wrong with you?"

"Come on," I tell her.

I sat with her in the bathroom. I could've left her there and let Oliver come back and do all the vile things he wanted to like rape her and probably even worse. I even took her to my table. I fed her, and with the noise picking me apart at the moment, I'm starting to get really tired of her shit.

She needs to be grateful. The way she's acting right now reminds me too much of my father, and it makes me feel dumb. If there's anything I hate in this world, it's people who make me feel like he does.

"Get away!" she shouts, louder this time, as the guards behind me start to yell.

"Get on the ground!" they shout at today's contestants. "On the ground! Now!"

"Come with me to the basement," I plead. "I'll make it all better."

"I'm not going anywhere with you," she hisses, the words nasty across her pretty teeth. "And I'm certainly not going with you down there. It's forbidden. You're trying to get me locked up in isolation, but guess what, creep? It won't work."

"I'm not trying to get you in trouble," I tell her. "I'm trying to help you get out of it."

She rolls her eyes, sniffling again.

What is wrong with her?

"What do I have to do for you to leave me alone?" she asks me.

I lean in, letting my breath feather across her face, as I force her to her knees in the middle of the hallway. I shouldn't do it. I'm drawing unnecessary attention, but everyone's distracted by the train wreck unfolding behind us.

"Beg me for it," I tell her as she looks up at me, wide-eyed, kneeling, and utterly perfect. "*Grovel*, baby girl."

It won't work, even if she kisses the toes of my shoes, but I don't tell her that. I want my power back—I *need* it. She's currently stealing it from me the same way my father does.

She scoffs at my words, refusing me, and slaps my hands away as she climbs to her feet.

I hate that she refuses me. It makes me feel stupid and weak, just like my father says I am. I lean forward a little and pinch her sides, trying to see if she's gained any weight.

She screams and goes absolutely feral.

And now there's way too much damn noise rattling inside my head.

I feel it shearing me apart, cutting me into tiny pieces, and it's too much.

Flashes explode in front of my eyes, but only I can see them.

My father raising his folded belt and hitting me across the legs when I stuttered.

My father bringing his cigar to the back of my neck and pressing it into my flesh when the words started to melt together.

My father calling me *a dumb sonovabitch* before he threw his whiskey decanter across the room at my face.

And my mother, weak and pathetic, crying as he made me scream.

I smile at my Firefly as I feel it tearing me apart. Then I turn around and throw a punch like a madman, catching some asshole in the face before I feel myself fracture in two.

11

GABE

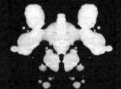

Where am I?

How did I get here?

I turn my head side to side, or at least I try to, but the world has gone shaky at the edges, and I'm a little woozy. It feels like something is strapped across my temple, holding it tight to the chair in which I sit. I try to turn my head again, and the back of my skull rubs against the strap and something hard behind me.

It's the chair.

And I'm in the room.

Fuck.

I look down as far as I can, which isn't very far given that I'm currently tied down like a rabid animal. What I do see confirms my suspicions, though. My wrists are tied with thick leather restraints to the armrests of a wooden chair, and I spot another leather restraint around my middle, at least six inches wide and cinching me in place.

Fucking fantastic.

I hate this place, particularly this very room and this very chair. Dr. Boucher put me in the damn sensory deprivation chamber again because of course, he would come at me with my worst nightmare. Hydrotherapy didn't do a damn thing to me, and neither did the drugs, but he sure seems to like to make me scream inside this room. Probably because it's the only time he can get a reaction out of me, maybe even a couple of honest words if I'm feeling particularly broken by the end of my time in here.

I look downward again, mostly with my eyeballs given the leather restraint tight around my skull. I try to move my feet, jerking them forward, but as expected, they're also tied, bound at the ankles to the chair. I know for a fact that the chair is bolted to the floor too, and no matter how much I wiggle or try to get free, I won't succeed. I've never been able to escape, not once during the sixteen—no, I think it's seventeen now—times he's caged me in here. I used to scream and throw a fit, trying to break the damn thing, but I know better than that now. He knows better too because there's no give in the restraints today. They're extra tight.

I stopped trying to escape six or seven visits ago. I don't know how long I tried to escape during my final attempt—there's not exactly a clock on the wall—but I know it was a long damn time. I was out of breath, my wrists rubbed raw by the leather, and my ankles bleeding by the time I stopped fighting.

I don't even bother this time. Maybe I will later when the room starts to get to me, and I lose whatever little shred is left of my sanity, but not right now.

I concentrate my energy to knock out whichever lucky bastard unties me from this fucking chair.

Is this the beginning or the end?

Have I already been in here and paid the price of my disobedience, or is this new today?

Damn disassociation makes it so I never know if I'm at the end of a match or if the first bell just rang.

I flex my hands around the wooden planks of the armrest, my fingers gripping the hard, thick wood. My shirt's been removed. For that matter, so have my pants, and I'm in one of those crappy hospital gowns that opens at the back with a tiny little tie that doesn't ever stay put.

It makes me sick to think about a bunch of people crowding around me and holding me down to strip me of my clothes and put me in this gown. It's probably good that I don't remember it. Maybe it's a small blessing in a place where God never answers your prayers.

I hope I gave them a hell of a fight, though, and by the looks of it, I think I did. There's blood splattered on the dark carpeted floor in front of me. It freckles the tops of my bare knees and the tops of my hands and forearms. I must have gotten in a good couple of punches at least. The pain shooting across my sternum and stabbing into my chest confirms it. They don't follow Hammurabi's Code in the hole. It's the Butcher's rules now, and that means you pay double for what you put out into the world. My chest feels like someone took a baseball bat to my ribs, and my collarbone's probably broken. Everything hurts, each wheezed inhale and every raspy exhale. Just sitting here is almost excruciating, but that's one thing my father taught me at least, how to deal with the pain.

I look around the room, though I don't actually know why I bother. Nothing has changed, not that I can tell. It's the same hell that has always been here. There's the thick black foam on the ceiling and on the walls and thick carpet beneath my feet. It blocks the world out and traps you in your own thoughts. At first, I thought it was a joke. I laughed when the doc turned off the light and closed the door, but it stopped being funny soon after. There's nothing normal about a room being so quiet you can hear your own heartbeat roaring between your ears.

Butcher must've waited to turn off the lights this time, no doubt wanting me to lose my shit and spill all my secrets as soon as I woke up. Everyone knows you don't talk to the Butcher, though. Anything you say can and will be used against you here. There are no laws in the Asylum, just verdicts and undue punishments.

I guess today the bad doc plans on picking at the one thread still holding me together. Maybe the next time when I disassociate, I won't come back. Maybe that's what he wants. If you can't cure them, make it so no one can, right?

The longer I stay in the chamber, the louder my breath becomes, as it always does in here. I hear the *tha-thump, tha-thump* of my own heart along with the *woosh* of my breath. They gain traction with each passing second, going faster and faster, until it's all I can hear. It's only me in here, but the noise is already nearly unbearable.

I hate this fucking room.

I concentrate on the feeling of the chair beneath me. It's cold against my bare back and ass. Would it kill the fucker to put a cushion on it?

The leather restraints are cold too against my bare ankles, wrists, and forehead. The one around my middle isn't much better. It chills me through the thin fabric of the gown, delivering cold knives to my chest.

I sit there a moment longer, listening to the whistle of my breath and the beat of my heart before I open my mouth and scream as loud as I can. I'd rather get this over with. I want them to know I'm awake, although I hate screaming in this room. The walls absorb the sound instantly, and it plays tricks with your mind. Did you really say something if you aren't certain you heard it? Somewhere, Butcher is watching the camera that records from the corner of the room nearest the door, and he sees me moving and must know I'm awake.

I look around the room again, trying to occupy myself, though I still find not much has changed. There is a chunk of foam missing on the only door to the chamber. Somebody must've gotten it good during a fight, and looking at the broken piece makes me smile. Someone fucked up one of Butcher's favorite treatment methods. Good for them.

The longer I sit, the louder my heart beats in the cavity of my chest. I don't know how long I'm there, waiting for the doctor to arrive, but I can feel it vibrating inside my brain now. I hate when the head doc locks me up with my thoughts and waits to see if I can break myself.

Sometimes, I do and disassociate.

Most of the time, I don't.

It could be minutes later. It could be seconds. Hell, it could be a fucking hour for all I know, but the door opens, and there's the butchering doc in the flesh. He walks inside the room, his white lab coat starched and pristine. Unfortunately, that means I didn't get a good hit in on him, not this time at least.

Whatever. I'm certain there will be more chances.

Dr. Boucher's got a face that reminds me of death with razor-sharp cheekbones, hollow cheeks, sunken eyes, and paper-thin lips. He could be fifty years old or a hundred, but personally, I'm guessing he's old enough to have met Noah and taken a ride on the boat.

"You're awake, Mr. Soros," he tells me as he steps closer. "Glad to see it."

I'm sure the fucker is not glad to see it, but I'm glad he left the door open because there's a commotion in the halls, and it drowns out the rapid fire beat of my own heart. He walks to stand in front of me, his hands clasped together in front of him.

"How are you feeling?" he asks.

"I'm reformed, Doc," I tell him. "You can untie me now."

Butcher laughs, and it's creepy as fuck on his skeletal face.

"I think not," he tells me. "You sent three of my guards to the hospital, and I don't even have a final body count on the number of students you hurt today. What exactly triggered you this time, Gabriel?"

Now we're playing this game.

Good.

"I must've disassociated," I tell him. "I don't remember what happened. I promise it wasn't me, Doc. It was one of the voices in my head."

He knows better than to think I hear voices, but I did disassociate this time, apparently, given I can't remember what the fuck happened. The best lies are based in truth, right?

I once fooled him for an entire semester when I told him I heard voices that ordered me to set shit on fire. No way is he buying that one again, and I catch the moment he realizes I'm lying to him. Dr. Butcher smiles, but the expression doesn't reach his dead blue eyes. I swear they get less blue and more clear every time I see him, like he's literally becoming less human and more specter with each passing day.

"I promise I'll be better," I tell him. I can barely hear my heartbeat with the door open, letting in the outside noise. I need it to stay that way. "You fixed me."

Butcher's smile falls.

"You used to be such a good boy, Gabriel," he tells me with a frown. "What happened? Did your father call?"

Butcher knows damn well my father called this morning, right after I tried to read and the words became hieroglyphics again. My day took the highway to worse after I spotted my Firefly crying in the hall. I don't know how he knows my dear old dad called me, but he does. Maybe I've shared too much when he's pumped me full of drugs and left me to ramble. It pisses me off, him immediately identifying the root of all my troubles. I used to be so good at fooling him, like the semester I told him I heard voices, and then there was the one when I convinced him the only way I could get my dick hard was by igniting fires. We explored my sexuality for a good five months back then. I must be losing my touch. He doesn't believe me anymore.

Oh well.

I cut the shit.

"How much blood was there?" I ask him, raising an eyebrow. Well, as much as one can raise an eyebrow when their head is strapped to a chair. "How many did I take down while they ripped off my clothes?"

Butcher smiles, but it's not real. If anything, it's a grimace, which makes me smile because that means I took down a lot of the bastards.

Good.

"Any fires?" I ask him.

One can hope, and there was that time I got lucky and grabbed my lighter before they found it in my pocket first. I never got my baby back after they finally ripped it from my hands, only after I set an orderly on fire. I guess they incinerated it afterward. Luckily, I have spares hidden away in my room because I like the aesthetic of my black Zippos.

Butcher shakes his head.

"No fires today, son," he tells me.

"Such a shame," I say. "How long ago was it?"

I'm actually curious about this one because I'd like to know if I did disassociate or if it was the drugs this time. Dr. Boucher steps closer, his hands still clasped. He reeks of old people and rubbing alcohol, and it makes my eyes burn.

"It's been long enough," he says, giving me a nonanswer. "Why are you so afraid of getting better, Gabriel? You can be more.

You could be reformed. You could control the urges and control yourself. You could live a normal life."

"Where's the fun in that?" I scoff.

Neurotypicals are so not fun, but beyond that, the truth is I can't be normal. The doc in front of me will never understand that at the end of the day, I can't be normal because what happens when I'm normal and my father still doesn't give a fuck about me.

"Don't feel like talking?" Butcher tilts his head at me. "Maybe you will tonight."

No.

No!

"Stop!" I shout, but he's figured me out after all, and he doesn't even pause as he heads to the exit, flips the light switch off, and closes the door, locking me inside the silent darkness.

It's sensory deprivation at its most cruel.

I blink, but there's no light in here.

There's no sound either, except for the rising panic of my own breath and the pounding of my heart vibrating between my ears. This is my punishment for not cooperating. I guess he thinks if he can't break me, he'll let my own mind do it for him instead.

Smart bastard.

My heart beats faster and faster until the hammering steadies into a resounding loud pulse. It's nearly deafening between my ears, and it might actually sever the last of my sanity before everything quiets, and I am brought back to the before.

I stare down at the book. I'm probably six or seven, sitting at the dining room table at my parents' house. My father walks in and says, "Read it to me."

I feel everything in me clench at the command, but I do as I'm told. I look at the first word on the page.

"Once," I read aloud, "there w . . . w . . . was a b . . . boy . . ."

The words jumble together, flipping up and around, melding into symbols I don't recognize.

I falter.

"I said read it, boy," my father barks, and I try again.

"Once, there was a boy . . ."

But that's as far as I get. There are no words anymore, just symbols, lines and squiggles jumbled together. He steps behind me, grabs the back of my head, and slams my forehead into the desk. The world goes black for a minute, and blood bursts from my nose onto the table.

"You really are one stupid little fuck, aren't you?" he says with a scoff before he decides I'm not worth his time and leaves.

Then I'm back at my old school, the one before Chryseum, but this isn't right. I'm not supposed to be here. I try to ground myself in the present. My thumb twitches in an attempt to roll the wheel and ignite the flame, but the lighter isn't here and there's nothing to ground me. Over and over again, I make the motion, but it's a lost cause.

I am lost.

I'm taken back to the before again.

I stand in front of books, dozens of precious books behind glass cases. The school staff says they're worth hundreds of thousands of dollars, specifically brought in during family visitation weekend to impress our parents. I play with the lighter as I stare at the books. I roll the wheel and press the button over and over again, on and off, on and off, until it slips on and stays there.

I take a piece of paper from my pocket and hold it to the flame, igniting it. The fire is so pretty as the red, yellow, and orange colors fuse together, gyrating and dancing on the page. I want to stare at it. I want to look at it until the flames eat it up.

It goes against every instinct I have, but I force myself to drop the paper. I watch as the flames spread to the rug and grow higher and higher, until they lick the glass cases of the books.

The heat is so intense I feel like I'm baking from the front, but I can't move. It's beautiful. The alarms are blaring, and if I hadn't cut off the main water line in the basement, the sprinklers would've already come on, but I've learned from my mistakes. I stand there until smoke billows around me and every breath is a struggle. Then finally, when the choice is either death or to remain, I choose to live.

It's the event that got me sent here.

Four million dollars worth of damages when it was all said and done.

My thumb hits the chair again, but still, I can't manage to ground myself. I'm flung ahead, further in time, and there she is, the person who made this hellhole livable, and her black hair turns almost blue beneath the flames and she's smiling as we set shit on fire in the basement just to watch it burn. She grabs my hand and squeezes it tight, looking over at me.

I don't want to think about her, the fucking ghost. She died and left me here to deal with all the bullshit. She left me here with him.

She. Abandoned. Me.

It's too late, though. I can't unsee it now, and she looks right at me and mouths something, but my mind is fracturing, pieces coming apart and sliding together in a puzzle that doesn't quite fit. The memory is leaving, and my heartbeat pounds louder in the darkness. I blink out at nothing, trying to remember, my hand flicking at the lighter that isn't there, and with everything in me, I take a deep breath and I fucking scream.

But the cry is lost, absorbed by the padded walls.

I am left in the dark, playing victim to my own thoughts.

12

AVERY

I take my meds like a good girl, swallowing my pills like my psychiatrist expects. From what I've heard, my doctor is better than the last one they had here because at least he hasn't raped anyone yet. Well, as far as I know, at least, though he doesn't seem like the type. Then again, when does anyone seem like the type? Still, the last time I saw him, he was barely awake enough to form words, or maybe he just didn't care enough to even pretend to care.

My meds include all the standard players, an antidepressant, a multivitamin, pills to increase my appetite, and so on. Every morning, I'm placed in line with the other students with eating disorders. We walk to the medication dispensary together, and each of us waits our turn before we head as a group into the dining hall, where we are still forced to eat together. I think some of them have to get pills at night too before they go to their dorms, but at least I only have to see the dispensary staff once a day.

Today, when it's my place in line, I step up to the thick sheet of reinforced plexiglass built into the wall that separates the staff from us. A man dressed in black scrubs asks for my name, and a moment after I answer, he slips a small white paper cup across the counter through a hole cut into the plexiglass. I estimate twenty calories in my multivitamin and another twenty in the handful of other pills as I take the cup and lift it to my mouth, tossing the pills onto my tongue. Then I swallow them with the cup of water they provide with the pills. My meds catch in my throat, and I choke them down with more water, the aftertaste bitter and leaving grains of sand on my tongue.

I grimace at the taste as the guard looks at me from his metal stool and orders, "Open your mouth and stick out your tongue."

I do just as he tells me.

"Dismissed," he barks a moment later with a dismissive wave of his hand. I push the empty paper cups back to him across the counter, and he grabs them through the hole cut into the plexiglass and throws them into the trash.

I join the other eating disorder students in line before we are walked like kindergartners into the dining hall and told to get in line for a tray. They make all of us get our own food now like they got tired of waiting on us. They still weigh my tray at every meal, which is expected, but it makes it harder to get away with not eating. If you eat, they stand against the wall and watch you. If you don't, they cart you off to the hole to the one they call the Butcher.

I don't think I want to meet him. I've heard the whispers at the table as one friend encourages another to swallow the slop in front of them.

You don't want the tube, do you?

I heard he didn't even sedate Rylan last time. They just held her down and started shoving.

Please eat. You know what the Butcher will do.

The creep is still with him. He's been gone for over a week, and his absence has been both a blessing and a curse, a blessing I guess, or that's what I tell myself at least. It's a blessing because I haven't had to sit next to him or see him in math class every morning and feel him staring at me, trying to pick me apart with his eyes.

But it's a curse as well because something in me—the insanity, I guess—misses his attention and feeling like I'm worthy because of it. Introspection is a cruel bitch, but I tell myself that thinking of him is not actually about him. It's about me.

Still, I can't get the last time I saw him out of my head. It's always there at the back of my brain, haunting me, like he's sent his own ghost to follow me around and shout, *Boo!* at the most inopportune moments.

The last time I saw him, I'd refused to give him what he wanted. I told him I wouldn't go with him to the basement, and I'm still not sure what mind-fuck he had planned for me down there. Then I refused to lower myself in front of him and beg for him to leave me alone.

Beg me for it, he had said. *Grovel*, baby girl.

He can eat a dick for all I'm concerned.

He's a creep.

I don't go places with creeps.

I don't beg creeps.

But then why does it feel like I did something wrong that day, like I caused him to lose his shit and start wailing on everyone before getting dragged to solitary confinement? He brought four students and three guards to the floor before they managed to restrain him. Bodies piled around him, moaning and wriggling on the stone like he was the altar, and they were sacrifices to his god. I can't forget it, no matter how hard I try—the image of his face and the front of his otherwise white dress shirt splattered with the blood of strangers, his thick hair slick and wet with it. He smiled, half of his upper teeth stained red, as the guards forced him to the ground, pinning him on his stomach, and latched the wrist hobbles into place.

I should be shouting for joy and celebrating the win, but I find myself looking across the dining hall at his empty chair instead. I catch eyes with his crazy friend, the blond one, and it sends a shiver skittering up my spine.

The creep's crazy, but that guy, I just know, is downright unhinged.

I think that I might miss my stalker, but then maybe I'm just crazy too.

I can't miss him. I *shouldn't* miss him.

He's a freak.

He threatened to set me on fire multiple times.

He fucking force-fed me.

And it shouldn't matter that he looks at me like I'm the center of his solar system or that he hangs on every word I say or that he actually seems to care about me in his own deluded way.

He's wicked and vile and . . . makes me feel worthy of a king.

What the fuck is wrong with me?

I can't want him.

I will not allow myself to want him!

This shit is just this fucked-up place messing with my head.

Two days ago, I had another session with the headmistress, and she seems determined to make this work. I guess my dad is paying her a lot of money to make it work. Well, I know he is because during our last session, she told me so.

Your father has promised the Academy a substantial donation should we fix you.

We have every intention of fixing you, Ms. Bardot.

We will not go easy on you like your previous institutions.

What-the-fuck-ever.

She can eat a dick too as far as I'm concerned. None of my previous rehabilitation programs or reformatory schools were easy. I've had over a thousand hours of cognitive-behavioral therapy. I've talked about my upbringing and my parents for hours until my voice cracks from use. Even the poshest of the places I've gone to always made me work for it. Group sessions, individual cognitive-behavioral therapy, medications, hospitalizations, intensive inpatient rehabilitation programs, if you can name it, I've almost certainly tried it. Now did any of them have a pyromaniac who threatened to set me on fire if I didn't eat all of my dinner? Well, no. No, they did not. But no one's gone easy on me my entire life, and this place is just a new swirl in my personal shit sundae.

Headmistress wasn't exactly happy at my last weigh-in with her, and the nurse wasn't happy this morning, which makes me very happy. God knows what my mother's probably saying about me. I don't know if Headmistress Graves talks to her after every check-in like she does my father, but even if she doesn't, my father's probably telling her everything in a wayward belief that she cares.

She's probably telling him some tried-and-true favorites like, *It's a cry for attention, Michael!* and *It's not my fault she couldn't handle the pressure!* My father, the bastard, is probably letting her do it too. He might've said one thing to her, something like *She's our daughter, Megan! She needs help!* but he won't ever come out and say it, right?

He won't tell her that she's the reason their daughter has an eating disorder. He won't say she should've never been allowed to be a mother, and that it's amazing the state ever saw her fit to raise a child. If he did that, he'd be forced to see his spouse as something less than the perfect wife and mother, and that would be unacceptable.

She can't be the villain when she's his queen.

Despite it all, I don't blame her for my current state though, not anymore. That's not to say that I have forgiven her either. I don't forgive, and I most definitely don't forget. I just move on, especially when the other person involved won't admit that they did anything wrong. I recognize, however, that I am an adult, eighteen years old and capable of making my own decisions.

She doesn't control my food choices anymore. She's not here to even see them. I choose whether to eat and what I eat. After all these years, I finally have the control, not her, not anymore. It may be her voice in my head, but I ultimately decide whether or not to listen to it.

I am in control.

The thought almost makes me smile as one after another, the cafeteria ladies fill my tray. I must be on some freaking list or something because I swear they give me more than everyone else. One piece of white bread, one helping of steamed carrots, one fish-looking substance, one of what may or may not be strawberry shortcake, topped with whipped cream, and one, well I don't know what that one is. I think it might be—I'm hoping it is—chocolate pudding.

At the end of the line, the lady weighs the tray, her hair net slipping from her bun and down her sweaty forehead. Then she hands it to me.

I take it from her and walk back into the dining hall. It's bright in here this morning, much brighter than normal, and the snow outside reflects the sunlight, tossing light across the gray stone floor and walls and up to the arched wooden beams criss-crossing across the ceiling. Even the guards seem to have taken notice and half of them look out the window rather than at the students in the dining hall.

It gives me an opportunity to get rid of some of the food on my tray, one I shouldn't waste, but I have to be careful about it.

I could slip on the way to the table. I got away with it one time, lobbing a roll underneath a nearby kid's feet. But then I was stupid and desperate when I tried it the next day. That day, they took me back for a new tray, and I swear the cafeteria ladies added even more food than they did the first time.

Shit, the guard with the beer belly is looking at me now, and my opportunity just disappeared, gone in the blink of an eye.

Per Headmistress's rule, I join the rest of the anorexic and bulimic students at a table. I've noticed that even when they weren't required, they often ate together anyway. I have no desire to be here with them, though. A blonde girl with a short pixie cut sends me a friendly wave across the cafeteria, which I return. I can't decide if she feels sorry for me or what after she introduced herself during my first week on campus and offered to show me around. I think she said her name was Trixie, but I declined her offer. I don't need to make friends here.

I don't need to know their names either because it will just make it harder when I leave. No connections always ensures an easy exit.

You know his name though, and he has a beautiful name.

Gabriel, the archangel who spreads God's message, the brother of the Devil.

And also a man with demon-colored eyes and fire fetishes apparently.

Don't think about him, Avery.

Focus on what's ahead of you.

I look at my tray and mentally assess the damage.

I count a single piece of white bread, eighty calories.

One piece of, well, I think it's fish, with a buttery-looking sauce, two hundred fifty calories.

A grotesquely pink dessert with an enormous amount of whipped cream that feels like a personal affront. I'll be safe and call it four hundred.

One helping of steamed carrots, sixty calories.

And also, what may or may not be chocolate pudding, one hundred fifty calories.

They also gave me an apple juice today, but that one is easy. It lists the caloric content on the side of the box with the rest of the nutritional information.

One apple juice, a hundred calories.

That brings the grand total to—I do the math in my head—1,040 calories.

It's more than what I would normally allow myself in an entire day. I finish looking at my plate and start with the least amount of calories first, like I always do. It seems like if I eat at least half my tray, the guards are happy with it. That way, I don't have to go for an extra session with the headmistress, and they can feel like they're breaking me.

Sometimes, I can hide the food, shoving it into a napkin and dropping it beneath a table, but I almost got caught yesterday. Plus, after the creep threw down in the hallway, it sounds like solitary might be worse than where I'm currently at. It has to be worse if it means being locked up with him. I can't get locked up in there with the creep. I won't survive.

After I eat the carrots that taste like absolutely nothing, I move on to the fish, skipping the glucose spike with the bread and swallowing one slow bite after another. I leave the strawberry shortcake untouched with the juice, but I think they'll be happy today. Just to be safe, I open the juice carton, take the tiniest of sips, and then *accidentally* knock it over, wetting the table, before I quickly right it again. The guards aren't paying attention, so that's a win for me today.

My mother would be proud.

I stand, taking my tray to the nearest guard, who accepts it and tells me to wait there. He takes it back to the cafeteria line to have them weigh it and comes back out a minute later.

"You're free to go," he says.

I bite the inside of my cheek to stifle my smile.

These people won't be too hard to fool.

I don't even purge on my way to class.

13

GABE

I walk into class late—well, *very* late, like *there's five minutes left and I'm only here for my Firefly* kind of late. Butcher finally let me out of the hole this morning. I guess he gave up on trying to perform a fucking miracle and cure me. That or he moved on to his next victim. On second thought, it's definitely that. I'm just one piece of the fucked-up pie around here, and Butcher likes to take his knife to every single slice at one point or another.

Last night, they finally untied me from the chair, dragged me to a cell with padded walls, and let me sleep in a horizontal position. Then this morning a beefy guard with a graying mustache dropped a fresh set of clothes through the hole in the metal door and told me to change.

They didn't even let me piss before they sent me on my way. They just shut the door to the unit in my face and told me to head to class, but at least I got a glimpse of Butcher's newest distraction. There was a commotion in the ward at the place where the hallway divides into a T, veering left and right. Three guards ran from the left side of the hall to the right as somebody screamed bloody murder. Actually, it was more like burnt murder because I've only heard someone scream like that when they were on fire.

The victim probably thought they were from one of the hallucinogenics pushed into their veins. It was probably Jenkins or one of the other intellectually challenged students here. Everybody knows they have it worse than the rest of us because the Asylum isn't equipped to deal with a manic teenager with the rational capacity of a child. Like children, they have tantrums, and, like a bastard, the Butcher is vile, so it almost always turns into a freak show with one of them trying to kill someone. Then again, when is there not screaming around here? It's like a daily occurrence at this point. If a schizophrenic doesn't lose their shit, has another day even passed, or did the matrix glitch out for a moment?

I leave, grateful it's not me in there again, and take the stairs down from solitary confinement to the second floor. Then I walk the halls until I reach the spiral staircase that leads to my dorm room. The winding maze of halls and passageways in this place doesn't make sense. I just have it all memorized at this point. The Academy's been through so many identities—a typhus hospital, a state penitentiary, an orphanage, and more—that it's almost got its own case of dissociative identity disorder, and each of its identities has left its own scars.

The secret tunnels in the walls, the ones Saint likes to walk, are from the Typhoid Mary days, when the building was a hope and a prayer to the people coughing up blood as they died.

The almost-finished basement is thanks to the state coming in after the hospital shut down and attempting to turn the building into something useful, a penitentiary.

And the orphanage, well, it's gifted Kill with some of his favorite hideaway spots.

I wish my Firefly would go with me to the basement, but she

already declined once. I could force her—I will if she doesn't come to her senses soon enough—but first, I have to get a shower and grab another lighter.

Every time I leave solitary, I feel like I took a deep dive into a sewer. The place isn't exactly clean, and Butcher has a way of making you feel even nastier just by looking at you. I drop my shit inside my room and scrub the last week off of me. Then I dress and before I leave my space, I kick loose the tile behind the toilet. It falls, clanking to the floor, and one of these days, it's probably going to explode into a hundred tiny shards, but today is not that unlucky occasion. I grab a spare lighter from my stash and put the tile back into place, pressing it flat to the wall.

I pay Headmistress's sidepiece, Marshall, very well to ensure I am kept stocked at all times. I don't know if they're actually fucking, but I know he follows her around like she's a bitch in heat, and she makes him do all of her dirty work. I buy it all from him, lighters, matches, cigarettes, flash paper, and more. I keep that lumbering rat's contraband business booming thanks to the guilt money my mother sends me every month.

The one I grab from the hidden hole in the wall is probably the twentieth lighter, maybe even more, that's either broken or been seized by the staff since I came here freshman year. I'm definitely not getting back the one they confiscated this time either. I'm pretty sure they incinerate all the contraband, and I'd like to see it, just once, all the shivs, knives, joints, glass, and other shit doused with gasoline before it goes up in a glorious blaze. As long as Butcher's in charge, I have no chance of that, though. The bastard would ship it all out of state just to make sure I didn't get the satisfaction of watching it burn.

Pocketing the lighter, I leave my room and head to class.

I'm hungry and pissed off that Butcher locked me in the sensory deprivation room for the past week. The fucker has to know it's my least favorite place on campus, well that and anywhere he's currently standing, but he left me in there for eight days anyway.

Eight. Days.

Time passes differently in that room, and I only know how long I was in there because I heard a nurse mention today's date to a guard this morning. I don't know how many times I disassociated or screamed into the silence or nearly broke. It's all one black, silent blur.

Weaker men have lost their shit in twenty minutes in that room, and the only thing that kept me from losing it this time was the breaks when the guards would take me out like an animal to piss and eat. I'd clean my plate slowly, chewing each bite of food until it turned to mush, and then I'd piss all over my clothes just to delay being sent back. Those brief moments out of the chamber grounded me back in reality, sewing me back together again when my mind fractured in two.

Thank the old gods that no one can be allowed to sully the Butcher's precious torture chamber, so no eating and definitely no pissing allowed.

It's disgusting what they let him get away with here. I wouldn't even believe the doc had a medical license if I hadn't looked it up myself once on the state board's website. It took me six hours just to get the damn page to load on the crappy network up here. I was new back then, still two weeks fresh, and I thought it would help me find something to get my father to cart me away from here.

It didn't, though.

It doesn't matter how many complaints and disciplinary actions the guy has before the medical board. There were a handful of them before he came here—the records are sealed— but they don't matter either. My father didn't care about the Butcher's transgressions back then, and he wouldn't care now either. The doc is way behind on the times, preferring hydrotherapy and drug-induced psychosis to more mainstream, civilized treatments. I guess the parents put up with it because Chryseum provides results when nothing else does. Hell, if you don't end up six feet under, you're almost certain to graduate from here. Then you can be sent to the Academy's sister school in Connecticut, Prodigum University, for college or to one of the insane asylums for the poor bastards who can't be trusted to care for themselves.

I don't plan on going to either, though.

I will disappear when I graduate. I know enough about incendiaries and explosives to start my own militia. I've studied it tediously—and I do mean tediously, because there aren't many videos out there that show you how to make a fucking IED. I've painstakingly read aloud word-by-word books on the subject. I've made plans, and I have enough money set aside to disappear, even considering the astronomical prices Marshall charges me.

You see most of the world's silicone comes from quartzite, a mineral mined in Latin America, particularly Brazil. And that's where I'm headed after I get out of here. No more cold winters. No more being berated by my father. Just warm weather and blowing shit up.

I'm hoping once I get there I can use my knowledge to work for one of the mining conglomerates. There's always a need for explosives and the accompanying flames in mining. Those plans can wait, though, because right now I need to see my Firefly.

I'm getting tired of waiting for her to come around and understand. I can save her if she'd let me, and she can save me from the noise if she'll cooperate. Otherwise, she's going to starve herself to death and stop her heart one of these days, and I'm going to split in two, forever disassociated and unable to cope.

Whatever patience I had for her died a slow and painful death in the hole. I swear to God if she is still on a quest to kill herself, then I'm going to lose it. I will tie her up and force-feed her if I have to. I'll do it to keep her alive.

She asked me before why I cared, and it was a good question, one that haunted me in the hole, especially during sensory deprivation when I wanted to think of anything but my own damned heartbeat. Dr. Cross, the dead asshole, would've probably said that my new obsession with her has less to do with her and more to do with me, that if I save her I'll somehow save myself. I don't think that's right though, not fully at least. In fact, I'd say I do okay in controlling my urges. Every morning I don't set fire to campus is a personal win.

No, I think it's more complicated than that.

Sure, there's the initial attraction between us. I wanted to fuck her from the moment I first saw her.

There's the added challenge too, the back-and-forth, the give-and-take, and the spunky fight she gives me.

But more than all of that, there's the one thing I never had, not really, and I crave it from her.

Control.

I think she wants it too, in her own way. She controls what she eats and in doing so, affirms her own self-worth. I need to control her in order to know mine as well. I have a plan that will get us both what we need, but first, she needs to come with me to the basement.

Sure, I already control the self-proclaimed pyromaniacs in this place. I can make them do whatever I want when I want, but it's only real control if you earn it, and I've earned nothing from them.

Kill would tell me to stop analyzing shit and that the drugs Butcher gave me must have gone to my head. Saint would say to shut the hell up and fuck her already. Maybe they're right, but all I know is that I *need* to fix her. I itch for it in the same way that I itch for the flame.

I hope she's gained weight because if she hasn't, she's going to regret what I'm going to do to her. As I walk down the halls, I flick my lighter on and off in my pants pocket. It's been too long, but it brings my already boiling blood down to a simmer. On and off, I roll the wheel and press the button, burning the inside of my finger while I keep it pressed against the nozzle for the flame.

On and off, on and off, and on again.

I need her to choose to come with me, or none of this works. She needs the illusion of a choice, even if it's forced, or her self-worth vanishes in an instant, and I lose her forever.

I can't risk that.

As I walk into my math class, the professor already packing up for the day, I take one look at her and know she's lost weight. She looks fucking terrible, half-asleep and staring at the board. She's an entirely new color of anemic this morning.

Goddammit!

She didn't obey, which means she has to be punished. Because this shit right here makes me feel weak, and I hate feeling weak. It reminds me too much of my own father.

I sit beside her, sliding into the chair. Kill glances over at me, but I'm looking at her, staring until she finally notices me. I guess what they have her on is strong today, but then again, I bet most medicines are strong if they're the only thing you're eating.

I reach over, across the aisle, and pinch her sides.

Sure enough, I can feel more of her ribs today. She yelps and swats me away, but the professor ignores it.

Anger, fear, disgust, it all blurs inside my head, growing louder and louder until the noise is blaring. Everything in me wants to grab her books and set them on fire, but I can't, not right now. I was gone for a little over a week, and she almost succeeded in killing herself. What happens when I'm gone for two?

I think about ways to punish her instead. I want her naked, bound, fucking *branded.*

Maybe I can take the lighter, shove it up her skirt, and let it heat her pussy.

Maybe I can take a cigarette and burn marks into that pretty, pale skin of hers.

Maybe I'll set her strawberry blonde hair on fire.

Then she'll know what it feels like to me when she hurts herself.

The professor drones on. I guess at least he tries, but he's got to be the most boring person on the fucking planet. Finally, the bell tolls, and the professor grabs his shit. He leaves with the students, one after another filing out of the room. She tries to leave too, but I'm faster. I grab her wrist, holding it tight between my thumb and pinky finger, squeezing it. Her eyes flare wide.

"Let me go," she tells me as the last of them leave the room, and the door closes behind them.

I stand, drawing to my full height as she sits at her desk, her hand still caught in mine.

"You've lost weight," I hiss.

"Maybe because you weren't here to force-feed me," she spits back.

I yank her out of her desk, and it's a messy exit. She jumps as the desk topples, and she lands against me, her small breasts pressed to my chest. While I like her there, I like it even more when I back her against the wall, trap her hands above her head, and make her stretch on the tips of her toes to look at me.

"Why do you insist on defying me?" I demand.

She scoffs. "Why do you insist on making everything about yourself? This isn't about you, creep! It has nothing to do with you!"

"It has everything to do with me," I hiss, letting my breath fall like ash raining from the sky across her beautiful face. "You are damaging what is mine."

She laughs, but there's no humor in it. If anything, it's angry.

"I am not yours, fire freak, and I never will be."

"You've been mine since the moment you stepped foot in class, baby girl."

"You truly believe that?" she asks, tipping her chin at me in defiance. "Then why are you trapping me here?"

Dammit.

She has a point.

I don't want her to have a point.

I release her hands, and they fall limply to her sides. She can call me a creep or a freak or tell me to stop, but she isn't running away. She feels it too, the flames licking between us, warming our skin.

I bring my index finger up, catching her bottom lip, and she doesn't move.

I pull her lip down, exposing her teeth, and she doesn't move. I drag my hand down over her neck, across her collarbone, over her breasts, and down her abdomen to that plaid skirt she's wearing, and she still doesn't move.

I watch as the pulse point at the base of her throat goes wild.

I continue down to the hem of her skirt and run my hand up and over her white tights.

"Don't," she murmurs.

"Then stop me," I tell her.

My fingers trail up her thigh to the lip of her tights, which sit low on her waist. Her skin is hot against mine, sweaty and burning up, as my fingers slip beneath the tights and her underwear and down to her cunt.

A flush blazes across her cheeks and she pants as she watches me. I breathe in the scent of mint toothpaste between us, and she sucks in a sharp breath as my fingers delve between her thighs.

Thank everything.

She's fucking soaked.

"I hate you," she whispers to me.

"Your pussy doesn't," I remark, and her eyes flutter shut as I push two fingers inside of her, watching her face as I stretch her wet heat.

The sound of her riding my fingers is gloriously loud.

I add another digit, thrusting in and out of her, slow and steady. Her lips part as her eyes remain closed.

"Faster," she murmurs.

I give her what she needs until she comes, throwing her head back and calling out my name.

Then I flatten my lips to hers and kiss her, savoring the nip of peppermint on my tongue.

"I can't let you die, baby girl," I murmur, "not when we could ignite the world together instead."

14

AVERY

What just happened?

I open my eyes and find the creep smirking at me, his hair messy and his dark eyes locked on me. His tongue peeks out from his mouth to taste his top lip. His fingers are still inside of me, the aftershocks of my orgasm fluttering around them.

This feels intimate. I don't do intimate.

I'm not even supposed to know his name. I'm getting out of here.

He removes his hand, and there's an obnoxious squelching sound that mortifies me.

Oh my God, could this get any worse?

He brings his fingers between us, and they are slick with my wetness. He puts them in his mouth, shutting his eyes on the taste.

I'm frozen to the wall, flushed and sweaty. The air smells like peppermint and sex as he sucks his fingers clean. They leave his mouth a long moment later with a *pop* that I feel sizzle across my flesh.

"Salted bones and caramel, baby girl," he tells me with a sala-
cious grin. "You're my favorite flavor."

Oh my God, it got worse.

I can't breathe. I can't even think.

"Meet me in the dining hall," he murmurs, pressing a kiss to
my temple. "I need to run an errand. I'm getting a surprise ready
for you, Firefly."

He releases me, turning his back to me, and walking out of
the room. I'm sweaty and out of breath. I can't believe I let him
do that.

Why did I let him do that?

But then again when was the last time I felt desired by
anyone?

A year ago? Maybe more?

And back then, it was just sex. My partner had made that
very clear before we ever fucked. He never cared enough to try
to force me to eat. He never cared at all because I was just a
means to an end, a way for him to get his rocks off, and nothing
more. I don't remember feeling desired when he pulled out of
me, pumped his dick, and came all over my chest. We were
convenient, and we both knew it.

Yet the King of the Asylum makes me feel wanted. He took
care of me, and that is a first. No guy has ever done that. Fuck,
most of my prior partners were content to screw me dry as long
as they could get their dick inside of me.

This was new but nice. It can't happen again, though.

I didn't even know my parts down below still worked. They
definitely do, though, because I can still feel the lingering aftershocks rumbling in my core and the slickness smearing my
thighs.

My periods have always been erratic, probably thanks to
having an eating disorder before I even got my first monthly
cycle. I don't think I've had my period in four months, though,

maybe more. I don't ever count the days. I'd figured all of my parts down there had withered and dried to nothing by now, just like they say the rest of me is doing too.

Salted bones and caramel, huh? It could be worse. He could have said I tasted like death.

He told me to meet him in the dining hall, but how do I face him after that?

How do I see him and his friends and pretend it didn't happen?

I could've run. He was right. I could've run.

He gave me a choice, and I chose to stay.

I messed up because this will go nowhere fast. I'm leaving. My father is no doubt already losing his patience with my lack of progress. The longest I've ever been enrolled anywhere was eight months, and that was because I spent the majority of it in-patient and not at the school. I've been here for almost a few weeks now, and that's when my father always starts asking the difficult questions. The higher the price tag, the more he demands, and no one ever meets his demands, except my mother.

Not me.

Not the places he hires to save me.

No one.

Right now I regret not running from the fire freak. It would've been easier. But it happened so fast, and before I knew it, his hands were on me, and it felt like tiny bolts of lightning shot through his fingertips, electrifying my skin and making me feel something I don't remember ever feeling, not for a long time. His touch made me feel alive.

Then he gave me that look—hooded, soulless eyes and a touch of hedonism—one that he's given probably countless girls before, and I was a goner. He didn't even have to say the words to let me know what he was thinking.

He wanted *me.*

Desired *me.*

And that made me feel something I didn't know I could feel anymore.

I felt coveted, craved even, and I knew my worth.

My mother would say he only likes me because I'm skinny. She'd congratulate me and take credit for the win.

I don't want to think about him, but I do. His smell, campfires and charcoal. His taste, cigarettes with a kiss of peppermint. His eyes, those two black pools that drag me close and hold me captive in their gravity.

I have no hope of escape, not now when I know the feeling of him on me, *in* me. I don't know if I ever did. Maybe before, when he went into isolation, the place the people around here call the hole, and I'm guessing it's because it's such a literal cesspit. I should have seen this coming, but I didn't expect him back so soon or with such an appetite . . . for me.

He acted like I was personally offending him by not taking care of myself and eating properly.

Doesn't he understand, though?

In a world that gives me no power, food is the only thing I have, my one way of controlling my value in the world. My mother drilled it into my brain since I could walk.

No one will love me if I'm fat.

No one will want me.

I will be abandoned and all alone.

I remember the first time I actually thought I would end up alone and discarded by eating the wrong thing. She'd been mad before, of course, but not like that. She was furious. I thought she was going to leave me there, seven years old and thrown away like trash. I remember that day like it was yesterday. Heck, it feels like it was yesterday.

As I stand in the classroom trying to not think of him, I think of her instead, and the memory brings it all back: shame, regret, and fear.

We were on our way somewhere, running errands. I can't remember exactly where, but the car needed gasoline, so my mother pulled off the highway and stopped at a convenience store with gasoline pumps out front.

"Ugh, it's hot out today," she complained, grabbing her billfold from the center console and taking out a five-dollar bill.

"Go inside and get a bottle of Evian," she told me, handing me the bill. "Or whatever has electrolytes. Not any of that flavored crap either. It's horrible for you."

I unbuckled myself, held the five inside my palm, and opened the car door, carefully shutting it after me. She didn't like it when I slammed the doors on her pretty new car. I watched for traffic, but the place was busy, cars darting in and out, and when my path was clear, I walked across the black asphalt and into the big building. People bustled about everywhere, walking here and there, over to the counter selling scoops of ice cream in the back corner and down the aisles that advertised treats my mother would never let me have.

Like a good girl, though, I minded my own business and walked straight to where the drinks were kept in the coolers on the side of the building. I scanned the drinks held behind the glass doors. They probably sold twenty different varieties of water, but they didn't have her favorite brand. I looked for the one I thought she would like the best. It said it was from natural springs, and she always liked things that said they were organic, natural, or whole. Also, it was unflavored, just like she said.

I plucked it from the cooler and walked between the aisles, my attention catching on something on the middle shelf. I stopped walking and stared at a display of Moon Pies. Mother would never let me eat them, but it said it had marshmallows in the middle. My stomach pinched. We had skipped breakfast. She said I could afford to skip breakfast, and it looked so good in the wrapper. It was even my favorite flavor too, chocolate. I only had a five-dollar bill, though, and if I didn't come back with enough change, my mother would know I bought something for myself.

My stomach pinched again and gurgled loudly as the smell of hot dogs turning over in the display wafted over to me. A man at the end of the aisle grabbed a bag of chips that crinkled in the cellophane wrapping.

My middle gurgled again, and I crossed my arms over my stomach. Without another thought, I snatched a Moon Pie right off of the shelf and shoved it beneath my shirt, the movement awkward and clunky. My heart beat like a thumping rabbit inside of my chest as I beelined to the counter and got in line. I waited until it was my turn, and then I sat the water on the counter in front of the register. I could feel the wrapper of the Moon Pie cool and scratchy against my skin. The clerk behind the counter blinked at me, frowning. Wrinkles piled on top of more wrinkles at her forehead, and her fake tan was blotchy at her temples.

"This all you getting today?" she had asked me, chewing on the inside of her cheek like she was a cow, and her cheek was the cud.

She scared me when I looked at her for too long, so I didn't look at her. I just nodded down at the counter and slapped the five-dollar bill in front of her. When she didn't pick it up and instead stared down at it too, looking disgusted, my heart thumped even faster.

"There's nothing else you want to add?" she asked me.

I should have known then. Hell, I should have known before then, but I was a kid, and I stupidly didn't realize.

My voice cracked as I shook my head again.

"No," I managed as a guy walked through the front doors and into the store, ringing the bell tied to the top of the doorframe.

"Where are your parents, kid?" she asked me, still chewing on the inside of her cheek. She let go of it with a loud *squelch*. Another customer joined the line behind me, and his phone rang, loud in the big open store.

"Hello," he answered, practically yelling. He sounded like my grandfather before he had died, when he couldn't hear anymore and shouted at everyone all of the time.

"Hey, kid," the lady behind the counter snapped her fingers in front of my face, her ruby red nails were chipped at the ends. My mother would snicker behind her back and tell her to take better care of herself. "Who brought you here? Your mom or your dad?"

I turned and looked out the window at my mother, still pumping gas into her convertible, an anniversary gift from my father. She was talking on her cellphone, as she finished pumping gasoline and put the nozzle back on the machine, where it was supposed to go.

"Billy," the lady said behind the counter, calling to someone in the back. She rang up the total for my water quickly and slid the change across the counter to me. "I'll be right back."

A man ducked out from behind a cigarette display.

"Watch the register?" he asked her.

"Yeah," she confirmed.

He nodded. "No problem, boss."

The old lady walked around the counter and grabbed me by the back of my shirt, reeling me in close. I could feel the people in the store looking at us now, and my cheeks flushed with heat. It felt like they were on fire as a bunch of strangers stared at us.

"I know you stole it," she hissed at me, "you little brat. Didn't your parents teach you any better than that?"

"I'll pay," I told her quickly, shoving the dollars back at her. When she didn't take them, I threw them at her chest, dollars and coins falling to the floor. A quarter rolled into the boot of the man on his phone, and he backed away a little from it, looking confused. The bottle of water went bouncing into a candy display.

The woman sneered, and I could see all of her small, yellow teeth. She had a smile better suited for a rodent than a human. She took one look at the money littered across the floor and scoffed.

"It's too late for that," she said to me before she gripped the back of my shirt even tighter and dragged me across the tile and out of the front double doors. The sun was bright when it hit my eyes, and the asphalt baked in the sun, steaming beneath the heat of summer. The air smelled like gasoline and evaporated rain as I struggled against the lady, the Moon Pie still plastered to my skin. The hot pavement caught against the toes of my sneakers as she dragged me across the pavement. She was stronger than she looked.

An excruciating moment later, she delivered me in front of my mother, who was still on the phone My mother's bright blue eyes went wide as she told my father, "Benjamin, I'm going to need to call you back."

"Is this your little brat?" the lady practically shouted as my mother hung up the phone.

The cashier shoved me forward so that my head hit my mother before she steered me to her side. Then my mother straightened, and she looked the lady in the eye as she said her next words.

"Yes," she answered her. "What did she go?"

"Stole something," the mean lady hissed. "Got it hid underneath her shirt."

Oh no.

I backed away from my mother, and I would've given anything in that moment to be able to disappear, but God didn't favor me back then, not that he does now either. My mother snatched my wrist and pulled me in close to her.

"What did you do?" she hissed. "What did you steal, piggy?"

Her hands patted me down, hard and fast. My sides, my butt, my arms, and my pockets, until her fingers hit my chest, and the Moon Pie crinkled. It felt like the entire world disappeared out from under me when she found it.

She shoved her cold, thin hand up my shirt and grabbed the treat before she dropped it to the pavement like it burned her. My face burned along with it.

The lady from behind the counter scoffed as my mother grabbed me by the shoulders and demanded, "Why would you do that? Are you a pig or a human, Avery? Can you not control yourself?"

I felt the tears prick at the corners of my eyes first, and I started to cry as my mother released me, disgusted.

"What does she owe you for this?" my mother asked as she stepped forward and crushed the pie beneath the heel of her pump.

"The rest of what she left inside will be enough," the lady said, looking at me and gloating. "I just wanted to make sure you knew what she did."

Even now the memory brings shame, but there's something there that covers it like a shadow stretching before nightfall.

Wetness slicks between my thighs as the lingering glow of my orgasm from the creep's hands fades. It makes me wonder if maybe I'm not a piggy, after all, that maybe I'm desired and worth it.

I push off the wall and leave the room to walk to the cafeteria. When I enter, I don't see Gabe at his table in the middle of the room with his friends. His throne still sits empty. I hold my head high as I walk to the line and grab a tray.

Maybe tomorrow I'll let my mother win, but right now I'm winning.

Maybe it's thanks to him.

Or to this place.

Or something inside of me that he has awoken.

I don't know, but I do know for the first time in a long time I don't hear my mother *oink* when I sit down to eat and stab at the salad on my plate.

15

AVERY

I finish the side salad on my tray, skipping the lump of spaghetti with a dinner roll beside it, and eye my mandarin oranges in a plastic cup. The rest of the eating disorder students at the table are avoiding the spaghetti and rolls too and instead poking at their salads and orange slices with their silicone forks. I look over at the table where Gabe normally sits, but he's still not there.

He said he was getting a surprise ready for me, but what is it?

No one ever surprises me with anything. My parents send me money at Christmastime and on my birthday, but it's always the same amount each year.

I'm actually kind of excited, and that's dangerous for a girl like me. I survive by not getting attached. No connections, no names, and no regrets.

Stop it, Avery.

You can't get all excited because a hot guy tells you he has a surprise for you. He's a psychopath with a fire fetish, which means it could be a bad surprise like a box of ashes, a severed finger, or, even worse, his dick in a box. For Christ's sake, you're in a mental institution, and he is crazy! Stop thinking about him!

Move. On.

You know where this leads, and it's a one-way street to rejection and pain.

You are leaving this place!

I suffocate the treasonous thoughts and swallow hard, pulling back the plastic lid on the mandarin oranges.

One slice in its own juice, five calories.

I plop one into my mouth and chew. I've eaten more at this meal than I have eaten in a long time, but I have an appetite for once, which is weird. I thought it had withered and died with all of my lady bits. I'm only ever hungry anymore when I'm about to pass out and hit the floor. Maybe his touch restarted that fire inside of me too.

Stop. It. Avery.

"You," a guard barks, coming up behind me, "walk with me. Headmistress wants to see you."

I stand as another guard takes my tray away to be weighed. My gaze immediately flicks to his table again, but his seat directly across from his probably-a-serial-killer friend is still empty. This time when I look, I catch the eyes of the only girl who ever sits with them, the one who wears the leather collar. Willow, I think her name is.

A smile haunts her lips as she looks at me, her laughter at something her creepy boyfriend has said dying in the cavernous room. She doesn't look disgusted by me, though. If anything, her gaze flicks from Gabe's empty seat to me and then back again. She just looks sort of sad as she does it, like she wishes he was there for me too, like she somehow understands why I'm looking for him. Is that what she feels for the boy who's currently playing with her collar? Does she crave his presence? I shouldn't care, just like I shouldn't crave the creep's touch, but I do.

Stop. It!

"Come on," the guard pushes, grabbing me by the elbow and steering me away from the table.

"I'm coming," I tell her, and she releases me, letting me walk beside her as we leave the dining room and start toward Headmistress Grave's office. It doesn't take long to get there, seven or eight minutes maybe, and then we're in the room that smells like moth balls again. There's an old lady behind the long desk that stretches across the space, her blue-tinged hair in a tight bun atop her head. She frowns at me as we walk inside.

"Name?" she asks.

"Bardot," the guard answers for me. "Headmistress said to bring her here immediately."

The old lady walks around, her foot hitching on the floor with a limp I don't remember her having before. She swings open the built-in door in the desk and steers me down another hall. We walk the distance to Headmistress's office, and I knock on the door.

The ancient woman side-eyes me. I guess she wanted to do that.

"Come inside," Headmistress barks from the other side.

I swallow the knot in my throat and resist the urge to wring my fingers together in front of me as I open the door and walk into the room. I wanted this, right? Surely, my father is taking me away from here and sending me somewhere else, far away from the creep with bottomless, inky eyes and sparks of fire in his fingertips capable of setting my skin ablaze.

Her office is just as it was last week, a large, cold tomb. The door shuts behind me, and Headmistress gestures to the leather chairs in front of her desk.

"Sit," she tells me. "Now Avery."

Well, this can't be good.

Normally, by this point, the administration is already being sickly sweet to me and arguing with my father about why he can't have his money back.

I take a seat, and Headmistress drags her office phone across her desk to her. The buttons on the phone light up like traffic lights flashing in the dead of night, blinking all at once.

"I have your parents on the phone," she tells me, her lips thinning into a wan frown. "It appears you've lost weight since you've joined us."

She hits buttons on the phone, and abruptly, I can hear my father breathing and my mother giggling. I know he's angry just from the air he's currently expelling. My mother only giggles when she drinks, and she only drinks at the country club.

"Mr. and Mrs. Bardot," Headmistress says, "thank you for joining me today. We are here to talk about your daughter. It appears Avery has continued to lose weight since joining us, and it is time to discuss the next steps in our treatment plan."

My father curses on the other end of the line, and I want to tell him that it's okay, I ate today. I saw the food, calculated the calories, and I ate it regardless. Well, some of it, at least, but I don't say anything as my mother scoffs, probably sipping low-calorie mimosas this early in the afternoon.

"What am I paying you people for?" my father nearly shouts, and there it is, the big question, the one that always gets me pulled from places like this one.

Headmistress glares at the phone and then over her desk at me. Her eyes turn into beady little cannonballs in the right light, and it feels like she's aiming them at me right now.

"You are paying us, Mr. Bardot, because Chryseum does not fail our students, ever. We will resort to the most extreme measures to make sure this doesn't happen again." She continues to glare at me. "Is that understood, Avery?"

"Yes, ma'am," I mutter through clenched teeth.

My mother cackles at something someone says. She's probably flirting with the pool boy. I'm sure her laughter puts my father in an even worse mood. He hates when he's confronted with the truth that she's not as nice and perfect as she looks.

"How much weight did she lose this time?" my father demands.

"Three pounds," Headmistress answers, looking down at her notes.

"It's just three pounds," my mother tells her, her laughter fading from her lips. "Calm down, Benjamin. She will be fine."

"With all due respect, Mrs. Bardot," Headmistress Graves murmurs, "your daughter didn't have three pounds to lose."

"She did the last time I saw her," my mother quips before she guffaws so violently she snorts. My father curses again on the other end of the line, probably planning to pour his own drink, a whiskey neat, soon enough.

"Do what you have to," he tells Headmistress, "but I expect results at our next check-in, or you can forget about the installment payment, Ms. Graves."

He disconnects from the call without another word while my mother laughs and snorts, somehow finding humor in his threat. Headmistress hangs up the phone.

This should make me happy.

This is everything I wanted, right?

Leave and let the cycle repeat.

No connections, no friends, no intimacy of any kind. I guess I already fucked that up this morning, though. I should have run from him.

Phone calls like this one are my father's own canon event at this point, only he's stuck, having to live his reckoning over and over again because he never learns and finds a way forward. He refuses to see the truth that I can only come home if she's not there.

Headmistress Graves glares at me from over her desk.

"From now on," she tells me, looking positively murderous, "you will not leave the cafeteria for one hour after consuming meals. If you are not showing progress by Friday, you will be transferred to the isolation ward to be observed by Dr. Boucher and to receive forced nutrition. Is that understood?"

"Yes ma'am," I answer as she reaches into her desk and pulls out a porcelain tea plate and a plastic bag of the things she called nutrition cubes. She leans back in her chair across from me, placing one cube after another onto the plate until it's stacked high with them. There has to be at least twenty of the cubes on it at this point, maybe even more. I'm going to be sick if she makes me choke down all of them.

"Eat," she tells me, and it shouldn't be a surprise. It isn't a surprise, but it still feels like a shock to the system just the same. My throat closes, my mouth goes dry, and my stomach pinches inside of me at the thought.

It's too much.

She leans across her desk, flattening her palms on the smooth, dark wood.

"If I have to get up from this desk," she tells me, "you will eat double what is in front of you right now, Avery."

I believe her. I grab a cube and pop it into my mouth. It's disgustingly sweet on my tongue, and I barely chew it before forcing it down my throat. I eat them as fast as I can, trying to think of anything but the calorie count.

Grab, chew, swallow, repeat.

I don't know what number I'm on, but crumbs stick to my chin and fall onto my lap as I eat the cubes, swallowing them faster and faster, desperate to get it over with until finally, the plate is clear. I'm done, but I think I might throw up. My stomach churns, and I bury the urge to vomit. If I throw them up, God only knows what she's going to do.

"Get out of my office." She waves her hand, dismissing me.

"And remember, Avery, if I have to, I will shove the fucking food down your throat myself."

The thought makes me shiver as she says it.

Unlike Gabe, I know she doesn't give a damn about me. Maybe he doesn't either, but at least he's not trying to profit off me and take advantage of my disease.

"What do you say?" she snaps as I stand, trying to not be sick.

"Yes, ma'am," I manage before I leave the room.

Maybe this is for the best. Surely, my father wouldn't let them force-feed me, not again, not after the last incident when the prior school sent me to the hospital and the nurse shoved the tube down into my lungs instead of my stomach and almost killed me.

Do they even bother to make sure it's in the right place here?

Or are you counted as a success story if they kill you instead of you killing yourself?

As I walk away from her office, tears blurring my vision, I tell myself that this is for the best. I don't care if I have to think about it a thousand times before I believe it. I don't need the creep to save me. I don't belong here.

The plan has always been to move on when my father got sick of paying these people and sent me somewhere new.

What do I have, realistically? Two, maybe three, more transfers until I graduate high school, and by then I think my father will be sick of me. He'll give up on this quest to save me. He'll have no choice but to give up.

I walk down the hall, my lunch and the cubes sitting like a lead ball in my stomach. Bile scrapes at my esophagus, and I cough and choke down the desperate urge to throw up. I'm walking down the hall, trying to not be sick, when the creep arrives at my side like he threw off his invisibility cloak to show himself to me.

"Come with me," he says, looking at the guard up ahead of us. "I have a surprise for you, baby girl."

"No, thanks," I quip, sniffling.

A clean break is easier for what's to come. I should have run this morning instead of giving in to him.

"Why are you crying?" he asks, looking over at me with a frown.

"I'm not crying," I tell him, my words a lie and my tone flat. "It looks like I'm leaving this place, fire freak. I'm happy."

He stops walking, catching my arm and dragging me to a stop with him.

"What did you say?" he asks me.

"My father isn't happy with my lack of progress," I tell him. "He'll send me somewhere new in a couple of weeks."

"Unacceptable," he murmurs. "We were just getting started."

"Listen," I tell him, damming up the rest of my unshed tears, "I'd love to say it's been fun, but it really hasn't been. Better luck in the next life, but it's time to face the truth. I'll never be one of your groupies, Gabe."

I shouldn't have called him by his name. It's too personal, and I shouldn't have mentioned the girls who fawn over him, smiling at him in the halls and practically throwing themselves at his feet.

I shouldn't have admitted that I noticed it.

He doesn't call me out on any of it. He just grabs my wrist, reels me in close, and lets his words pepper my face with heat.

"No," he murmurs down to me, "you're worth more than any of them."

There it is again, that fire shooting through me at his touch.

"Let go of me," I say to him.

"No." With one hand, he pushes open the door to my left and drags me inside an empty classroom.

"What are you doing?" I ask him, wrestling free of his grip and backing away from him. "I told you I'm leaving this place."

"The hell you fucking are," he snarls, stepping forward. "The game's just getting good, baby girl."

"What is wrong with you? Do you not understand the English language? I am leaving. Why are you so obsessed with me?"

"Don't pretend you don't feel the pull," he says with another step. "I will set your pretty ass on fire. Don't think I won't." He reaches into his pocket, grabs his lighter, flips the lid, and starts the flame. "You are mine, Firefly."

It makes me laugh.

"The hell I am. I'm not your property. I'm nothing to you. You don't even know my last name."

"Bardot," he guesses correctly.

When the hell did he learn that?

He grabs a discarded piece of paper off a desk and holds it up to the flame. My eyes go wide as I watch the piece of paper blaze, and then even wider as I watch him continue to hold it.

I stare at the burning piece of paper and so does he before he tears his gaze away to watch me instead.

Memories live in the flame he's holding.

Of a car wreck.

And the crackle of glass.

And me begging my mother to wake up.

Fuck. I'm definitely going to be sick.

"Do you think I won't do it?" he asks me.

"I think you're crazy," I tell him. I take a step back, and he takes a step forward. "I think you shouldn't care what I do to me or my body."

"I care," he hisses, still holding the burning paper, "because you disobey me. You drive me nuts. You make me work for it, and then you dare damage what is mine."

Finally, he drops the smoking paper with a hiss as the flames reach his fingertips.

"I'll never say yes," I tell him as he swallows the distance between us.

He yanks me around the middle, pulling me flush against him.

"It's okay. You don't have to say the words, baby girl," he tells me. "Your pussy already did that for you this morning."

He flattens his mouth to mine, kissing me brutally. He sucks the air out of me and fucks my mouth with his tongue until my chest aches for breath and all of me burns for him. Only then does he break the kiss and say, "You taste like sugar, Firefly."

It's ironic, I think, for me to taste sweet.

He thinks he's won. But he's playing a game he doesn't understand.

I can't be his because I won't even be here in a few short weeks.

16

GABE

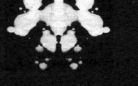

This girl with pretty bones and hair the color of fire is quickly becoming a massive pain in my ass. The day after she tells me her parents are going to pull the plug on letting Headmistress try to fix her, she disappears for a week.

A whole *fucking* week.

I feel personally offended, attacked even.

I barely even muster the energy to laugh my ass off when Dean and Zane beat the shit out of each other in the hallway again, making the floor look like bloody Carrie just transferred in and hasn't had a chance to shower yet. One of them is going to need a transfusion after that shit.

While she's gone, I burn through a lighter every forty-eight hours, which is impressive but also has me questioning the quality of Marshall's contraband. Then again, I've only been igniting them every ten seconds or so for hours on end. The bottom of my fucking finger looks like it got toasted extra crispy by the fire nozzle, and I think I smell fried chicken now every time I light up.

I can't eat.

I can't sleep.

I can't even jerk off because my pansy ass is worried that they're going to steal my Firefly away.

There's too much fucking noise, and it all revolves around her. I smoke a carton of cigarettes and then have to raid Saint's stash to get through until the end of the month when Marshall can bring in more again. My bro's going to freak when he realizes his cigs are gone, and it's a good thing we aren't roommates. Else he'd probably try to suffocate me with a pillow or some shit. On second thought, the dude would definitely use his hands so he could see my face and feel the crunch. That's what I'd do if I were him.

One week feels like ten weeks, and it's driving me insane, even though I know where she went. Her daddy must be paying the Asylum a lot of money for all the bells and whistles they've rolled out for her. She has no free time between classes anymore, or very little of it, at least. Guards are with her from the moment she steps foot into the line for meds each morning, always carting her off somewhere else and onto the next thing.

I've sat back and watched as she's been taken to group therapy and cognitive-behavioral therapy with the mind docs and then nutritional counseling sessions with the nurse. They even brought in Dr. Boucher one day to do a consultation or some shit. I hated it for her. It's not fair to meet his ancient ass outside of the hole because it's like watching a lion behind the fence at the zoo. You don't realize how dangerous the lion is because he's not in his natural habitat. He looks tame by comparison, but if he jumps that fence, he's going to eat you alive.

God knows what her father promised Headmistress if they cured her. I can't remember the last time they pulled out this many stops for anyone, not even that heir to the English throne who graduated last year. Granted he had like one hundred forty-nine people in front of him who had to all perish before he could be the King of England, but still, he had royal blood, even if it was only a teensy, tiny amount only visible under a strong microscope.

If all that wasn't bad enough, the administration is still forcing all the rexie students to eat together too, though they now keep her an hour after she's done with her tray, probably to make sure she doesn't send their hard work directly into the nearest toilet.

Every minute of her day lately has been pre-planned and all of it designed to ensure she will be cured, which is stupid. These fucks don't seem to understand that I'm the only one who can fix her now. They've tried and failed, and it takes one broken person to understand another, and despite what Avery may think, I do understand her.

At the end of the day, we both lack control. She needs to control what she eats, and I need to control her. Maybe her parents fucked her up like mine did me, I don't know. But I'm sick of her pretending like we aren't the same.

She measures her self-worth in calories. I measure mine by how many words I can figure out on the page. She hates herself, but I hate myself even more. She regains control by controlling what she puts into her body. I regain mine by controlling her.

We both need a fresh start, and the best way to do that is to cleanse all the bad shit away with the flame. This time I think when I get her alone, I might actually light her ass on fire because my patience is wearing thin.

I need to fix her, but I'd prefer if she agreed to come with me voluntarily. If I force her, her paper-thin self-esteem might incinerate in an instant, and if that happens, she'll be lost to me for good.

It's a fine line I'm walking, giving her a choice to come with me to the basement, while also not giving her one at all. I'm the worst type of good guy, the one who tricks you into submission before you even realize you've been misled.

She'll call me more than a creep before this is all said and done. I'll be a freak, a bully, a sadist, and more. I don't care, though. She can believe I'm the devil itself if it stops her from killing herself.

The school staff is wasting precious time I could be using to save her.

I just need to get her alone.

At the thought, my hand reaches into my pocket, and I play with my Zippo, opening the lid and starting the flame, over and over again. I hold my finger against the flame nozzle as I roll the wheel with my thumb and hit the button at the same time, burning that spot on the underside of my finger again and again, like I always do. Either the skin is going to get even tougher by the time I manage to get her alone, or I'm going to burn a hole down to the bone.

I don't have much time to act, but I think my best chance might be during shift change when the dumbass guards from the first shift fill in the dumbass guards from the second shift. I'm in the deserted hallway outside her group therapy class with my back against the wall as I wait for her to come out with all of the other students who like to starve themselves. Speaking of, I'm fucking starving, having skipped breakfast and lunch to stalk her like an actual creep since six this morning. I snatched a bag of salt-n-vinegar potato chips from the vending machines twenty minutes ago, but they taste like they're original to the building. I'm going to chip a tooth on this trash, but I shove the last of my chips into my mouth and toss the wrapper in the trash bin. I know from the cigarette butt incident in the bathroom on her first day of school that she doesn't like it when I litter on the floor.

Why do I care?

What is happening to me?

I stand there some more, feeling like a dumbass as I stare at the doors and start to wonder if her session is ever going to let out. Then the doors finally open and out she walks, the first one to flee therapy. The light from the windows that line the exterior wall hits her just right, sending starbursts dancing through her hair. Her bright blue eyes are pinned straight ahead, oblivious to me, as I press off the wall and walk until I arrive behind her.

"Hey, baby girl," I tell her, throwing an arm around her shoulders and bringing her in for a side hug.

She yelps, and it's like music to my ears. It's nice catching her by surprise. I didn't realize how much I missed the thrill of doing that.

As I hold her tight, though, I notice that her shoulders feel even bonier today. I reach over with my free hand and pinch her side. I hit a rib.

Fuck.

I think she might've lost even more weight.

"Let go of me!" she hisses, trying to pull away from me.

"No thanks," I say, tipping my chin at her. "Offer rejected."

She tries to dart away, but I hold her a little tighter and murmur my next words against the shell of her ear. Her hair smells like strawberries today, and I suck it in greedily.

"I will burn this goddamned place to the ground if you don't stop it," I tell her.

She looks at me like she's not sure if I'll do it. She should know better than that.

I grab the lighter—rolling the wheel and pressing the button at the same time—and bring the flame to her abdomen, a couple of inches away from her. She stops struggling. Well, technically, she stops moving entirely. She falls victim to Elsa and freezes to the floor. I stop walking too, and it becomes a whole thing.

What is her deal with a little bit of fire?

I've got to rid her of this asap. She's missing out.

"How long do you think it'll take them to find a fire extinguisher?" I murmur down to her, letting my breath tickle her hair. "Remember to stop, drop, and roll, baby girl."

"What in the actual fuck is wrong with you?" she hisses, snapping out of it to cock her head at me.

"What do you think happens when you don't comply around here?" I clap back. "Do you think you get to go home? No one leaves this place, Avery. They will tie you down to the table and force a tube down your throat to feed you. They will set up IVs. They will bring in doctors and specialists. I don't know how many more ways I can say it, but you aren't going home, not unless it's in a cap and gown or in a pine board box."

"My father will take me out of here," she tells me.

Lord, is she really this dense?

Apparently so.

"If it comes down to it, Headmistress Graves will lie through her bleached teeth. Look at all the stops they're already pulling out, baby girl. They will make sure your daddy finances the next wing in this place. She'll tell him you're making progress, that you are doing better, until they can figure out what to do with you. You think you're the only person who's tried to leave the Academy? No one leaves, not unless they graduate or they die. End of story."

Her mouth drops open like it hadn't even occurred to her that Headmistress would lie to make a buck, my sweet, naïve Firefly. It always takes a baseball bat to beat that lesson into the new students' brains. Chryseum isn't like the standard preparatory or reformatory schools. No one here follows the same rules or abides by the same standards. This place is literally the last resort, and they take advantage of that fact.

"Now come with me," I tell her. "We're going to the basement."

"No," she shakes her head, "it's forbidden."

This again?

I shrug. "It's only forbidden if they find out. And they're not going to find out."

She doesn't move.

"What's wrong?" I ask her with a grin. "Afraid of being alone with me?"

"You've threatened to set me on fire enough, I should be," she deadpans.

Ouch . . .

Burn.

Ha!

"I'm not going to set you on fire in the basement," I tell her.

Not until you beg for the flash paper, and I light you up.

She doesn't look convinced, so I add, "There's no open air down there, and I don't feel like suffocating today, m'kay?"

It's a half-truth, but she doesn't need to know that. It's true that there are no windows in the basement, but I've set plenty of fires down there, just like I used to with . . .

Don't think of her.

Too late.

Aisling's face detonates in my brain, and I hate her for haunting me. She's dead and gone, and it's her own fucking fault. Avery reminds me of her—ninety percent attitude and ten percent infuriating—except Avery is afraid of the flame, not enchanted by it. And Aisling never could quiet my noise. If anything, she made it even louder.

"I don't trust you," she tells me.

So her IQ is in the triple digits. Good to know.

"What's the worst I can do?" I tease with a wink.

For the record, I can do a hell of a lot, but she doesn't know that, not yet. I see her imagination try to run wild and watch as it trips over its own two feet. That's okay. My imagination more than makes up for it.

Cages and cells.

Mirrors and mirage images.

Floggings and flash paper.

Branding and burns.

It almost makes me cream my pants thinking about it. I bite my tongue to bury my moan.

Like I said, there's a hell of a lot I plan to do with her. I watch as she mulls it over. She's curious, but she knows what, proverbially, killed the cat.

The longer I stare at her, the more I'm certain she's going to make me do it.

That's all right, though.

I'll be the villain. Heroes haven't done a damn thing for her anyway.

17

GABE

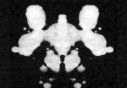

I wanted her to have her choice, but she's forcing my hand. I can't wait for her to decide to go with me. I may never get another chance. I don't have time to give her the illusion of control. I have to find another way.

"Don't make me do it," I tell her.

When she looks at me stupidly, I repeat my statement, the words flat and dead, just like my soul. "Don't make me do it."

Now I have to say I don't care if she makes me do it. I'm just feeling remarkably lazy and very hungry. I need a snack, a nap, and to fuck her. Well, not in that order.

She blinks her guileless blue eyes, the color of spring rain, at me.

She's going to make me do it.

Sighs.

The guards normally wouldn't care, but they've been so far up her ass lately that I'd rather not blatantly draw attention to ourselves, even during shift change. I can't risk being sent to the hole, not now, when she could be gone before I have a chance to make sure she stays. Sure, Headmistress would lie to her father first, if necessary, to continue milking the cash cow, but who's to say her father isn't a total moron and sees right through her bullshit? I'm not willing to risk everything.

I always try to use the empty classrooms, the abandoned hallways, and the places where I know the staff isn't looking. Shift change is almost over, though, and our little homestead in hell is getting crowded. The hall fills with students and staff members, and I pocket the lighter in an instant before one of them wakes up and notices.

She's making me do it. It's her own fault.

Ugh, fiiiiiinnnnnnnneeeeeee.

In one second flat, I capture her by the arm and yank her down the hallway. In another two seconds, we're around the corner. Three seconds later, I have her between me and the stone wall, in the spot where the light doesn't quite reach and the shadows take over. I've got one hand pressed tightly against her throat, almost but not quite cutting off her air. I pluck my lighter back out of my pocket, and in one fluid motion, I roll the wheel, press the button, and ignite the flame.

It's mesmerizing.

I shouldn't look.

It's too late.

I bring it to the bottom of her chin, and she squirms, trying to get away. I'm already there, though, at the spot where her head meets her throat, and she goes utterly still. I let it singe the nearly invisible hairs there. She hisses as I watch it broil the flesh. Tears spring to her eyes, and she tries to scream, but I'm holding too hard. She doesn't have enough air to yell for help.

The flame is gorgeous, dancing in front of me as it licks her flesh. Orange and yellow melt together, gyrating in a slow dance, against her pale skin. I'm in awe, amazed, and my cock is rockhard as I watch it lave at her skin, burning its mark and cooking her. I watch it spread.

Repress, Gabriel.

I watch a moment longer.

Fucking repress!

With some effort, I release the button and let the flame die. She sucks in a breath between her clenched teeth as I force her head up, admiring my handiwork.

There, along the bottom of her chin, a pink welt starts to blister. It makes me want to whip out my dick and come all over the disfigured flesh. It would only take a couple of pumps before I exploded.

The mark defiles her.

It screams she is mine.

It is *everything.*

The air smells like barbecued meat and smoke and her.

Fffuuuuccccckkkkk.

She whimpers, and I realize she's shaking. I may be a psychopath, but on a scale of one to sadist, I'm like an eighty-five on the antisocial personality disorder chart. I'd love to watch her burn. I want to watch her burn. But I also want her to *want* to burn with me.

"Shh, baby girl," I tell her as I move my hand from around her throat to her hair and yank it down, further exposing the wound to me. I force her head to the side and press my lips to her skin, sucking on the burn. She tastes like ashes and salt as I lave my tongue against the wound.

She squeezes her eyes shut and goes completely and utterly still.

The fuck?

I back away a little and look at her.

This is unexpected. Sure, I knew she was afraid of a little fire play, but why does she have doll eyes now and look dead inside?

"Avery?" I ask her.

No response.

I let go of her and repeat her name.

Again, no response.

I snap my fingers in front of her face.

Still no response.

Uh oh.

I can't believe my Firefly went fucking catatonic. Saint and Kill are never going to let me live this down. On second thought, they don't need to know.

There are guards and students walking down the hallway, and I've bought myself a little time. I made sure the cameras were still down from the last time a student torched the server room before I came here.

Is she breathing? *Yes.*

Is she blinking? *Not that I can tell.*

What the fuck.

I shake her a little, and there's nothing. Avery's gone, and she left her shell behind.

Note to self, maybe warn her next time before you whip out your lighter and mark her with it. I was just trying to make her a little more agreeable, though I didn't mean to make her *this* agreeable.

I snap my fingers in front of her face again. Still, there's no response.

Goddammit.

This complicates matters, and the noise at the back of my skull is getting louder with each passing second as the buzz of students and guards fills the hallway. Somebody laughs, and it feels like nails to the chalkboard of my brain.

I have to make a decision.

I'm either going to have to leave her here or do something with her. Since the guards will be looking for her soon enough, my decision is made for me.

Well, I guess a little sightseeing never hurt anybody. She can

agree when she wakes up, and we aren't both in the hole. I grab
her hand, and thank everything she can still walk as I steer her to
one of the employee-only passageways kept under lock and key.
There's only one way to the basement, the others having been
sealed off ages ago, and the way down begins here.

I pull out my badge, stolen from the employee locker rooms
on the fifth floor, and swipe it across the card reader. The door
unlocks with a click and a green light on the card reader. I push
her inside and down we go, our shoes loud on the stone stairs.

I send a quick text to the boys to take care of shit for me. I
make sure it goes through before we descend farther. The
already limited cell network doesn't work at all underground.
Most of the tunnels that wind through this place, snaking
through its seams, don't go to the basement. Hell, no one goes to
the basement if they know what's good for them.

We head down the stairs until we reach the end of the line.
From there, I push open a door and drag her with me down the
dark hall. Down here, it's just old emergency lighting on motion
sensors, and as we move, the lights click on, illuminating the
next twenty or so feet. One of these days, the light at the end of
the hall is going to click on, and I'm pretty sure a clown with
sharp teeth is going to show his face and smile.

That would be cool.

We could make plans together.

We veer into another damp dark room, and Avery starts to
snap out of whatever state she's in and starts to struggle. She
takes a lazy swipe at me as I force her down the hall and through
another door. Most students don't even know this place exists,
but I've explored every inch of it. The tunnels are Saint's terri-
tory and the graves are Kill's. Me, though? I like the darkness and
the smell of wet decay like I've entered a catacomb.

We go down another flight of stairs, and this one doesn't have
the motion sensor lights like before. A single line of incandes-

cent bulbs hangs from the ceiling. They turn on with a buzz when I flip the light switch.

Her breathing is loud with panic seeping into each breath, as I drag her farther into the depths with me.

I push open the heavy metal door at the bottom of the stairs, and it screeches noisily. The lights are scattered now, some of the bulbs broken, and a patchwork of shadows stretches across the stone ceiling.

"Where are we?" she asks slowly. "How did I get here?"

"The basement," I say, giving her a half-answer as I tug her forward.

"Why?"

I don't need to explain. She'll figure it out.

Cells line the walls on either side of the massive room, their rusting metal bars touching the ceiling. They're finished on the north end but unfinished on the south.

I throw her a bone.

"In the early 1900s," I tell her, "after the typhus hospital shut down, this building sat vacant for years, but then the state came in. They wanted to convert it into a jail, and they put a lot of money into it before the Great Depression hit and everything went belly up. This building has had many lives, baby girl. We're just in its newest reincarnation."

"I don't want to be here," she says. "It's creepy."

She can't leave yet. She hasn't seen my surprise.

Her shoes clack against the stone, echoing in the massive space, as we reach the north end of the basement. I steer her into one of the empty cells, its steel bars flaked with rust.

"We'll go upstairs in a minute," I lie. "It's beautiful, right?"

"More like terrifying," she murmurs.

She steps inside the cell, curiosity winning out, and somewhere far above here, I think I hear one of the forgotten souls in solitary scream.

She ventures farther into the cell. Her fingers trail the bars that comprise three of the walls before she reaches the stone wall at the back and stops touching things. I grab the lantern I had Marshall smuggle in ages ago and light the flame. It starts instantly.

She reaches the bed hidden in the corner where the light from above doesn't quite reach, and she stops walking.

"I think I've seen enough," she says, abruptly starting for the cell door.

With one hand, I shut it behind us, lock the bolt, and pocket the key.

Her eyes go wide, and she walks over to the cell door, pulling on it. It doesn't open. She gapes at me.

"What have you done?" she pulls again, panic bleeding into the words.

She pulls again and again until she groans with the force and digs her heels against the floor. I stand there and watch her until, many minutes later, she finally tires her frail frame. Out of breath and defeated, her hands slip from the bars, and she falls back onto her ass, *hard*.

It must hurt. It's not like she has much back there to pad the fall. She starts to cry, and maybe I should feel bad, but I don't. Only one thought passes through my mind.

She's gorgeous when she cries. She'll be breathtaking when she burns.

"Let me go, Gabe," she murmurs, looking at me, bleary-eyed from her tears. "*Please.*"

"I can't do that," I tell her, leaning against the metal bars behind me. "You know I can't do that."

"Why?" She jumps to her feet, bolts to the nearest panel of bars, and pulls with all of her might. She's playing a game of tug of war she has no hopes of ever winning. It doesn't even budge.

"You can't leave until you're cured," I tell her, stepping away from the wall. "They're going to take you from me, and I can't allow that. You want to live, Avery. You don't want to die. They will let you die, eventually, but I'll never give up on you, baby girl."

She roars with her anger, raises both hands, and bounds forward to push me.

"Let me go!" she shouts. "Let me out of here!"

She hits me, pummeling her small fists against my chest. I barely even feel the blows.

"Not until you're better," I tell her.

She continues to strike me, again and again and again. I let her. She pummels at my chest, arms, shoulders, and pectorals until finally, she exhausts herself, which isn't long. She drops to her knees in front of me, sweating and out of breath.

"What do I have to do?" she asks me, crying.

"Beg me for it," I tell her, repeating the words I murmured to her once before. She looks up at me again. Only this time she isn't perfect. She's snot-nosed, teary-eyed, and red-faced. "*Grovel*, baby girl."

She looks like she might actually do it this time. I'll be disappointed if she does, but she never disappoints me. That fire ignites inside of her again, just like I want it to. It's going to keep her alive while she's down here. She scrambles to stand in front of me, looking positively manic.

Good. I want her feral and fucking unhinged.

"Fuck you!" she screams at me.

She tries to hit me again, but I don't let her this time. I spin her around, pin her arms flat to her sides, and force her head back to admire my surprise. I hold her against me, letting her appreciate my handiwork for herself, and I know the moment she realizes the full extent of it. Above us, painstakingly hung and suspended, are a hundred mirrors, maybe more. Some are true mirrors, hard to come by in this place, and others are just reflective surfaces, sheets of metal and thick plastic that bend and distort our bodies.

"What is this?" she asks me, still breathing heavily as we look up at a hundred versions of ourselves, our bodies cut and diced like lunch meat.

Half of me holding her.

One eye and a slice of her face staring down at us.

Her skin and bones held in place by me.

"See us together, baby girl," I whisper against her hair as I stare along with her. "See yourself for what you are."

"I can't," she squeaks, but there are too many of them. She can't fool herself in every single one. She starts to shake against me.

"You are more than your reflection," I continue as she starts to unravel. "You are mine."

Then she looks at the hundreds of faces of herself and screams.

18

AVERY

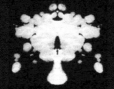

I don't know how long I'm there, held by the creep and caged inside his prison. I stare with him, his arms wrapped around me, as we both look up at the quilt of mirrors blanketing the ceiling. Where are my chubby cheeks and the roundness of my face? What happened to my belly and the puffiness around my throat? The longer I stare, the more I don't recognize what I see.

Is this how he sees me?

Blue eyes made even bluer by the dark circles beneath them?

Hollow cheeks that curve around the bone?

A skeleton of my former self?

What happened to me?

When did I start to die?

It hurts to look at and know the truth, to not see the image of the overweight girl staring back at me. I think I preferred her over this.

We stand there, one of his arms around my middle, holding me in place, and the other beneath my chin, making me look at the mirrors.

The images distort and change, dysmorphia ebbing and flowing with the tide of each of my breaths. He lets go of me eventually and walks over to the bed in the corner of the cell on a rickety metal frame that looks like it might collapse at any moment. I don't know how I didn't see it before, but I watch him as he opens a black backpack that's atop the gray blanket. Does he sleep here? My heart skips a beat. He unzips the backpack and starts to unpack it across the bed.

Bottles of water.

Prepackaged cookies and crackers.

Two oranges and two apples.

Something wrapped in butcher paper that looks like a sandwich.

It's all food. Why is he unpacking so much food?

It hits me all of a sudden. Of course, he doesn't sleep here. This room isn't for him. It's for me, a cage designed just for me. I'm going to be sick.

"Eat," he tells me.

"What?" I ask him.

He raises an eyebrow like he's unimpressed with my question, but still, he repeats himself.

"Eat," he says again.

"No." I shake my head at him, my mind whirling with everything he has done. The urge to vomit almost wins out this time. "I'm not hungry."

He cocks his head at me, his eyes like two black orbs in the dim light of this scary place.

"You seem to have misunderstood the assignment, Firefly," he tells me. "Why exactly do you think I brought you down here?"

"Because you're a psychopath," I tell him.

"And you think I'll do exactly what with you down here?"

"I don't know." I scoff, angry, confused, and afraid. "You're the psychopath, not me."

He clasps his hands together in front of himself, like he's a priest patiently waiting to take my confession.

"Baby girl, look at the bed and figure it out."

I look at the food on the bed.

"I see food," I say stupidly.

"And what do people normally do with food?"

"Eat it," I tell him, crossing my arms over my chest. "You already said that."

"Would I tell you to eat the food if I took you all the way down here just to harm you?"

He cocks his head at me again, and I can't take the way he's looking at me right now with the fire playing in his hair and the dim light of the room tanning his otherwise pale skin. He's both gorgeous and frightening. I swallow hard and bury the attraction. I'm not about to develop Stockholm Syndrome in this bitch.

"I don't know what you plan to do with me," I say. "You're the one who trapped me in here."

"And you're the one who's intentionally acting obtuse." He blinks at me. "I've always tried to help you, Avery."

"Why?"

"Call it altruism."

"I think I'll call it kidnapping instead."

It doesn't even faze him.

"Why are you fighting this?" he asks. "Why are you so scared of being saved?"

"I'm not scared of being saved. I'm scared of you."

"And everyone else apparently," he scoffs, his palms hitting his knees. "You've never once let anyone help you, Avery. Why is that? Do you not believe you are worth saving?"

The barb stings.

"You never answered my question," I deflect. "Why help me?"

He looks up at the ceiling and the mirrors there that reflect a hundred faces I don't want to see.

"Fine," he says, before his gaze snaps back to me, "a question for a question then."

"I'm not answering anything from you."

He laughs. "I don't think you're in any position to negotiate."

Touché.

"Fine," I say, holding myself even tighter. "Agreed. So why me, Gabe?"

He smirks at the name and maybe I shouldn't have let it slip. I should have called him Gil or pretended to not remember it. Because we don't care about each other, right? I don't care about him.

"I don't give a fuck about saving you because of altruism," he admits. "I care because something about you quiets the noise."

What does that mean?

"The noise?" I ask.

He shakes his head. "One question at a time. Now it's my turn. Why won't you eat?"

"I'm not hungry."

His *tsk* hits his teeth. "The truth, Avery."

"I . . ." I swallow hard. "My mother used to oink at me when I was little." I shrug. "It fucked me up."

"You hear her do that when you eat?"

"One question at a time," I remind him. "What do you mean the noise? What exactly do you hear?"

"It's hard to explain." He thinks a moment, looking out at the cavernous room, and I'm glad he's here with me at least because if he wasn't, I think I'd be terrified. Darkness crowds the space, leeching across the stone floor and toward the light bulbs that hang from the ceiling. I look back at him quickly.

"You walk down a hallway, and you hear, what?" he says. "A guy laughing with his friend? A guard on the radio, and that's all you pick up, right? My brain isn't like that, though. It picks up on everything until it's so loud it feels like I'm going to explode."

"So you have ADD or something?" I question.

"I think that's enough questions for today, baby girl. I want to see you eat something." He pats the bed beside him. "Come here. Eat with me."

"You aren't going to shove it down my throat?"

"I wasn't planning on it."

I stand and walk over to the bed. Not because I want to eat, or plan on doing so, but because I feel better being with him, especially now in this cold basement where water trickles in a corner every so often. I sit on the bed on the opposite side of him with the food between us.

"What's the plan?" I ask. "To keep me down here until I obey you?"

"Something like that," he murmurs, gesturing at the food. "Pick something."

I look it all over. "No, thanks."

"It wasn't a suggestion." He shoots me a glare. "I said I didn't plan on shoving the food down your throat. It doesn't mean I won't."

I grab an orange and start to peel it. I'm slow about it, but he doesn't say a word until I'm finished and there's a neat pile of orange peelings where the fruit used to be and a pile of orange slices in my lap. As he watches me, I pop one into my mouth and start to chew. Not because I want to eat, but because I want him to stay, at least until I can figure a way out of this hellhole.

"You chose the thing with the least amount of calories," he tells me. "Well, except for the water."

"Technically the apple is less," I tell him. "It's probably seventy-five calories to the orange's eighty, but I don't like Granny Smith apples."

He smirks like he's learned something about me, and I realize

I've said too much. I pop another orange slice into my mouth and look at him to keep my mother's oinking at bay. He's still staring at me by the time I finish the orange.

"Okay," I tell him. "You can let me go now. I ate something."

He shakes his head. "You gotta eat a lot more than that, Firefly, to get out of this cage."

"What's the plan?" I ask him. I know I'm goading him, but I don't care. The fucker kidnapped me. I did what he asked, and now he won't let me go? Screw him! "The guards are eventually going to realize that I'm missing, and they're going to come looking for me. What will they do to you when they find out you fucked with the headmistress's cash cow? You think the doctor will go easy on you this time?"

Gabe leans toward me, flattening his palms across the bed.

"They aren't going to be looking for you in here, baby girl. They're going to be too busy searching the woods outside."

"What?" I blink at him. "What does that mean?"

He laughs. "You're a smart girl. You'll figure it out."

"I'm dumber than I look. Enlighten me."

"It means," he quips, "that while your ass went to la-la land earlier, I texted my boys to make sure your space looks like you up and left in a hurry. Told 'em to leave a note and everything."

He has to be lying. "You're lying"

"Just because you say it doesn't make it true." He laughs, his teeth appearing even whiter than normal in the low light. "They're going to scour the woods for miles looking for you, Firefly," he tells me. "It'll come to no one's surprise. What number is this rehabilitation program for you? You gotta be in the double digits by now, right? And your father was already talking about shipping you off to another one? Baby girl, that's got to hurt, and that's what your note will say too. I'm sure Kill will make it look good. He'll be meticulous about it, and by the time he and Saint fuck up your space, there will be no doubt you left in a hurry."

"My father will never believe I ran away," I lie, but won't he? After I tried to run from the last school too?

"You're mine until I fix you, so eat up. The faster you rehabilitate, the faster you can get out of here."

"Keep your fucking food and your fucking lies!" I snarl at him. "You will never fix me, fire freak."

Maybe it's my defiance or maybe it's my words, but I watch the moment when the last of his patience snaps. He leaps across the bed, and my head hits the bed rail as he flattens me beneath him, food going everywhere.

A clang sounds between my ears as my head starts to pound.

"You will learn your worth," he snarls above me, his body heavy and hot against me. "I don't care if I have to cage you in here for a thousand days until it gets through your thick skull."

I spit at him, and it lands hot and sticky on his face, but he doesn't seem to mind. Instead, he runs his tongue over his lips and says, "Tastes like oranges."

Then he flattens his lips to mine and sucks all the air out of me. He's massive, his tall frame crowding me and pinning me to the bed, as his tongue dives into my mouth.

He tastes like salt-and-vinegar chips but smells like campfires and charcoal. His fingers skim my sides, and my heart beats fast, knocking against my ribs. I want him to stop, but I don't want to let him go. I kiss him back. Despite it all, I kiss him back, falling victim to the con of feeling wanted.

I kiss him until I can't breathe, until everything in me burns for his touch, and wetness smears between my thighs. I arch beneath him, pressing against his cock, and start to rub. The friction is glorious between us, and the ache is impossible to ignore. It feels like I'm going to explode.

"No," he tells me with a groan, rolling onto his side. "You only get that when you take care of yourself. I'm not giving my cum to a dead girl."

He stands, and I watch him. I should move. I should do something, but I am frozen as he undoes his belt buckle and then his pants, dragging the zipper down slowly. He pulls down his black boxer briefs and frees his cock a moment later, and it's beautiful. Big, large, and intimidating, just like him. All of me aches to touch it, but I'm afraid if I do, he might put it away.

He strokes himself root to tip, watching me, before spitting into his hand. Then he moves his hand back up to the thick mushroom head of his dick and back down again, his eyes hooded as he watches me.

"Lift your shirt," he commands, the words guttural.

I do as I am told, and a moment later, he comes, exploding onto my chest with a roar.

His eyes shutter, but when they open and find my flesh marked with ropes of his cum, he says, "That's all you get, baby girl, until you treat yourself the way you deserve."

He puts himself away, zips up his pants, redoes his belt, and walks to the cell door. He unlocks it in a flash and then locks it back just as quickly.

"Where are you going?!" I call after him. "You can't just leave me here!"

He looks back at me, illuminated by a halo of light falling from the bulb above his head.

"You can't leave me here," I tell him, shivering with my words. "If you feel something for me, you *won't* leave me here."

He cocks an eyebrow at me, his expression deadly. "Who said I felt anything at all?"

"Liar!" I hiss. "You feel something for me."

He ignores the jab, and I leap off of the bed, pulling my shirt back into place, and grab the bars of the cell, panicking.

"When will you be back?" I call after him.

"I have to attend class, but I'll be back this afternoon. In the meantime, eat and look in the mirror. Learn who you truly are."

With that, he leaves me, even as I yell and scream at him, begging him not to go. He disappears up the stairs, and I hate this place. It's creepy, but I'm lucky the bed's in the corner where I can tuck myself away, and he left the light on, though it feels like the walls are looking at me.

I walk back to the bed, taking the lantern he left as well. I huddle on the bed in the corner of the cell, my back pressed against the stone wall, trying to not freak the fuck out. I can't even look at the lantern for too long without thinking of the car wreck and almost panicking.

I choose something else to focus on, and I spot all the food he's left behind, the water, and the disgusting bucket in a corner that I will *never* use. I try not to think about the purpose of that bucket as I look at the food again, where it has spilled across the bed and rolled off to the floor.

I reach into the backpack and find a washcloth and a roll of toilet paper. I use the washcloth to wipe myself and ignore the toilet paper.

I think I'm going to be sick.

He caged me like an animal and locked me away like a secret.

My mother's voice comes back to haunt me as I look at the bright green apple that's rolled onto the dirty floor.

Oink, oink, piggy. You know you want to lick it clean.

19

AVERY

It could be minutes or hours or even days. I'm not sure how long I lay there, curled in the dark corner of my cage and hoping for Gabe to come back. It feels like he's been gone too long. He said he would come back this afternoon, but there are no windows to tell the time by.

Is it afternoon or evening? Has night already come and gone?

I've paced the floors of my cell, pulled at the bars, and looked beneath the bed searching for a way out of here. There's no secret tunnel out of this hellhole, and if he doesn't come back, I'm convinced I'm going to die in this place. If he does come back, I might kill him for leaving me here.

On the bed, beneath the blanket while I try to keep out the cold that needles at my skin, I go through all of the horrible scenarios in my head.

The first one is that he left me here intentionally and that I'm going to be stuck here until, at some point, the bulbs overhead finally burn out, and I'm alone in the dark. The thought sends a shiver bolting up my spine as something scurries just out of sight.

What was that? And why do I not want to know?

The second scenario is that something has happened to him. Maybe he fell and hit his head on the way back up to civilization or maybe he got in another fight and he's been taken to the hole. Maybe he either doesn't remember to come back for me or can't come back, so I'll be left here, screaming into oblivion.

The third one, and the scenario that I hope for, is that Gabe never left. He's just been standing there at the top of the stairs, waiting for me and not really leaving me in the creepy basement by myself. I prefer that one, but the more I yell for him to come back, my shouts echoing against the stone walls, the less I believe that he is up at the top of the stairs, ready to walk down and come back to me.

It makes me cry. I'm not proud of it, and I'm not afraid of the dark, but I definitely don't appreciate being locked down here, where it feels like things lurk in the shadows that I can't quite see. Even worse than looking out at the massive space is looking up at the mirrors piecemealed to the ceiling. He even put them above the bed, so that I can't escape them. When I glance up, I see my blue eyes blinking back at me, though I'm contorted. My face slices across the uneven surfaces, but the more I look at the mirrors, the more I think I might actually see my true self. I don't know the last time I saw me for, well, me, but now I spot the blueish bags beneath my eyes, the hollow beneath my cheekbones, and the skeletal look that seems to have taken over me. There can be no dysmorphia here beneath his hall of mirrors. There are too many of them, and my brain can only fool me so much.

When I look up at the ceiling, I cry even harder until I'm sobbing on the bed, shaking beneath the blanket, and begging for him to come back.

How long is he planning on leaving me down here?

Will he come back today like he said he would, or will he wait until tomorrow?

I can't be here until tomorrow. I don't know if I'll make it.

I stare at the other orange he left for me, untouched and rolled onto the floor next to the apples. I guess it fell when he leapt over the bed and kissed me. Or maybe it fell when he pulled away from me, took out his dick, and jerked off all over my tits. I still can't believe that happened. Most guys prefer pussy in my limited experience, but what did he say? Oh yeah, that he wouldn't give his cum to a dead girl.

Whatever.

He gave it to my tits instead, spraying rope after rope across my bra, my chest, and my abdomen. He looked like a man possessed when he came, his eyes closing with his orgasm. When they opened, his delicious mouth fell open, and he stared at me, breathing hard, as the twin pools of ink in his irises captured me by the feet and pulled me under.

I shouldn't be thinking about him.

Or his cock.

And definitely not the way the cords in his neck jutted out and his jaw clenched when he came.

Shit. Well, what else am I supposed to be thinking about down here?

It's not like I want to think about him, but between the most likely haunted basement, the mirrors above the ceiling, the food, and him, I choose him. He's the only choice that doesn't involve a surefire hit to my sanity.

The creep—or should I call him a kidnapper now?—is beautiful in a way that men should not be beautiful. He's the villain you can't help but root for because of the way he makes you feel when he stares at you for way longer than acceptable and sets your skin aflame. He's the anti-hero who shouldn't earn a second look from the heroine, except for that invisible pull between them that demands it.

Everything about him screams at me to run away, but I can't, even if I wasn't in a cage. I'm a deer frozen in the headlights of an oncoming car, only he's the car. I want to run—I *need* to run—but I can't, and we're both going to be damaged even more before this is over.

He has dark, chiseled features and inscrutable eyes that never give away what he's thinking, not unless he wants you to know.

He's tall, six-foot-three, maybe even taller, and massive compared to me. He knows how to use it too, dipping his head to whisper in my ear or rising to his full height when he wants to intimidate. When he was on top of me, flattening his hard body to mine, it felt like he could break all of me without even trying, and there wouldn't be a damn thing I could do about it.

He's a king—a psychopathic mad king—who locks undeserving girls in dark places and defiles them for his own pleasure. And for theirs too, I guess.

The burn mark he left on my throat hurts like a bitch, and I know I should hate him for it. I am trying to hate him for it as I rub the mark absentmindedly and try to not think about him. I figured I had at least a few good days in me before my brain fucked everything up for me.

Apparently not.

I tell the voice inside my head to stop thinking about the mad king. It doesn't matter if I enjoyed him coming all over me or not. It's not like there's a time requirement for Stockholm Syndrome. Well, not one that I know about at least, and that's definitely what I have. I'm already losing it, reliant on him, and at his mercy. It would be crazy to not develop an attachment to him.

Or at least that's what I tell myself.

Locked in the basement and curled in a corner on the bed, I

hope and pray for him to come back. It was bad enough I got pulled from class this morning to meet with the psychiatrist, the one who's new here and has the personality of a rock.

"Tell me about your parents, Avery," he had said like he didn't already know the root cause of my problems.

All of these places correctly guess at one point or another, but then they keep that knowledge to themselves. In the end, right before my father pulls the plug, some of them try to mention it in an effort to save themselves. But my father never wants to hear any of it, no matter how many times it's flung in his face.

He loves his wife.

His wife is perfect.

I'm the problem.

End. Of. Story.

It's almost like if he recognizes that she's the problem, he might have to admit his own fault in choosing her.

After I met with Dr. Boring Rock, I had to attend group therapy, which was even worse than talking to the psychiatrist one-on-one. It, too, was headed by the man with the personality of a stone, and all of the eating disorder students were there going through the motions of giving a shit. The doctor wanted me to talk about my parents in group therapy, but I refused. Well, I actually told him my mother was dead, and the dumbass believed me.

Now I'm here, and I'm feeling like I got tag-teamed by bullshit this morning. The boring doctor was bad enough, but then the creep kidnapped me and took me down to the basement for his special surprise.

Also, worst surprise ever, for the record.

I hate this place, and I don't care if I have to shout it to get it into my skull, but I hate him too. I don't care about his reasons. I don't want to hear any more about them. He could have the intentions of an angel, but they can't make up for what he's doing to me.

He locked me in here like an animal, the bastard.

Fuck him!

At some point, I fall asleep on the bed, still wrapped in the blanket, my head cradled on a small but clean pillow he must have brought down here, especially for his torture chamber. I don't dream or at least I don't think I do. I fall into the black of nothingness.

I wake to the sound of clanging and the cell door scraping against the stone floor. I peek over to watch him lock the cell door behind him. Everything hits me one after the other.

Relief first that calms my shaking bones.

Happiness, second, that washes over me.

Anger last, incinerating all the good feelings away.

He left me here, but I know he has a key. I've seen it twice now, and if I can just overpower him, I have a chance of locking him in this shitty place and getting out of here myself. I screw my eyes shut again, sliding the blanket a little farther up my cold arms, and a moment later, I feel the bed dip beneath his weight.

He sits in front of me, his body so close to mine that his thigh grazes my forearm. Every hair on me stands up all at once.

I can't think about him or what he did just hours—days?—earlier. I can't remember how he came all over my tits and made me feel like the most important thing to him in the world during that moment. Feelings like that are dangerous.

Focus! Get the key!

"I know you're awake, Firefly," he tells me, blowing hot air down the side of my face.

I open my eyes to glare at him, but I find him already staring at me, looking less than entertained.

"Sleep well?" he asks me. I can already tell from his tone that it's the only pleasantry I'm getting from him this time.

"I hate it here," I say to him. "Let me go."

He cocks his head at me. "You know I can't do that, baby girl, not unless you see your worth yet." He looks at the untouched food and says, "And by the looks of it, you don't."

I prop myself up on my elbow, glaring at him and trying to ignore how close we are.

Focus, Avery! Get out of here!

"What do you want from me?!" I demand.

He leans forward, swallowing the space between us.

"I don't want," he murmurs. "I *need*, baby girl, and I need it all, your every thought, breath, and heartbeat. I need everything, and I need it devoted to me."

He shouldn't say those words. He shouldn't say any words like that because they heat my skin, steal my breath, and stop my heart mid-beat. Words like that give girls like me false hope. I don't want false hope. False hope equates to broken promises and pain. No attachments and no intimacy means leaving my heart intact.

"You put me in a filthy, disgusting room and expect me to see my worth?" I cackle at him, but there's no amusement in it. "You're treating me like trash. You have to know how ironic that is, right?"

"No," he leans in close, so close I can smell the peppermint lingering on his breath. Did he chew gum before he came down here, or is it already morning? This shit is already screwing with my head. "I'm treating you like you treat yourself. You lock yourself in your little world, and you refuse to interact with the rest of us. You haven't made a single friend since you arrived here, Avery. Why is that? Do you think you're better than us? Or do you think you're not worth it? Which one is it?"

"None of your business," I snap.

He slides a cigarette out of his pocket and lights up, taking a long drag.

"How about your worth?" I bark back at him. "You sit there sucking down cancer sticks. If you saw your worth, you wouldn't be trying to kill yourself, would you? You hate yourself just as much as I hate myself."

His glare slides to me. "Avery, shut the fuck up. You have no idea what you're talking about."

I don't care that he's right.

I don't want to listen to him any longer.

I want him to feel how I feel: disgusted and angry.

I sit up in bed.

"No, let's talk about you," I deadpan.

"You're angry," he cuts those unreal dark eyes to me again. There's something dangerous in his gaze, some threat I can't quite read. Still, I don't back down. I want to push all of his buttons until he redlines and starts to spark. He takes another suck out of his cigarette and blows smoke rings into the air.

"What makes you so weak that you can't control your noise by yourself?" I demand. "You say you need me to do it, whatever that means, but it's pretty pathetic that you can't cope with it at this point, right? Like are you stupid or just so self-absorbed that you think everyone should bow down and do as you command? Well, I got news for you, sunshine. Wear some headphones because whatever shit you hear in your head is a you problem, not a me problem. I don't give a fuck about helping you."

"You're one to talk," he hisses. "You're so fucked up you can't even eat, Avery, so don't you dare sit there and pretend you don't belong here with me."

A flush warms his cheek, and the boy who loves the flame burns with his anger as I lean in closer.

"Yeah, but at least I don't pretend to be better than everyone else like you do," I snarl back at him. "I don't walk around doing whatever I want like I'm a god. They got your name wrong, you know? You aren't an archangel, *Gabriel*. You're as fucked up and as human as the rest of us. And I'm betting you can't stand knowing you are as worthless as we are and that your parents locked you up in here."

He roars, picking up the lantern and throwing it against the cell wall. It shatters and sparks fly everywhere as he strides to the cell door and hurriedly leaves, locking the door back behind him. I move to follow him, but the world sways, and I sit back down on the bed.

"What?" I taunt after him. "You don't like hearing the truth?"

He keeps going, walking straight ahead, and I'm afraid, shaking even as I see my one hope of getting out of here disappear, but even more than that, I'm angry.

Fuck him for bringing me down here.

Fuck him for locking me up.

And most of all fuck him for wanting me to confront my demons while he pretends his don't even exist.

I hate him. I hate him. I hate him!!!

Part of me hopes that if I think the words enough times, my wish will be granted, and they'll become true.

20

GABE

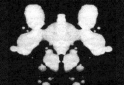

I bolt up the stone stairs that lead out of the basement and run through the maintenance hallways and into pitch black. The gurgle of water and the buzz of electricity from somewhere close by intertwines with my uneven breath as I run. I move so fast that the motion-sensor lights don't even turn on until after I'm already past them and farther down the hallway. I've been here so often, it doesn't matter, though. The power could go out, and I'd find my way back to the surface in the dark.

My knuckles prickle with the urge to hit something, and I ball them into tight fists, trying to suffocate the urge. I can't give in to it now. Stone bricks and thick steel pipes surround me, and I can't split open my knuckles today or risk breaking the bones in my hand. The administration has already started searching the woods for Avery, bringing in search parties and hunting dogs. Not the police, though, not yet at least. She isn't even considered missing for forty-eight hours, and I'm sure Headmistress doesn't want the attention that comes with a missing student. Right now, I imagine they're still combing through the woods like they have a hope of locating her. Still, a broken hand would raise questions, and I can't risk them looking inward and zeroing in on me. I need time to fix my Firefly.

I tighten my fists, feeling my knuckles pop, and bound through the maze of hallways until I reach the flight of stairs that wind all the way up to the ground floor. I hadn't planned on leaving her so soon, but if she said one more word about my failures, I was going to prove I wasn't a failure . . . well, at killing her, at least.

She has food, water, and a bucket, and I left the lights on for her. What else could she need? Whatever. It doesn't matter anyway. I need time to decompress before I fucking explode.

Stop thinking about her, Gabe!

What is it about her that always makes me lose my cool?

Normally, the flames would keep the noise at bay, but not today, not with her. If I had taken my lighter out in her cell, I wouldn't have found it to be calming. I wouldn't have calmed until I watched her sizzle.

Fuck, I let her get to me. She's *still* getting to me, hammering away at my ability to repress. If she gets through, I'm going to kill her, and that won't be good for either one of us.

Control yourself, Gabriel!

I shouldn't have let her get to me. She's angry and afraid, which is understandable, given I locked her up so many feet underground that the devil has a better chance of hearing her than God. The basement is about as isolated as it gets at the Asylum, even more secluded than the cemetery on the outskirts of campus and the overgrown mausoleums that stand watch there.

The basement isn't really a basement. It's more like a cavern. It's deep underground, below even the morgue and doctors' offices originally built during the typhus outbreak, and all the way down to the old root cellar. The cellar was converted to the maintenance tunnels when they installed electricity in the mid-twentieth century and then central heating and air conditioning thereafter. Or that's what I've been able to learn on the rare occasion the internet works.

I locked her up in a place where no one would hear her screams or find her body. She knows it too. I can see it in the frantic jitter of her gaze every time something skitters in the dark. My Firefly is scared, and she's taking it out on me. I guess that's expected too. I am the one who locked her up down there, after all. I could take her snarky comments, her sarcasm, and her eye rolls, but I can't take her sounding like my father.

She said I was too weak to keep the noise away, and she's right, goddammit. I walk around campus, letting the pyros worship me, doing whatever I want, and acting like I'm better than everyone else, but I'm not. Outside these walls, I'm just another fucked-up guy with a mental illness that society doesn't know what to do with. I'm a number, not a name, no matter how much I pretend otherwise. I'm not special, and my father knows it, just like she does. That's why he sent me here.

She even talked to me like my father does, using the *exact* same tone, the one that makes me feel lower than dog shit. My father compared me to my mother's dog once, a Pomeranian that she decorates with different colored bows depending on the occasion. He said that the dog was smarter than me because at least the dog could follow commands. It didn't matter that I couldn't follow his commands because he was breathing down my neck and ordering me to perform like a trained monkey. When I couldn't read the words on the page and they all jumbled together, he extinguished his cigar against the top of my hand. You can still see the scar when the light hits it just right. I'd like to see my mother's dog keep its cool under those circumstances.

The backs of my thighs burn like a bitch as I exit the stairwell and find the hallway blissfully empty. I really need to step up my cardio if I'm going to be making multiple visits to my Firefly every day. I walk it off and beeline to my dormitory. My knuckles are still craving a good punch or two, and my lighter isn't doing shit to quiet the rising tide of noise at the moment.

I roll the wheel, press the button, and burn the inside of my index finger like I always do.

It does nothing to quell the furious drumming of my heart or the replay of her insults like I'm listening to Avery's Top 40 hits.

... are you stupid or self-absorbed ...

... you're just as fucked up and human as the rest of us ...

... it's pretty pathetic you can't cope ...

Shut up, shut up, shut up!!!

Her taunts grow louder with each step like she's right beside me and not buried dozens of feet below me.

Roll and click, on.

Roll and click, off.

I don't know why I even bother. The fire does nothing to douse the noise.

I head straight for the boy's dormitory and beeline up the stairs. I don't go to my dorm room, though. I go to Saint and Kill's instead. Any later in the day, and I'd have to jimmy their pain-in-the-ass window to get inside, but it's still early enough that curfew isn't in place yet and the door's unlocked.

I enter without knocking. Neither one of them is even bothered by it. I think it would annoy them if I started knocking at this point.

Both are on their beds, stretched out and looking bored, as I take a seat behind them, at Saint's desk. It's a miracle I don't break the chair with how hard I land, which is so unlike me. I'm graceful and light on my feet, not a stampeding buffalo.

Get your shit together, Gabe!

"Wanna talk about it?" Kill offers, not even glancing at me as he flips the page of his book.

"No," I grumble.

Saint looks up from his phone, probably texting his girl-friend, and reaches a hand back behind himself and over his pillow to pass me his lit cigarette. I accept it with shaky fingers and take a puff. I close my eyes as the nicotine hits my blood-stream and starts to calm my nerves.

"Wanna fight?" Kill offers, sending me a grin over his shoulder as I pass the cigarette back to Saint. "You know you always feel better after you kick somebody's ass."

"Yeah, hit him," Saint says with a laugh, sucking on his cigarette like it's a lollipop.

"I didn't mean me, dumbass," Kill retorts with a rare laugh that shows his teeth. "Let's go fuck some shit up like the old days before you two went all feminist and got woman problems."

I look to Saint, who's currently sucking on the cigarette again, but his blue eyes are trained on me.

"What the fuck does he think a feminist is?" I ask Saint, cocking my head in Kill's direction.

He laughs, expelling smoke from between his teeth and hands the cherry back to me. With anybody else, cigarette swapping would probably be nasty, but not with my brother. He's the equally fucked-up family I never had.

Kill sits up in his bed, reaches behind himself, and smacks the back of my head, but there's no force behind it. He's in a good mood for once. Either he hit his skull on a wall and concussed himself recently or he found a virgin and popped her cherry. Kill's got a thing for virgin, preferably deeply devout, blood. I like my pussy less uptight and more experienced but to each their own.

"Funny," Kill says to me. "Also, I know what a feminist is. I'm just saying you two are whipped. You by the dead girl, and Saint by Willow."

"Bro," I look at him like he's crazy because he *is* fucking crazy to say that shit. "You know I have Avery locked up in the basement at the moment, right? Like in an actual prison cell?"

Saint snorts, and I look to him for help. "How am I whipped?"

Saint's gaze slices from me across the room to Kill. "G's got a point."

Then he steals the cig back right from between my fingers and takes a puff.

Fuck, I need Marshall to replace our stash asap, or I'm going to have to resort to stealing and smoking the Virginia Slims Headmistress sneaks when she thinks no one is looking.

"Also," Saint says to Kill, "keep my pet's name out of your filthy mouth or I'll break your teeth for it."

The words are all soft corners and sanded-down edges, but Saint is serious. Nobody talks about his perfect pet. Hell, nobody looks at her if they know what's good for them.

Kill turns around to me this time, running a hand through his dirty blond hair so that it points out every which way.

"Daaaaaadddd," he pouts, "he's threatening me."

Saint rolls his eyes, and I laugh.

"Hold up," I say, looking back at Saint. "What if we have to say your girl's name in class or something? Are you saying that we can't talk to her at all anymore? What about at meals when you bring her to *our* table? Or when you sneak her in here? And what about now when she's not even here? We can't say her name?"

Saint nods. "Exactly."

Killian snorts.

"Dude's whipped," I agree with Kill. I point at Saint, sitting on his bed, looking like he doesn't give a fuck what we think. "You're whipped. Next thing you're going to say is don't even look at her."

"That can be arranged," Saint murmurs, and the fucker is one hundred percent threatening to remove my eyeballs without so many words.

Kill smiles, and oh fuck, that can't be good. He's about to say something really naughty and start a battle royale in this dorm room. It's creepy as fuck when he smiles like that, when he's looking off into space and suddenly a grin pours slowly across his features like he's getting the expression painted on him at a fair. Never have I once seen Kill smile like that, where his blue eyes light up like he's been shot full of electricity, without shit going to Armageddon-level fucked in a matter of minutes.

"Hey, Saint?" Kill says.

Oh for fuck's sake.

"'Sup," Saint responds, texting on his phone again.

"I know I can't talk to your girl or say her name," Kill says, "but it's cool if she talks to me when we cuddle, right?"

And there it is.

We're fucked.

Saint goes still in his bed, but I'm certain he only caught the tail end of Kill's words or one of them would already be bleeding.

"What the fuck did you say?" he demands.

Saint takes jokes at Willow's expense about as well as most people take a bullet to the brain.

"I asked," Kill replies, apparently jonesing for a fight today, "if it was still cool to talk to her after we fuck."

Saint is off the bed in less than a second. It's a blur, but I manage to make out that he almost catches Kill by the lapels of his dress shirt. He would have, too, if I didn't shoot to my feet and put myself between them.

"What is wrong with you two?" I look at Saint and push him back with both hands. "You know Willow ain't riding anyone's dick but yours." I glare over my shoulder at Kill. "Stop trying to start shit to meet your bloodletting quota."

Saint grumbles and I'm pretty sure threatens murder, but he

knows Kill ain't doing shit with his pet. Kill relaxes a little and laughs in his bed.

"I need to get out of here," Saint barks a second later, looking at me. "You still want to fight?"

"Fuck yeah," I agree.

Kill grins.

"Let's go," I tell them both. "I need to fuck something up before I burn that little brat in the basement."

Kill laughs, and just as we are about to leave the room and start the hunt, there's a *ping* against the window. We all turn to see Saint's girlfriend on the edge of the building, her brown hair whipping every which way in the howling wind and looking absolutely terrified. Saint walks to her, opens the window quickly, and helps her inside.

"My heart is beating so fast," she says to him, her cheeks rosy from the cold and snow sprinkling her hair. "I hate having to sneak in here."

Saint loops his index finger around the ring at the front of her collar and pulls her in close. "I'll come to you next time, pretty girl."

Then he kisses her, and I want to yell at them to hurry up so I can go knock someone's teeth out.

"How's your father?" he asks the moment they break apart, her breathless and with her cheeks flushed.

"Still a jerk," she says to him. "He hung up on me after I mentioned doing a memorial service for Mama on her birthday. He still won't say her name. I guess it hurts too much. How's yours?"

"I'm sorry," he says, and to his credit, he does look like he's trying to empathize. "My father's fine. He's still a dick." He cuts his eyes across the room to me. "Gabe's got girl problems. Wanna help him out?"

"What?" I say, frowning as Kill snickers. "You just said we

couldn't talk to her?"

"You said *what?*" Willow's brown-eyed gaze slides to Saint, and he gives her the creepiest smile I've ever seen. I guess he's trying to put on his human mask today, but it slips and he doesn't pull off the adorable boyfriend look he's going for. Instead, he looks like a cannibal who just cut out a human-sized pate. Even I can do better than that.

"I said you're beautiful," he tells her.

Willow barks with laughter and playfully slaps him on the chest. Then she turns back to me.

"Okay," she says, "I want to help. You're having problems with that girl, right, the one who sat at our table?"

"Yeah," Kill nods for me, "the dead one."

"Dead?" she asks the word carefully as Saint plays with her hair, letting the smooth strands slide between his fingers.

"It's because she smells like death," he explains. "G didn't kill her. Wait," he looks at me, "did you kill her?"

"No."

"Would've been easier," Kill murmurs.

Now that, I agree with.

"What's the problem?" Willow says, making herself comfortable on Saint's bed.

"She's infuriating and stubborn and won't listen and . . ." I lose the words.

Willow looks to Saint and something unspoken passes between the two of them before her attention returns to me.

"Hmm," she says, thinking. "Well, it sounds like you can't reason with her, right?"

"Right," I agree. "There's no reasoning with her."

She shrugs. "Then the way I see it, you only have one option. Give her a choice, one where you're happy regardless of how she chooses."

"And if she won't choose?" I ask.

She shrugs. "Then make her."

She says it like it's the easiest thing in the world, and as Saint nods with her, I wonder what impossible choice he gave his stubborn girlfriend to make her say yes to being his pet. If I know Saint, though, it had something to do with the fucking morgue.

21

GABE

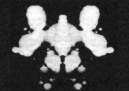

I let Avery stew all goddamn night and well into the next morning before I stuff a bunch of shit from the vending machines into my pockets and start for the basement. My bulbous pockets look suspicious as fuck, but the staff's so busy at the moment that even if there were any in the hallway, I don't think they'd notice me. The staff is still searching the campus grounds, and we're coming up on the forty-eight-hour mark, but I know Headmistress is going to put off getting the police involved. She won't want the attention that comes with the government poking around up here.

Saint and Kill were smart about Avery's disappearance, though, especially on short notice. They dropped just enough clues in her room and around campus, that have the staff running around the forest in circles.

Literally, from what Kill overhead between a couple of guards this morning.

Time isn't on my side, though, and I need my Firefly to learn to cooperate and quickly. I need to step up my game.

I swipe the key card, open the door, and disappear into the winding stairwell. It takes twelve minutes from the time I open the door until I reach Avery, and when I do, I spot her tucked into a ball on the bed, her back against the wall. I unlock the cage, and she looks up, lifting her head out of the fetal position. She looks terrible, and I immediately regret not coming earlier. She's got dark circles under her eyes and a faraway look. Her skin is ethereal, so pale it's almost unearthly even in this dark space.

Kill would take one look at her and say she looks actually dead today.

I don't disagree.

I glance at the untouched food on the floor and on the bed. She even found the granola bars at some point last night, but they're untouched too, and a couple of them are just outside of the cell, like she got tired of trying to throw them out, and finally, started carefully pushing them through the spaces in between the bars.

What the fuck is she doing to herself?

What the fuck is she doing to me?

A tidal wave of noise slams into me until it's all I can do to stand there and take it. Everything is loud. Her breathing, the drip in the corner of the room, the grumble of her stomach that she pretends isn't there. I could snap her neck and bring us both less misery. I'm going to if she doesn't start obeying me.

I start snatching shit from my pockets and toss it on the bed around her.

"No thanks," she tells me, barely even glancing at it, as she flicks at a thread on the blanket.

How pathetic. It makes me even angrier.

"Oh, we ain't playing this game today," I snarl at her as I lean over the bed, pressing my palms flat to the blanket she has tucked around herself. I don't know what I'm going to say. She smells like sugar-coated strawberries and sweat, and the anger is loud now, pulsing against my eardrums and thrumming inside my brain like the reverb of a guitar that never stops. I can taste my disgust as easily as I can hear my rage. It lays thick and bitter on my tongue as my fingers cinch the blanket around her body, wanting the scratchy fabric to be her throat instead.

There are a lot of things I can tolerate, but this isn't one of them. Pathetic is a bad goddamn look on her. I'm going to kill her. I'm going to set her skinny ass on fire and stop this torment. I'm going to . . .

Give her an impossible choice.

I blink as it comes to me. I figure it's either that or adding a murder charge to my impending rap sheet. I yank a chocolate bar from where it landed above her head and I punch it into the mattress inches away from her face. She flinches at the hit.

"Eat it," I snarl, "or get on your goddamn knees. Do neither, and I'll make you eat it before I fuck your face, and I don't care how many teeth you have to swallow, baby girl, to choke it all down."

The impossible choice.

Either way, I fucking win.

I don't want to win, though. I want her to win, goddammit! Why is she doing this to herself?!

She sits up in bed slowly, the blanket falling around her to the bed, and she crosses her arms around her chest. The bones in her hands and wrists flex as she does, and the rage inside of me broils even hotter.

"No," she says flatly.

She even sounds dead today.

GODDAMMIT!!!

I tear open the chocolate bar with my teeth, spitting out part of the wrapper, and I don't warn her or ease her into it. I shove the fucking thing into her mouth until she's choking and coughing on it. She tries to spit at me and loses a little of it, pieces of candy falling down the front of her shirt and into her lap. I force her head up by her chin and pinch her nose shut with my other hand until she has no choice but to swallow if she wants to breathe. She tries to scratch at me, raking her nails over my skin. I feel them catch on my flesh. That's going to be a bitch to explain, but I barely feel the marks. She screams into my hands, but I hold tight, forcing her to swallow.

One swallow, then a second, and then a third, until finally, I yank my bleeding arms away from her, and she sucks in a deep breath. Her drool is speckled with chocolate dust, and she looks like she's going to be sick. I don't give a fuck, though. I warned her. She refused to choose, and now I'm choosing for her. I told her I'd never lie to her, and I meant it.

I raise my hands to my belt, and she bares her chocolate-stained teeth at me.

"Bring your dick to my face," she warns, "and I'll bite it off!"

"On your knees," I hiss as I step forward, and she holds her ground. I grab her beneath her chin and heat her already flushed skin with my words. "On your knees, baby girl. Let's see you try to count the calories of my fucking cum."

She spits at me, and it lands hot and sticky across my face, tattooing my skin with her anger.

Good, I want her angry. Anything is better than dead.

I lean in, eating up the space between us and crowding her. I let my words slither across her lips.

"More," I snarl.

She tries again, and this time, when her saliva hits me, I catch her by the throat and crawl astride the bed, my knees on either side of hers. With one hand around her throat, I roll the wheel of the lighter with my free thumb. I bring it between us and watch the delicate flame dance in the air.

"Don't," she croaks, wincing with the word.

Tears prick at her eyes, and she looks like she's about to cry. Such an attitude adjustment for the little spitfire. I don't fucking like it.

"I hate you," she tells me.

"You're a terrible liar," I say.

She sniffles.

"What are you afraid of?" I ask her, forcing her to look up at me.

Her blue eyes blink twice before she answers.

"You," she murmurs to me, swallowing against my hand.

"Good," I say. "Then you can stop being afraid of living."

I kiss her, and it's not sweet or gentle. It's a punishment for everything she's put me through, for her continued refusal to see herself for what she is, and to care whether she lives or dies. I hope it conveys everything I haven't said to her yet. I hope it screams that I want each and every part of her, her robbed childhood, her insecurities and doubts, her fears and nightmares, *everything*. I need them, and I'll burn the answers out of her if I have to.

She raises her hands, trying to push me away, but I'm too strong, or maybe she's too weak. I keep her there, pressed against the wall, and I know I should make her choose, but there's something in the way she smells, like ocean water and strawberries that makes me ravenous. I kiss her again, only this time I reach between us and tear at her underwear and her skirt, yanking them off and sending them to the floor. It's messy. Elbows and knees hit as our arms and legs tangle. I kiss her again, and she fights me. She pushes me away with two hands in a brutal shove that lands like a baseball bat to my sternum. Then she pulls me to her, reeling me back, kissing me once again.

"I hate you," she tells me against my lips.

"Only because no one else has given a fuck about you before, and you don't know how to feel about it," I clap back.

She forces me away again with a snarl, and she's gorgeous, her lips swollen and puffy and her blue eyes swimming in unshed tears. She yanks me back a second time, kissing me.

"I want to hate you," she says as she pushes me away again.

"Now that, I believe," I agree.

I feel the exact moment she gives in to me. The taste of victory mixes with salt on her tongue as she flattens her mouth to mine and tugs me even closer.

"It doesn't mean anything if we fuck," she says, panting and out of breath.

"Liar," I hiss.

Her shirt and bra go next until she's gloriously naked in front of me. I prefer my women with a little more meat on their bones, literally, but fuck if the light isn't hitting her strawberry blonde hair just right at the moment, transforming it into churning rapids of fire. Strands fall to caress her shoulders and tickle her rose-colored nipples where they've wrangled free from her ponytail.

I thrust two fingers inside of her pussy, and she nearly comes off the bed.

"Gabe!" she shrieks.

"That's my name, baby girl," I murmur against her lips with a growl. "I expect you to scream it by the time we're over."

I thrust in her again, bringing my thumb to play with her clit. I'm not gentle about it, but she's already soaking wet and ready for me. I fuck her hard and fast with my fingers until she's writhing between me and the bed, her body covered in a sheen of sweat despite the cold.

"I'm going to come," she says, arching her beautiful spine.

"Not yet, baby girl," I tell her. "First I need this perfect little pussy to strangle my cock."

I undo my belt, shove down my boxers just enough to free myself, and shove inside of her in one brutal thrust. She screams, her mouth catching open at the sound, and I tear the rest of our clothes off as the mirrors show everything. The sharp edge of her hipbone, her narrow waist below her ribs, her small breasts starved to almost nothing. I fuck her hard, and she screams again, her nails reaching up to scrape at my back. The bed jolts and creaks as I punish her.

I don't want to stop. I don't want to ever stop. But more than that, I want her to feel the heat of my body and the brutal impale of my cock, my balls hitting her taint, and how angry I am.

I'm angry too, even angrier than before because now that I've had her pussy, I know that there's no coming back. Not now, not for me, not ever.

She will *never* take it away.

"Goddamn," I tell her, "your pussy is heaven, baby girl."

She murmurs something on a breath, but it's unintelligible. She doesn't get it. She can't because girls like her get the stars and the moon, and I get the rot and decay far below. Heaven isn't attainable for a man like me. I don't get to go to those pearly gates, not in this life or the next, except when I'm with her. Now that I've had a taste, I won't ever be able to give it up.

I yank one of her legs over my shoulder, grabbing behind her thigh, and pound into her even deeper. She cries out, and I feel her walls start to flutter around me. She's about to come, and I want to let her. My balls tighten, and it takes everything in me to not follow her, but I don't. I stop moving. She's been bad. She doesn't deserve to come, not yet.

"Don't stop," she pleads, lifting her hips off the bed and trying to fuck me from below. I press my hips forward, bottoming out inside of her, and pin her to the bed beneath my weight.

"You've been a bad girl, Firefly," I murmur, reaching an arm up to smooth her sweat-slicked hair away from her forehead. I thrust in and out slowly, starting a lazy rhythm. "You don't get to come on my cock, not yet."

She rakes her fingernails down my back, and I continue my slow torturous thrusts, sinking in inch by inch and then pulling back even slower. Everything hurts, my balls, my ass, my hips, and my abdominals. I need to come so badly that every bit of me aches, but I don't. I dig down deep and find the last crumbs of my self-control.

I fuck her for what feels like hours, and it's beautiful torture.

The sound of us, sweaty and panting in the basement as we rut like animals, ingrains into the gray matter of my brain. Even when I'm old, I don't want to forget the sound of our skin slapping and sliding as she pleads for me to let her come.

"Oh please, Gabe. Please, oh, please . . ." she begs.

She cries and hits me. Still, though, I don't give her what she wants.

I pound into her hard and fast and then hit the brakes, sinking between her legs slowly.

She wraps her legs around me, squeezing with her thighs and kicking at me with her ankles, but I don't give in. The bed creaks as I slide for home and bottom out inside of her. Sweat covers both of us, and she shakes beneath me.

I continue my torment. The air tastes like sweat and smells like sex as I edge the both of us. Her pussy grips me like wet lace, and fuck, I need to come.

"Please, Gabe," she says, her voice hoarse. "*Please . . .* I need to come."

"Who's pussy is this?" I tell her, sinking home once more.

"Yours," she says.

"Goddamn right," I growl.

I give her false hope and adjust. I pull out and climb to my knees before I swing her legs over my shoulders, one over each one, and start to really fuck her. The whole bed shakes now, the metal joints screeching and squealing, as I jackhammer inside of her.

"F-f-f-f-f-f-f-u-u-u-u-u-c-c-c-c-k-k-k-k," she says, her curse cutting into vowels and consonants with every impale.

Her entire body shakes with the ferocity of our fucking. Hell, I think the world shakes as her ass bounces against my balls. I hold her in place with one hand still atop her legs as I snake my other hand around her thigh and to her clit. I don't slow down. I just start flicking it in a furious rhythm to our fucking.

A savage satisfaction comes over me when I feel the moment she starts to quake. This is the thirteenth time now that I've almost given in, and each time, it gets even harder to stop. My thighs are shaking, and my dick feels like it's about to explode, but she's been bad and bad girls don't get to come until I tell them to.

"Yes, yes, y—!" she cries.

I stop abruptly, pulling out and letting her ass fall to the bed. She bounces on impact and looks up from the mattress at me, confused and then pissed.

"What the hell?!" she hisses, but I don't give her the time to continue her tirade. I grab her at the hips and flip her over, putting her on all fours before I slam into her again. She shrieks on the impale, and I know I'm even bigger at this angle, but I don't care. I want her to feel sore and used and know that I was the one that brought her there. I pound into her from behind a few times before I pull her top half off of the bed and against me as I rock back onto my heels. Her head falls to my shoulder, her cheek pressed against my jawline as her hair—her ponytail long gone—skims my back. I continue that slow pace inside of her again.

"Look with me," I murmur against her jawline, breathing in

the chocolate that still lingers on her breath. "Look at you, baby girl, and see how beautiful you are."

I fuck her slowly, thrusting in and out lazily, as we both look up at the mirrors suspended from the ceiling. Her eyes are glossy as she stares along with me, enchanted and watching as I take her from behind, massive compared to her small, pale frame. One of her hands reaches behind her and runs up and across my shoulder and around my neck, tickling my hair there. She's beautiful to behold, and I am lost, transfixed by the way her mouth falls open as she looks upward and her breasts thrust to the ceiling. She's a firefly beneath the mirrors, creating sparks of magic as we move together.

"Oh my God," she breathes as I continue to thrust into her.

I bring a hand around to her front to play with her clit.

"You're gorgeous, baby girl," I tell her, as I continue that lazy pace again. My fingers find her swollen nub, and I begin to rub, lightly at first and then harder, until she trembles against me.

"We're gorgeous," she breathes.

"Are you going to be a good girl?" I ask her, my words pressed against her cheek as we fuck. "Will you eat for me?"

"Y . . . yes," she murmurs, and I'm not sure if she hears me or if she's lost in the sensations. I reach across the bed and grab another chocolate bar. I tear the wrapper open with my teeth and shove it inside her mouth. She chews without hesitation, and I pick up speed.

"That's right, baby girl," I tell her, forcing her head back to look at me. "Be a good girl for me. You can't take heaven from me, Firefly, not now after I've had a taste."

And she is so good after what feels like—and might actually be—hours of edging, and she finally eats without me forcing her to, watching us as she does. The more she chews, the faster I go, until I'm hammering into her wildly, and she's staring up at the ceiling, enchanted by the reflections of us. She finishes the bar, and I fuck her even harder, watching her mirror image as she bounces on my dick and comes, calling my name as she does.

Her walls clench around me, and I follow quickly after her, spilling inside of her and coming harder than I ever have before, desecrating her perfect walls with my cum. I feel it begin to leak out of her as my eyes roll back into my head, and I'm lost in heaven.

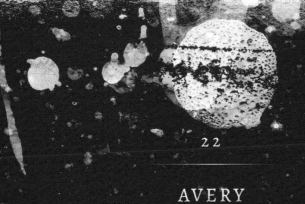

22

AVERY

G abe says I've been down here for four days now. I can't tell if he's lying or not, though. It could've been four days, or it could've been forty too. Time is measured when I see him, and the rest of it is spent sleeping, staring at myself in the mirrors, reading the books he brings me, or blocking everything out. I used to hate looking in the mirror, and if I'm being honest, it still makes me uncomfortable, but at least I think I'm starting to see myself for who I really am now. I don't hate my body when I look up at the hundreds of reflections puzzled together across the ceiling. I don't see the bits of fat and cellulite stuck here and there across my skin. I see him holding me, the muscles in his back rippling as he rolls his hips and drives inside of me. I see him buried to the hilt, wanting me and going crazy for me. I see his brown hair colored black by his sweat as I make him unravel. I see us, together, and the beautiful picture we create.

We talk. We eat. We fuck.

Gabe lets me out of my cell to use the restroom, but that's only because I refuse to use the bucket. We had a lengthy, loud debate about it, which ended in me convincing him that making me go to the bathroom in a bucket wouldn't exactly be good for my self-worth or whatever. The same argument did not work in my favor, however, when I tried to use it to get out of being caged in my cell like I'm his own personal zoo exhibit.

There's a small bathroom on the floor just above us, where the maintenance rooms, the boilers, and the big pipes that feed this place all reside. The bathroom isn't anything fancy, just two porcelain sinks and two stalls, each with a toilet, but I relish the times he lets me out to go up there. I find myself looking forward to them.

The first time he took me there, I tried to run.

The second time, I tried to kick him in the balls and then run.

The third, when he threatened to make me use the bucket if I didn't learn to behave, well . . . I learned to behave.

Speaking of bathrooms . . . *ugh.* I look down between my legs and sigh.

I got my period this morning. It's been so long that at first, I thought I peed myself, but then I spotted the red stain on the bed linen and it hit me.

Gabriel Edward Soros kicks my ovaries into overdrive, apparently.

When was the last time I got my period?

Six months probably, maybe even more. My monthly gift is sporadic on a good day, but when I barely consume enough to keep a Chihuahua breathing, well . . . it skips out entirely. I wadded up toilet paper and stuffed it into my underwear, but I'm feeling remarkably gross by the time Gabe arrives at lunchtime. Well, he says it's lunchtime when he walks into my cell, shuts the door behind him, and places a tray full of food onto the bed beside me.

"What's wrong?" he asks, stealing a grape off of my tray and popping it into his mouth.

"I need a tampon," I tell him. "Well, tampons actually. I need a box of tampons."

I don't give a shit if it makes him uncomfortable. Menstruation is a normal bodily function. He can suck it up. My last fuck buddy was freaked out by periods. He said he preferred being with me so he didn't have to deal with that "disgusting shit."

Like my suffering made his life easier, the bastard.

I refuse to be made to feel that way again.

Not now, not after everything, and especially not with Gabe.

Gabe chews his grape slowly as he does that unblinking stare thing I'm getting used to before he swallows the fruit.

"Tampons?" he asks, arching an eyebrow.

"And clean bed sheets," I tell him. I pull back the gray linen blanket on top of the bed and show him the stained sheet. He blinks at it for a long moment, plucks another grape from the tray, and feeds it to me. I chew, swallow it, and open my mouth for another.

Somewhere deep down, I hear the count begin.

Five calories per grape.

One down, another incoming.

I tell it to shut the fuck up.

"Okay," he says to me.

"Okay?" I ask. This is way too easy. "That's it? You aren't going to try to use it against me or something? Make me do your bidding, King Gabriel?"

"My bidding?" He grins as he cocks his head at me and *finally* blinks again. "Nah, I'm good. Would you like me to make you do something?"

He feeds me another grape, his gaze dipping to my lips as he watches me pluck it from between his fingers with my teeth.

"No," I tell him.

Maybe.

He stares at me, watching me chew. His gaze is pensive as he says, "I do have one request, though."

"What's that?" I ask after I swallow.

His tongue flicks across his two top teeth, and he should never be allowed to do that again. People have started wars over less, I'm sure.

"Show me," he tells me, his dark gaze locked on me.

Wait . . . what did he just say?

"What?" I ask, certain I heard him wrong.

"Show me, baby girl," he murmurs, still staring at me, his dark eyes painted black in the low light of this room. No person should have eyes that dark like two black pools that catch you by the feet and pull you under. Yet I can't look away from him.

My heart batters my sternum like a hard rain falling to dry earth as a flush creeps from the top of my cheeks and down my throat. I swallow, feeling it burn across my flesh as it does.

"Why?" I ask him.

"I told you that I want all of you," he says to me like that should explain it. "And that means all of your bloody parts too."

His words don't explain anything, though. People say that sort of shit all the time, yet they don't want to go full-on gynecologist and see what's going on in my panties. I swallow again, trying to unstick the lump that growing in my throat and turning off my air.

"Or I could go to the bathroom," I manage.

"I'll let you go after . . ."

"I know, I know," I interrupt. "After I eat something."

He grins, giving me a glimpse of his white teeth. "Smart girl, but not just that, not today. You're doing so well. I want more than that now."

"More than that?" I murmur as he steps forward, stealing the space between us and claiming it for himself.

He nods, stepping forward again before he tips forward so that we're at eye level as he utters his words.

"I want three things actually," he tells me.

My heart is going to hammer itself right out of my chest to flop like a fish on the floor any minute now. He's so close that it assaults all of my senses.

I see, hear, taste, smell, and *almost* touch him.

Chiseled cheekbones and demon-colored eyes.

Campfires and charcoal.

Cigarettes and peppermint.

Radiating warmth that peppers my skin.

It's too much, and he's not even touching me . . . yet.

"Three?" I manage with a squeak.

"Mhmm," he tucks a strand of loose hair behind my ear. "I want to watch you eat, and I want to taste that bloody pussy of yours until you scream. Then I want to light up your pretty flesh with flash paper and watch you sizzle, baby girl."

Oh my Gabriel.

"Flash paper?" I cough-slash-choke. It's more of a garbled sound than words, but he still gets the point.

"Shh," he assures me, running the pad of his thumb across my cheek, "it won't hurt, I promise."

"It won't?"

It sounds like it'll hurt.

"No," he tells me, "and it won't last long. There's a reason they call it flash paper."

I try but fail at swallowing the knot that's clogging my throat.

"Why's that?" I whisper.

"Because it's not on there long enough to hurt you. It'll tickle, and then it'll be gone in a flash."

He smiles as if to comfort me, but the gleam of his teeth is less comforting and more stroke-inducing at the moment.

"It's not going to burn me?" I ask.

He shakes his head. "It won't burn you, Firefly. It won't even leave any ashes behind. It's special paper, the same kind magicians use. We can test it out before if you want. Would you like to do that?"

I nod.

"Gabe," I swallow again, but the lump at the back of my throat won't unstick. Memories of the overturned car, the stench of smoke, the heat of the fire, and the panic as I screamed for my mother to wake up replay inside of my mind. Only one thing in the whole wide world used to scare me more than gaining an ounce.

Fire.

He's demanding a payment I can't give, not yet. Maybe not ever.

"I don't think I can," I tell him, shaking my head quickly. "Ask me anything else, Gabe. Anything at all."

My heart hits the stone floor, leaving me hollow and empty in my middle.

"Yes, you can, baby girl," he reassures me. "I'll be right here. You trust me, don't you?"

It's a loaded question. He kidnapped me to save me. He feeds me to make sure I live. I believe him, but I'm terrified, scared of him, of what's to come, and most of all, the flames.

"I trust you," I admit.

"I can work with that," he says to me before he wraps both of his hands around the back of my thighs and tugs me abruptly to the edge of the bed.

"What are you doing?" I yelp.

"I believe I was promised pussy," he says with a lopsided grin, "medium rare."

Holy fuck.

"You did not just call my lady bits medium rare."

"What would you prefer I call them?" he smirks. "Bloody and still beating?"

"I'd prefer you not use steak terminology when describing them," I manage with a cough.

"Hey, Firefly?" he says, his grin splitting even wider.

"Yeah?" I ask.

"You're stalling."

I don't get out another word before he drops to his knees on the floor and yanks my panties down, the wad of toilet paper falling to the floor with his tug. Lord Almighty, I don't think I've ever been so embarrassed.

What is wrong with me? Is this a dream? A nightmare?

This can't be happening right now.

Before I can react, he buries his head between my legs. By buried, I mean he full-on disappears as he thrusts his tongue inside of me.

I'm mortified.

Embarrassed.

Ablaze.

"You taste so good, baby girl," he says between thrusts of his tongue. "Absolutely fucking perfect."

He looks up at me, lifting his head, and I see that his nose, his chin, and his lips are all smeared with my blood.

Oh. My. God.

Then he disappears between my legs again, and I shudder the moment he flattens his tongue to me. It smells like blood, sweat, and sex in this cage. I need a shower—a real shower, not just one in a sink—but he doesn't seem to mind. He pushes his tongue inside of me again, fucking me with it, and I lose track of all my thoughts. There's just him, scraping his tongue inside of me, groaning as he does it, and my head lolling onto the bed as his strong arms force my thighs open even wider.

He pins me to the bed with his hands, but even if I wasn't pinned down, I don't think I would move. My fingers tangle in his hair of their own accord as his tongue sweeps across my pussy and screws me mercilessly. I shake, quivering against the bed when he adds a finger on my clit and goes to town, rubbing it faster and faster until everything in my core tightens like a spindle being drawn too tight until the string snaps and it unravels all at once. Marvelous heat scorches my veins, and I call out his name, looking up at the mirrors above us and my god on his knees before me.

He sits back on his heels and smiles at me, and I tip my chin down and look at him. I shouldn't have looked, though. I knew I shouldn't have looked. It nearly ends me on the spot.

The lower half of his face, the tip of his nose, and his teeth are all stained red with me. The wicked sight sucks all of the air straight out of my lungs.

"Fucking perfect," he praises before he leans up and over the bed to kiss me, flattening his lips to mine and letting me taste everything.

Sugar.

Salt.

Pennies.

I'm horrified yet on fire as he deepens the kiss and thrusts his tongue inside my mouth just like he did between my legs a moment earlier.

He pulls back a moment later, and I feel something shift in the air as the room buzzes with invisible energy. Is this what the girls who follow him feel too, the power that seems to radiate off him at a moment's notice?

I think I understand now. I think I finally see it, for once.

He reaches into his back pocket and pulls out a roll of bandage wraps that smell kind of funny, like chemicals and gasoline.

"Lay flat," he tells me. "On the floor. Take off your clothes."

I stand and start to undress, dropping what's left of my clothes onto the floor before I move to lie on the cold stone floor. He unravels the paper and wipes his face with it, and then cleans me between the legs gently until the wrappings are stained with blotches of red.

All of me shakes, and I squeeze my eyes together tightly to try to stop my shivering. He has to notice. I can almost hear my teeth clattering, but he says nothing as the stone cools my back and he begins to cover me in the paper. He lays the wrappings carefully, draping them atop my feet and continuing up to my legs and further still. I watch him as he drapes the fabric over my stomach, crisscrossing it back and forth as it climbs to my nipples.

"Is it going to hurt?" I ask him with a swallow. Screams are echoing in my head now—my screams from long ago, begging my mother to wake up before the fire kills us both. Blood rushes to my head again, just like it did before when the car was overturned. My breath comes and goes faster and faster until it's so fast I'm having a hard time catching my breath. It feels like I can't breathe, like I'll never be able to get enough air.

Gabe reaches for my hand and squeezes it tightly.

"There's nothing to be afraid of, baby girl," he murmurs to me. "Don't you want to go back upstairs?"

I look at him, my teeth chattering. "What?"

"This is it, Firefly," he tells me. "You've come so far, baby girl."

"What?" I ask him. This is too soon. He said a week, maybe more. Four days isn't long enough.

"The police are being called in. Saint's girlfriend, Willow, overhead a couple of guards in the girls' dormitory talking about it. I guess your dad is insisting on it. They are going to start searching the campus. Headmistress can't keep them out much longer, and eventually, they will find this place. I don't know how many days we have left together."

"Left together?" I ask, my shivering becoming even more violent beneath the chill of his words.

"Well," he tilts his head at me, "I'm pretty sure I'm either getting sent upstate to one of the permanent asylums or to prison when they find out what I did."

"That's your plan?" I gawk at him. "To fix me and then abandon me?"

"Not by choice," he says.

But that's not acceptable. I *need* him.

"I won't tell them it was you," I blurt. "I'll tell them I came down here by myself."

"Why would you do that?" he asks me, looking down the line of his nose at me.

"You know why I would do that," I murmur.

"I'm going to need you to say it."

My teeth chatter even louder, filling the silence, and I bite down hard, silencing them. "Because I . . ."

"Because you what?"

"Because I like you, I guess," I manage. "I'm grateful for you as fucked up as that is. No one's ever gone to the lengths you did, not for me, not ever. Even though what you did was colossally fucked up, at least you tried.

"When it gets hard, my dad just ships me off somewhere new, and the docs don't care, not really. They barely learn my name before he decides it isn't working and transfers me. I'm just a dollar amount to everyone—the schools see what they'll earn and my father sees what he'll spend. You did all of this for me, and for once in forever, I can finally look in a mirror and not hate myself. I can eat something and not hear my mother oinking at me, well, at least most of the time. Maybe I'm developing Stockholm Syndrome. I don't know, okay? I just know that I sort of don't think you're a total creep anymore."

He laughs, throwing his back, and the sound fills the room. I think I like it when he laughs.

"Don't discredit yourself," he shakes his head, sending stray tendrils of hair into his eyes, which he swipes away. "We both know you are too strong for that shit."

"What do you mean?"

"I mean that whatever you're feeling, you're feeling it willingly." He pins me with a stare. "Thank you, Firefly."

I giggle. I can't help it. Of course, the psychopathic pyromaniac would respond by thanking me. I confess my maybe-feelings, and he *thanks* me.

Awesome.

"You sure you don't want to add anything else to that?" I manage through my chattering teeth.

"I said I'd never lie to you, Avery," he warns.

I'm not going to lie. It stings.

"Oh o . . . o . . . k . . . kay," I say, biting my teeth together once more.

He frowns at me. "You misunderstand. I'm saying your words are inadequate. I'm saying I feel more."

He feels more, and I feel like the air has been sucked out of my lungs.

Who cares whether a guy likes you when you can have *more* instead?

"Gabe?" I ask him a moment later, reaching for his hand and holding it tight.

He looks down at me from his seated position at my side. "Yeah, baby girl?"

"I'm glad you're my creep."

He smirks. "Is that your way of thanking me for saving you?"

I laugh, and the paper wriggles with my flesh when I do. "Don't get a big head about it. I'm not saying I'm cured. You didn't just invent some fucked-up anorexia treatment. You know that, right?"

"I don't need you cured, baby girl." He leans up, still holding my hand, and with his free hand, pets my hair. "It will always be a struggle, and there's not a single thing I can do to stop that. All I need is for you to know your way back to me."

"I know my way back to you."

"Good," he releases my hand and stops petting my hair to stand. He's so tall beside me as I lie naked on the cold stone floor. My breath spills from my lungs even faster as he pulls the lighter from his back pocket, flips the lid on the black Zippo, and ignites the flame.

"Ready, Firefly?"

"Ready," I squeak.

My heart batters my chest, and my stomach somersaults as I look at him. I'm having a hard time breathing.

Broken glass, smoke, and ash.

I start to cry, blinking away the tears as fast as I can.

Screams, bleeding cuts, and the groan of crushed metal.

His image wavers behind my tears.

Fire, screeching tires, and the pressure of the seat belt against my chest.

Through my bleary vision, I watch as he drops the Zippo, and it hits my side. The flash paper ignites instantaneously and all of me goes up in blinding orange light.

I'm hot, burning, and on fire for a fraction of a second, but then cold again in an instant. I'm still crying when I look down and find that I'm naked with tendrils of smoke curling in the air above my bare skin.

"Oh my God," I tell him, trying to catch my breath.

He grins wickedly down at me.

"I knew you would be beautiful when you burned, baby girl."

I feel beautiful as I look back up at him, smoke dispersing in the air, and find him still staring at me.

23

AVERY

I t's strange seeing my parents in person. I knew my entire world was about to be engulfed in hellfire after Gabe let me out of the basement, but I couldn't stay down there forever. Even without the police about to show up at my father's behest and storm the campus, I would've had to eventually leave.

Gabe led me out of the basement, and I walked down the halls, headed back to my dorm room. Staffing was thin—almost transparent—as I navigated the hallways. It was just as he said. They were so busy looking for me outside that they couldn't turn their gazes inside and find me. I almost made it to the girls' dormitory, too, before a guard spotted me.

"Hey!" she called after me, a gobsmacked expression blasting across her round face. "Hey, you!"

I kept walking, and she reached for her radio. "I have the lost student with me on level 2, northwest quadrant. Requesting backup immediately."

Then she ran forward, bolting after me, and caught me by the elbow.

"Avery?" she asked. "Avery Bardot?"

"The one and only," I told her before she steered me into an empty classroom and onto an empty seat to wait for more guards.

It took them eleven minutes to arrive, or at least that's what the clock on the wall told me. I was restrained in wrist and ankle hobbles and walked like a dog on a leash to Headmistress's office. I thought the lady was going to blow a gasket when she saw me in person. I don't recall ever actually seeing a human being turn that shade of red, but she put a lid on her anger for now. Granted, it's probably going to bubble up and hit the ceiling at some point.

At her direction, a guard steered me into a chair in front of her desk. She didn't waste a second in calling my parents to let them know I had been located. I could hear my father on the other end of the line yelling as another guard knocked on the door, informing her that the sheriff's department had advised them that they were on their way to campus. She told my parents she had to call them back and moved so fast I think she might have even traveled at lightspeed before she telephoned the police, letting them know my disappearance was, as she put it, *a giant misunderstanding*, but that I had been safely located.

As my parents boarded the first plane here, Headmistress made me recount where I had gone. I recited the story Gabe and I practiced, one that would line up with everything his friends had done to frame my disappearance. I told her I had run away, and at first, I had gone into the woods, but that I wasn't prepared for the weather. I knew it would be cold, but not that cold, and I had to come back inside the building. I explained how I had heard about the tunnels beneath the Asylum and how I thought they might lead me somewhere away from this place. I told her I had found the door to the stairwell unlocked and said I had gone down there, looking for a way out, and finding no way, I stayed until I ran out of food.

It won't be hard for her to confirm the story, at least the part about staying in the basement. Gabe and I disassembled almost everything that he had put together down there. The bed frame is torn apart and scattered into pieces, and the mirrors are gone, smashed to bits throughout the room. The mattress and the bucket remain in the cell. We're going to have one thousand years of bad luck for breaking the mirrors if you believe in that sort of thing. I don't, though. Plus, if luck is real, then mine's always been fucked since the day I was born to my mother.

Headmistress asked a few questions but appears to have bought my story. It helps that I'm still dirty. I have rust from pulling on the cell bars caked beneath my fingernails and my clothes are torn, not from the forest surrounding campus or surviving in the elements, but from Gabe. She doesn't know that, though, or if she suspects it, she doesn't call me out on it.

When they cordon off the entrance to the basement, Gabe will lose his access to the lower levels of the Asylum, but he said that was all right and that it was worth it for me to be here with him instead. Still, I'd like to be there—or anywhere—with him right now rather than locked up in the administrative office about to meet with my mother and father. At least they took off my restraints, I guess.

Hell, I'm surprised my parents cared enough to board a plane. Then again, it's only an hour flight from Massachusetts, and their only child was missing for the past four days, so really, it was about the least they could've done.

I can't remember the last time they both came to see me or even sat in on the same video chat with me. My father visits me in school occasionally, but even Christmas isn't a guarantee anymore. He says my mother has a hard time at home when he's not there with her, and she never comes to visit because, I'm guessing, I remind her too much of her failures. Or maybe she just cares that little. Now that I think about it, it's definitely the latter.

"Sweet pea," my father says as I'm steered from the waiting area and back into Headmistress's private office. He's frozen for a moment. By the looks of it, both of them are, apparently, before he jumps to his feet and walks over to me. He wraps me in his arms and squeezes me tight enough to wring the water out of a sponge and leave it bone-dry. He hasn't called me that in years, probably since I was six or seven years old.

"We were worried about you," he tells me.

I doubt that. Maybe he was.

He pushes away from me and looks me up and down as if to check that I'm still here in front of him. Then he brings me in for another hug. I stand there unmoving as he holds me. He smells like coffee and soap as the fabric of his pea coat scratches at the side of my face.

"Are you okay?" he asks me, backing away from me again but keeping his hands on my shoulders. He looks me over once more, assuring himself that I am in one piece.

Headmistress closes the door to her office as my father continues to study me.

"I'm fine," I tell him as Headmistress walks around her desk to sit in her tall leather chair.

"As I explained on the phone, your daughter is quite fine, Mr. Bardot," she says as my mother remembers she's supposed to act like one, stands, and walks over to us. She brings me in for a tight hug that I also don't reciprocate.

"Avery, dear," she says, her thin arms firm around me, "we were so worried about you."

To her credit, she does actually sound worried, which is impressive, well, for my mother, at least. I wasn't sure she had the emotional capacity to worry about anyone except herself.

"Are you sure you're feeling well?" my father asks.

"I'm fine," I tell him. There's no emotion behind my words. I want this over with.

They haven't cared for years, but now when they think I ran away, they act like they give a shit. Fucking figures.

"As I said on the phone," Headmistress says, "your daughter is fine. However, there is the issue of what we should do with her now."

"Now?" my father goes rigid as his face flushes to the color of ripe beets. "Now? Are you kidding me, Ms. Graves? You lost her! There is no now! Our arrangement is over!"

My heart plummets to my feet and keeps on digging. I can't leave Gabe, not after everything. I need the fire freak, and the fire freak needs his firefly.

"Please," Headmistress says, gesturing at the chairs, "sit. We are adults. Let's be civilized."

There's nothing my father hates more than someone implying that he's acting unreasonably. He bristles, and his face reddens even further. I think I spot the moment when a capillary bursts across the bridge of his nose.

I sit first, choosing the chair farthest from Headmistress.

My father falls into the chair beside me, landing with a murmured curse. My mother moves to sit in the seat beside him.

"Now I understand your frustration, Mr. Bardot," Headmistress says, clasping her hands on her desk in front of her, "but rest assured, we will not make the same mistake with your daughter going forward. From this day on, she will be placed on 24/7 watch within our isolation unit until a plan can be established to ensure this does not happen again. And, as a small token of our sincere apologies, we will waive the next one hundred and twenty days of your daughter's tuition. I think you will find that remuneration to equal a considerable amount."

"One hundred and twenty days?" my father remarks, and although it stops my heart currently digging through the core of the Earth, I feel the familiar rage inside of me rise again. My whole life has been boiled down to dollar signs—how much my father will spend and how much the administration will earn.

Anger bleeds from my father's ruddy cheeks, bringing them back to their normal color, as he slowly calms.

"Yes, of course," Headmistress says. "It's the least we can offer after such an unfortunate event. And, of course, Avery will continue to receive the best care money can buy including group therapy, individual therapy, medication management, and more. I think you'll find our head psychiatrist, Dr. Boucher, to be more than capable of helping your daughter."

"And she will be in 24/7 observation for the time being?"

"Yes," Headmistress nods. "Our isolation unit is impregnable. Never once in all my years has a student managed to escape it."

I watch as he considers it.

"Well, that is good," my father says, and my mother nods, playing the part of an agreeable wife.

What the fuck?

I should be happy I'll remain here with Gabe—I *am* happy— but I'm also pissed off because it always comes down to money, doesn't it? It's the question that got me taken out of so many reformatory schools before this one.

What am I paying you for? my father would ask.

The words are there, living on the tip of my tongue, but I can't actually say them, not when so much is at stake, not until the deal is solidified.

Headmistress pushes a document across her desk toward my parents.

"If you'll just sign here, we will transfer Avery shortly."

My father reads the document and signs the thing. My mother doesn't read it at all but follows suit. The deal is done. Headmistress reaches for the paper as my father leans over and squeezes my knee.

"We love you so much, sweet pea," he tells me. "Your mother and I just want you to get better."

"Of course," my mother echoes.

"Please," Headmistress stands, "let me show you the way out."

They stand, and I can take it anymore. I'm going to explode if I don't get it out.

"Are you delusional?" I murmur to the two of them as they walk toward the door.

"What?" my father turns, squinting at me.

"Are you delusional?" I repeat, looking at him and then at my mother. "You must be if you actually think showing up here makes you decent parents."

"Your father and I have flown a very long way, Avery . . ." my mother begins.

"And there it is," I cut her off, "the guilt trip. It's not enough that you ruined my life, is it?"

"Avery!" my father shouts at the same time Headmistress exclaims, "Mr. Bardot!"

I don't back down, though.

I'm worth more than that.

Gabe taught me that.

Let's burn the lies and the false pretenses all the way down to hell so we can finally see the truth.

"You should've protected me," I tell my father. "You should have protected me from her."

I look at my mother, who gapes at me, her perfect face flushed with her embarrassment.

I want her more than embarrassed. I want her mortified and absolutely ruined.

"And you," I hiss at her, "you're pathetic. I don't want to see you ever again. You bullied me when I was three years old, and you still bully me now. What the fuck is actually wrong with you?"

"Language, Ms. Bardot!" Headmistress nearly shrieks as she presses a button on her phone and barks, "I need two guards immediately!"

My father gawks at me as the guards arrive and quickly open the door to the room.

"Avery," my father begins, stepping forward. He reaches for me, but I don't want him to touch me. "I love you."

"No, you don't!" I nearly scream, the words shredding my throat and cutting me apart from the inside. "Maybe you think you do, but you don't. I can assure you of that."

I reach for my mother and pinch her sides *hard*. She yelps and tries to get away, but I don't let her.

"How's it feel?" I ask her, grabbing her hard enough to bruise. "How's it feel, piggy?! Huh, piggy? Huh?"

She slaps me. It happens in the blink of an eye, and I feel a blossom of nettles across my cheek before I laugh in her face.

"Restrain her!" Headmistress yells at the guards.

"I knew I was right about you!" my mother sneers. "You always were a disgusting pig. Do you know much money your father and I pay . . ."

"I don't care!" I shout, raising my hands. "I wouldn't be here if it wasn't for you! And you're too self-absorbed to even admit that. I'm just a casualty in the mind game you've been playing with yourself for years, Mother."

"Oh my poor sweet piggy," she coos, sarcasm dripping like venom from her lips. "Your life is so hard!"

She pretends to wipe her tears away.

"Megan!" my father snaps, his tone severe.

"Like you care!" I snap back at him. "You don't give a fuck about me. You won't even be out the door before you've forgiven her. You will never ever see her for what she is!"

"And what is that?" my mother demands.

"A bully, and the worst kind too, the kind who does it to their own child. You're pathetic. The both of you are. You deserve each other."

"Enough!" Headmistress says, bringing her fist down to her table. The *bang* is loud in her large office, echoing in the space.

Her gaze cuts to my father. "You see what we've been dealing with? Now I'm afraid I have to ask you to leave so we can do our jobs, Mr. and Mrs. Bardot."

"Of course," my mother says, grabbing my father by the elbow and steering him toward the door.

My father nods and follows numbly behind her.

And isn't that fucked up too?

That they'll go on as business as usual when they leave and forget my words, but I can't leave and I can never forget what they've done to me.

24

GABE

I learned at a young age as I watched my grandfather light his fireplace that the flames had the ability to burn away all the bad feelings I kept bottled up inside of me. I sat and watched that fire for hours as my grandmother tried and failed at ushering me to bed. I was transfixed, and it was an absolute miracle I didn't stick my hand into the pretty orange and yellow tendrils crackling in front of me and try to capture them in the palm of my hand.

Even before I knew the meaning of the word, I didn't feel my father's disgust when I looked at the flames.

I wasn't the stupid son who couldn't do anything right.

I was just a boy enchanted by the liquid light.

Much later, the compulsion developed into something more, a safety blanket that hid me away from more than just the antipathy of my father, but also protected me from the noise that was always present between my ears and the bad thoughts that murmured I wasn't good enough for this world. Over time, the draw to the flame grew into something even more, and I realized I needed more than warm willing pussy to satiate my needs. Sex was boring without the fire, and no matter how much I tried I always came back to the flame, feeding the compulsion before I was finally able to come.

Sex wasn't boring with her, though, even when I didn't grab the lighter, roll the wheel, and press the button. It was a beautiful, tortuous mania that nearly sent me over the edge before we had even begun. I didn't have to imagine the flames licking her flesh to get my cock in the game. I stared at her when she came undone, and it was enough, more than enough, to explode inside of her.

Watching her beneath that ceiling of mirrors, her gaze hooded, her body contorted as she accepted what I gave her and took even more, it was pure bliss.

It's not normal. Pussy shouldn't be that good. I'm like an addict when it comes to her, shaking and sweating before my next hit when I can bury to the hilt inside of her and feel her perfect cunt clench around me like a glove.

I don't think about them again after I fuck them either. One and done isn't a motto for me. I'm not that kind of guy, and there are only so many options in a place like this. I'm more like one and move on. I do what I have to, fire play, branding, flash paper, and more, to fill whatever hole with my cum, and I don't think of them again—well, not until they come back and ask for more.

Yet I can't stop thinking about *her*, my firefly, who called my name like I was her lord when she came, spilling a hundred perfect reflections across the mirrors above us. I can't move on from her, and that has never happened, except once before with the girl who craved the burn as much as I do.

Aisling, who cooked herself to a crisp while I shouted at her to stop.

For months, I never wanted to come back to this place. It reminded me too much of her and her betrayal, yet I'm drawn here again, to this hideaway hole in the tunnels beneath the

Asylum. They boarded it up after she barbequed herself, but they'd need to fill the entire thing with concrete to keep me out.

There's a pile of ashes stretching across the stone floor in this dark tunnel. The flashlight from my phone doesn't provide much light, unlike that night, when the fire burnt brilliantly against the dark. She started with paper and then added rags and bits of pieces of wood until she created her own miniature fire in here.

I told her to stop adding shit or she was going to suffocate us to death. Aisling never did know when to stop, and more often than not, I had to hit the brakes on her off-the-rails plans before she killed both of us. I remember her reaching into her back-pack, smiling at me as she laughed. She hid it behind her back before I could spot what it was, and she made me ask nicely before she showed me. She pulled the aerosol can from behind her and waggled her eyebrows at me in a challenge.

Fuck, I had thought when I saw it, *not this again.*

She always did try to take it further, but she was careless, stupid even, and didn't understand incendiaries, not like I did at least. She didn't care either. She had one Neanderthal directive.

Big boom, pretty fire.

"Don't do it," I had told her, panic slipping between the words.

I liked the crackle of the flames and the roaring heat as much as she did, but I knew better. That shit could kill us when it blew. She should've known better, but Aisling was never good at learning her lesson. The gnarled flesh on her right forearm, stretching to the elbow, proved that.

She had a dangerous compulsion, but I was smart about it. I always reeled her back in, or I tried to, at least.

In response to my warning, she stuck her tongue out at me.

"It's empty, Gabriel." She rolled her hazel eyes. "Unwad your panties, sir."

She laughed, throwing her head back like what she said was hilarious. It wasn't. And I didn't laugh.

I hated when she got this way. It made light of the compulsion. It made it seem something it wasn't: fun and carefree. I didn't understand then, and I still don't now. The calling has never been blithe for me. It's a necessity, like air to breathe or water to drink. It demands respect.

"Don't throw that shit in there," I told her, shaking my head. "You'll fucking kill us both."

For some reason, she thought my words made it even funnier. I wanted to strangle her for it. She disrespected the one thing I cared about more than anything, the one thing that burned all the bad shit away when no one else protected me.

"Aisling," I growled, the flames in front of her casting orange and yellow shadows up the walls.

"Oh my God," she crooned, dancing around the fire. "Did I scare the big bad Gabriel? Is the wittle boy afwaid?"

I would have strangled her had she not been holding enough compressed propane and butane to blow us to smithereens. She laughed.

"I'm not scared," I told her, taking a step forward. She did a little twirl and nearly fell into the fucking fire. "I'm being smart. Don't do it, Aisling!"

She grinned, the light of the fire reflecting off the white glint of her teeth and her freckleless cheeks. She always wanted to go bigger without regard for the consequences.

It was too much, and I knew it. The canister would explode and maim both of us. She probably wanted to perform her party trick, like she always did, where she ran from one side of the fire toward me, killing off the lingering flames as she laughed. Only she never got the chance to run through the flames that day, and she didn't come out the other side unscathed.

She was on one side of the fire she had started, and I was on the opposite side when she pretended to toss the can before catching it out of the air.

"Don't throw it, Aisling! It'll blow!" I shouted, but she just laughed again as she danced around the pile, the can remaining in hand this time.

"Put it down," I yelled at her, and she just flipped her black hair over her shoulder, smiled at me, and sent me a little wave.

Despite it all, I never thought she would do it. She should've known I was serious. I've always been serious when it comes to the flames. Yet she laughed in my face when she threw the fucking thing, and at that moment, all I could think was goddammit, I told her not to fucking throw it.

"Get down!" I screamed at her, backing away for the door behind me, but she never even moved from her spot a couple of feet away from the flames. She was still standing there, grinning at me, as the can hit the fire, and the world stood on end for just a moment. I held my breath, and in the blink of an eye, it detonated, engulfing her in a ball of white fire. Her laughter ceased to be, extinguished as it turned to screams instead.

There was nothing I could do.

She was one big fucking fireball. I tore off my shirt and tried to get close to her, but she was so hot that it burned my skin from where I stood and popped sweat across my brow. She screamed and flailed, running wildly down the tunnel. It took less than seven seconds for her to fall to her knees and collapse face-first against the stone.

"Goddammit!" I yelled as I ran around the original fire and to her, using my shirt to try to extinguish the flames as best I could. Piece by piece, I tried to save her, suffocating the flames. It went against my every instinct. I didn't start the fire. I didn't add to it. I didn't watch it burn. I just doused it out as best as I could, and it still wasn't enough to save her.

A chunk of stone is missing in the wall from where the can

blew and ricocheted down the tunnel. Aisling died down here, and one day, I think I'd like to show Avery the exact same spot. Not because I want to recreate the blaze, but because she is my salve, the only person in the world I've met capable of calming the twitch in my fingers and the tingle racing up my spine that's desperate to set the world ablaze.

Avery is my new compulsion.

Aisling was compelled with me.

Maybe I grieved her. I don't know.

I hate thinking about her now, though, because thoughts of her remind me of my failures. Her death didn't stop my compulsion. If anything, it fed it.

I wanted to understand her disregard and her lack of respect, but even after all of this time, I don't understand a damn thing.

I wonder what my Firefly is doing right now. I skipped class today to come here, not that my professors will mind. Everything's pass-fail anyway, but I had to come. Something about this place calls to me when the world doesn't quite make sense.

I know that if they try to send Avery anywhere, I will follow her. I can't be without her, not now.

I play with my lighter in the dark, watching the flame flicker on and off, plunging me into darkness and delivering me from it again. I light a piece of paper and drop the burning page onto a pile of rags in front of me, catching them alight. The flames stretch toward the ceiling, but they're not even halfway there, not yet. I could burn the whole school down if I wanted to, but I don't. I need to protect her. I walk over to the burning pile and stomp it out beneath the heel of my loafer. It catches the bottom of my pants leg on fire, and I quickly smother the flame out with my hand.

My phone vibrates inside of my pocket, but the noise is too much today. I'm worried, and the letters and numbers jumble together and create something new on my phone screen. Still, I take it out and try to read it aloud to no avail. I even run my fingertip along the bottom of each line, but it doesn't help.

There's too much damn noise. It hums in between my ears, growing louder and louder, until I drown in it.

I take a deep breath and see Avery's face, and the noise quiets to a low rumble. Finally, when I run my fingertip along the line once more, I can read it. It's the group chat with Saint and Kill.

> **KILL**
>
> Your girl make it out of Headmistress's office alive?

> **SAINT**
>
> Doubtful. She looks like she'll break her in two.

I leave them both on read.

They underestimate her, but that's fine by me. They don't need to estimate anything when it comes to my Firefly.

I hope she's giving Headmistress and her parents hell right now. God knows Headmistress will try to send her to Butcher before the day is out. You can't disappear like she did and not expect repercussions, but everybody knows Butcher doesn't like to fuck with the eating disorder kids. They probably aren't enough of a challenge for him. He likes the ones who hurt others, not themselves. Members of the thinspo club get force-fed if they end up in isolation, but that's about it. Still, I'm hoping she can avoid meeting his ancient ass on his home turf.

I tear my eyes away from the still smoldering pile in front of me, turn on my heel, and head out of the tunnel and toward the administrative office.

I don't care if I have to wait all day. I need to see her face. And if they send her to the hole, I'll blow her a kiss and tell her to give Butcher a big *fuck you* from me when she arrives.

25

AVERY

A guard sits with me in Headmistress's office while she walks my parents out of the building. I don't know why the asshole beside me just won't go ahead and get it over with. He could've already taken me to the one known as the Butcher. From what I understand, that guy's the one who really runs this place, not Headmistress Graves. But the guard doesn't move. He doesn't even say a word to me. I'm only certain he's alive because he's breathing, a sharp whistle sounding from his nose on each exhale. Otherwise, he just sits there on the leather chair like a human seat cushion.

I sit in the chair on the opposite end of the row, leaving the one in the middle empty.

I'm tired of sitting here. I want to find Gabe and tell him every glorious detail about how I finally stood up for myself, how I made my parents face what they've done to me, but who knows when I'll be able to see him next? Even if I had his number, my phone is still in my dorm room unless Gabe's friends, Saint and Kill, did something with it too.

I don't care what the scary doc does to me at this point. The look on my mom's face when I pinched her fat and made her confront her own worst demons was worth whatever he tries. I'll replay her shriek whenever I feel like I'm going to break in the hole. It will make me stronger and get me through whatever else these fucks throw my way.

Who knows what they have left at this point?

Since I first arrived, I've done *everything* they've asked of me. I weighed in every single day. I met with the headmistress once a week. I attended cognitive-behavioral therapy, group therapy, and nutritional counseling. I took my meds and watched as the staff weighed my food before and after every meal. I even sat in my designated spot, lumped together with the rest of the eating disorder students. I stayed in my lane. Well, except for when Gabe kidnapped me, but whatever. That is not my fault.

I don't care anymore. Whatever they throw at me next won't break me and certainly won't fix me. No one can cure me, not even Gabe, but at least he reminded me what it was like to look in a mirror and not hate myself. He gave me hope when the world took it away, and with him, I don't calorie count with every bite or hear my mother oinking at each meal.

I sit there in the leather chair, waiting and listening to the whistle of the guard's breath, until finally, Headmistress returns.

The guard startles like he's been asleep with his eyes open. It wouldn't surprise me at this point. Nothing would. She walks into the room and around her desk, the stained-glass window behind her throwing bursts of color across the stone floor. Her black hair is more salt-and-pepper than true black today, but her spine is still as ramrod straight as ever as she begins digging in her top right-hand drawer.

"Henry," she barks at the guard before she tosses him something, "help me."

A blink later, Headmistress is at one side of my chair and the guard is at the other, each of them zip-tying me by the wrists to the wooden armrests.

What the fuck?

"Stop," I say as they both tighten the zip-ties simultaneously, so hard that the plastic band indents into my skin, digging against my bones.

Ow.

"What are you doing?" I ask, looking down at the ties and trying to lift my arms. I barely get my elbows three inches off the armrest before everything starts to go numb below the zip-tie, and I have to stop.

"We're doing something I should've done a long time ago," Headmistress barks at me. She looks up and over me to the guard with a beer belly and the whistle as he breathes.

"Henry, you may leave," she tells me.

"Ma'am." He nods before he walks to the door and leaves the room, closing the heavy wooden door behind him.

I swallow down the prickling fear that's needling up my throat. Something is different about Headmistress today. Sure, she's angry, but this is more than anger. She's always been . . . *off*, but right now with her gaze wide and slightly unfocused and her hair a little messy, she nearly looks manic. It's odd for a woman who never looks anything but pristine.

"I will not be made a fool of by a student," she snaps at me, shaking her head violently enough to throw off mud. She makes no move to go back around the table. "I especially won't be embarrassed by a weak little bitch who's afraid of her peas and carrots."

Well, I've already had enough of this today, and it's probably a bad idea, but I'm all out of good ones. I'm going to need to go ahead and get this over with.

"I'm not afraid of peas and carrots," I say, cocking my head at her and not blinking when she stares right back at me. "But you are a fool."

My comeuppance for the insult is damn near instantaneous. The bitch slaps me across the cheek so hard that the whole chair shakes like it's afraid of her too. The imprint stings, sending prickles and needles bolting up my forehead and down to my jaw. Tears spring to my eyes, but I blink them away.

I won't cry because of her if I have any say in it.

"I don't know what your plan was, Miss Bardot," she hisses, showing teeth too small for her smile, "but I will not have you sully the name of our Academy. No one ever pulls their students out of my school. Do you understand me?" She laughs dryly, and the sound carries in the large room, echoing a little, but it's the look that solidifies that she's gone batshit crazy. She's wide-eyed, pulling at her hair, and muttering to herself.

A thought barrels into the station as the pieces come together, interlocking in my head.

She didn't give my parents free tuition to appease them or even as a way to apologize for losing me for four days.

No, she gave it for one reason. She's got irrefutable proof in case word gets out that this is all one big misunderstanding, just like she claimed to the police. It can't be that bad—can it?—if you still leave your only child enrolled.

"It would've been easier if you had died in the woods," she says, peering down her hooked nose at me. "At least, I can explain that. But you tucked yourself away in your little hidey-hole on campus grounds, and it's downright embarrassing. You made a mockery of this place and of me."

Her second slap is worse than the first, but that's probably because my face is still on fire from the last one. This time, tears fall from my eyes no matter how many times I blink as the pins and needles spread like tumbled dominoes across my cheek and down my jaw.

She smells like peppermint tea and fury as her beady eyes latch onto me with another sneer.

"I should have ended you myself," she says before she walks around her desk, and adds, "I'll put an end to this nonsense right now, though. Let's cure you, Ms. Bardot."

"What?"

She doesn't answer, and I see her grab something from her desk.

"Drink it," she snarls at me, placing a can of soda on her desk. "Drink it, or I'll make sure Dr. Boucher places a feeding tube down your throat. They will pump you so full of sedatives, you won't remember your own name. Then they'll tie you down to a table and let the force-feeding do all the work. You should be grateful, Avery, at least you won't have to chew."

Oh God, I think I'm going to be sick. I don't want to be sick.

She looks like she might actually tell him too, and maybe it's the repeated heavy knocks to the head, but I renege on everything. I'm not unbreakable, and I don't want to break in the fucking hole.

She looks up and over me at the door, her expression going slack and pensive.

"What did you say your mother used to call you?" she murmurs. I can't tell if she's really trying to remember or just being a bitch.

"Oh yeah," her eyes light up like she won the lottery. "Piggy, right?"

She leans in close and oinks at me.

I can't stop the shudder, and Headmistress looks at me with such disgust I think she'd actually stab me right now if she could get away with it.

Her cash cow bit back, and she got offended. Well, too fucking bad.

She laughs before she walks behind her desk with the can of

soda. She places it back on the desk and lets me look at it for a moment.

It's pure liquid calories. It's not the diet version, but the full-fledged, high fructose corn syrup kind.

A drink so sweet it'll rot your teeth.

My mother would gag and pretend to throw up if she saw it.

Carbonated garbage, she would say, as Headmistress walks around the desk, taking the can with her, and grabs me by the chin. I try to wrench free, but she cinches tighter, and it hurts. It feels like she's trying to break my lower jaw off.

"Open up, piggy," she tells me with an oink.

I keep my lips shut even tighter.

She oinks again, over and over, wrinkling her nose before she abruptly stops, pops the top with one finger, and brings the can to my lips. I try to spit it out, but she won't let me. She starts to pour, oinking and snorting as I choke on the sugary soda she's forcing down my throat.

It reminds me of my mom.

The oinks.

The snorts.

The way she grabs me so hard it's like she wishes my bones would crack.

I swallow one gulp and then another, going faster and faster, but I'm not fast enough. I start to gag, feeling it run down my chin and throat.

I can't breathe.

"Stop!" I try to shout, but it comes out as a gurgle that makes me cough even louder.

"What's the matter, piggy?" she asks, taking the soda away for a moment. "You want some more?"

"No," I wheeze, but if she hears it, she doesn't care. She brings the can to my lips again and forces me to drink.

I'm trying to not think about the calories or the sugar content, but she's still oinking, bringing me back to my mom.

I hate her for it.

One can, one hundred fifty calories.

Each swallow, twenty calories.

What am I up to? Seventy at least, maybe even more.

Stop thinking about it, Avery!

I start to cough, but she doesn't pull away this time. If anything, she holds me even tighter, nearly breaking my neck to force my head back and my mouth open. The back of my neck rubs against the wooden chair, and I cough, or try to at least, but nothing comes out.

My lungs are burning.

My throat is burning.

My entire top half burns with the fizz.

I try to think of Gabriel and his stare, his smile, his *anything*, but she won't stop pouring. I can't breathe, and I can't think. I manage to wrench my head free of her, spit the drink to the floor, and take another breath, but then her hand is there again, gripping my chin, and forcing me to look at her.

She snorts, contorting her features into something disgusting.

"Is this what you were afraid of, you brat? A little drink!" She pours again, and I can't free my head this time. Her fingers cinch around my chin, pressing tight, and I'm choking, coughing, and trying to breathe. I think I might be sick. I don't want to be sick.

It clogs the back of my throat, and I can't swallow it fast enough. I can't find a moment to breathe. She's going to kill me!

I rear back in the chair, trying to get away from her, but it just screeches against the floor. I gulp in a breath, but she keeps on pouring.

"Swallow it, fatso!" she sneers before she grabs the back of my hair and yanks, forcing my head back. She starts to pour again, and the can has to be almost empty by now.

I still can't breathe, though! I can't even swallow it before she's waterboarding me with another, pouring liquid into my throat and down my nose.

I can't breathe.

I try to breathe, but there's nothing there except sugary liquid.

She's going to kill me. My throat makes an awful choking sound, and black specks mar my vision. I push against the floor with two feet and tip my chair backward, but it's not enough.

I still can't breathe!

The world is staggering, erasing to nothing in choppy bits and pieces. I push again with everything I have, and her fingers finally rip free of me.

The chair falls backward and lands hard against the floor with a *crack* that sounds like a gunshot and jumbles my brain. I scramble to stand, bits of wood surrounding me and the world rolling as I stagger. I swing blindly, still coughing and choking as I try to keep her away from me. She says something to me, but I don't hear it over my mother's torment.

Did you like that, piggy?

I bet you did, lard ass.

Oink, oink! No one loves a fatso!

I can't get enough air, no matter how much I gulp. I make an awful retching sound, but nothing comes up.

The room smells like spilled soda and the sting of fading peppermint.

I was wrong. I don't know if I can take this.

I need to get out of here. I need to find him.

I bolt for the door.

"Where do you think you're going?" she asks me as I run out of the room, my wrists still indented from the broken ties and the rest of me on fire, hot and dizzy after my confrontation with Headmistress. "You won't make it back to your dorm room before my staff catches you. You should have stayed gone, Ms. Bardot!"

Her cackles follow me as I leave.

As I stagger into the hallway, all I can think is that I don't think I'll make it if the Butcher is worse than that.

26

GABE

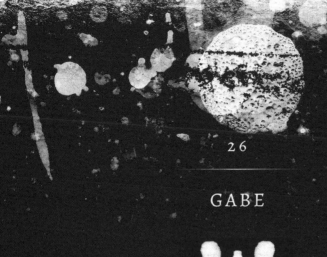

I lean against the wall, watching as snow piles up outside, collecting on the stone windowsills and inching up the glass. It's probably up to a couple of feet on the ground by now, maybe even more. Baby girl brought an extra carry-on with her when she arrived, an early winter, but I'm not complaining.

I love the cold, and I love the snow.

Fire looks even brighter against a backdrop of white.

Kill walks past me, giving me a salute and a shit-eating grin as he does. I'm surprised he's not scratching at his forearms like he's desperate for a fix at this point. He gets all itchy when he's trapped inside the Academy for too long, and old man winter has been saying fuck you to his outdoor plans for the past month. Each time the snow rolls in, it gets progressively worse. I don't think Saint gives a fuck if a blizzard drops by, especially now that he has Willow, but Kill prefers the outskirts of campus.

Sure, Kill can still sneak out of the dorm as long as he's careful to not slip on the ice and fall off the roof as he does it, but he can't see shit or enjoy anything outside right now. Most of the gravestones he likes to visit at the low spot of the cemetery are buried. Hell, even the damn pool is closed until further notice because I guess the guards said fuck it to even walking us across the courtyard.

Speaking of . . . I look out the window, letting my breath fog the glass. Everything outside is white save for the speckled stone of the building and the naked bark of bare trees. You can't see the stone walkways that crisscross the courtyard. Hell, you can barely spot the shape of the evergreen hedges at this point. Yeah, there's no way any of the lazy bastards around here are getting out in this shit, even if it does mean a massive fight is coming, probably a damn riot if I'm lucky.

No exercise plus cooping us up like barnyard animals at a petting zoo always means a good brawl, but at least it gives me something to look forward to. I reach for the lighter in my pocket, roll the wheel, hit the button, and suffocate the fire nozzle with my finger. It nips at my skin for a moment before the flame extinguishes.

Roll on and off.

Roll on and off.

It's not enough.

The noise thunders in the distance, and when the halls fill as class lets out, it's going to take every bit of my self-control to keep me from setting some shit on fire.

I hate waiting, especially when I know bad news is on the horizon. It's certainly headed my way now. This is about to be the last time I see Avery for a while.

Whatever went down with her parents couldn't have been good.

Her mother cried as she scuttled like a bug down the hall and her father about broke a tooth, clenching his jaw and his fists like he wanted to kill someone, as Headmistress walked them out earlier. I guess that means Avery hit them where it hurts. If so, I'm going to shake her hand and congratulate her.

I haven't even been able to do that with my father yet, but then again, our parents are not the same. Hers think they can buy her redemption. Mine prefer to shove it down my throat and see if I'll choke. Her father uses money to get he wants, but mine uses violence. If I did whatever she did to get a rise out of her parents, my father would go full conservatorship on my ass and make sure I never saw the sunlight again just to prove a single point.

That he has power over me. That he controls me.

Granted, I'd try to kill him for it, but if I didn't win, well, that would suck for decades, literally, while he let me rot in a cage somewhere just to spite me.

My old man would shit himself if he understood how far I've come. I'm no longer the scared little boy sitting at the dinner table hoping to make Daddy happy. I'm a man with a firefly who burns bright and quiets all the nasty urges that roll around in my skull. With her, the noise dies, and I can focus. She kills off the thousand fires in my brain and takes them down to a controlled burn.

My father's spent well over a million at my various boarding schools, and he could never buy me what she offers.

Is our symbiotic relationship fucked up? Probably.

Is having a human coping mechanism a *good choice* as the new, boring as fuck psychiatrist would say? Absolutely not.

Would I do it all over again? Fuck yes.

So, I stand in the hallway, watch the snow inch up the windowsill, and wait.

And wait . . .

And oh-my-God-is-this-what-Saint-means-when-his-crazy-ass-rambles-about-the-bordeom?

I'm about to burn through the last of my paper-thin patience.

Or something else.

Maybe the short twat with greasy hair who walks by. Fucker looks like he'll crackle before he pops.

Or maybe the guard who waddles after him, shouting something I don't give a fuck about, before the door to the administrative office opens and Avery bolts out.

She's wet all down her front, staining her dirty shirt even further. Her strawberry blonde hair has gone to frizz, and her gaze is bulbous and bleary-eyed as it searches the hallway.

It's like watching a caged dog scramble when a gate is left open. She's not graceful about her exit, nearly hitting the opposite side of the wall, before she rights herself to stagger down the hall.

I push off the wall and start toward her. I realize as I get closer that I've been near-sighted. She's not a caged dog. She looks like the human equivalent of a train that derailed, tumbled off a cliff, and then blew up at the bottom of the ravine. The closer I get, the worse it becomes. Her face is puffy, and her cheeks are flushed with her rage. She's wet not just on her shirt, but down to her chin, her throat, across her belly, and down to her wrinkled skirt. Even her eyes are the wrong color, tinted red with her anger.

I grab her by the shoulders, and in a very un-Avery like moment, she flings herself into my arms.

"What did they do to you?" I ask her when she starts to sob even harder. I hold her tight, squeezing her against me. Part of me wants to stand here and comfort her, but another part wants to go back and make this better for her. We can rot in the hole together.

"She . . ." she sobs, "s . . . she p . . . poured it down my t . . . throat, and I couldn't breathe," she wails. It takes her a minute before she composes herself enough to add, "She kept oinking at me, just like my m . . . mom used to."

She coughs as if reliving the moment, and I realize now why

all of her is wet with sticky sweetness. Headmistress Graves fucking water-boarded her.

All the progress I've made, everything I've done, and this bitch oinked at her and tortured her.

It's a bad idea to interfere. I never interfere, not for someone else, but she's my Firefly and I've never been good at following directions anyway. I steer her by the hand back to the administration office, and she goes rigid before she tries to pull on my wrist and stop me.

"What are you doing?" she sobs.

I look at her and offer a smile.

"I'm going to fix it," I tell her. "Let me make it better, baby girl."

I have to make it better for her. I take it all back. It's different now, having to see her like this, breaking apart because of what Headmistress did.

I can't watch her go to the hole, not now after seeing her like this.

She's strong. She'll survive. But that doesn't mean I will. I'll burn this fucking place to the ground before I'll let it happen.

I yank her into the office. The old lady who sits at the front isn't there, not that I'd care if she was. I hop the desk and help Avery over.

"Gabe," she tells me with a swallow, "I don't want to."

I grab her face in between my hands.

"Do you trust me, baby girl?" I ask her.

She sniffles and nods.

"Then let me help you."

Before she can argue further, I drag her down the hall to Headmistress's office and open the door unceremoniously. She's on the phone with someone and yelps when she sees me. I rip the phone off its cord and throw it across the room.

"Lock the door, Avery," I tell her.

I hear it shut behind me as I arrive in front of Headmistress.

"What are you doing in here?" she shrieks. "Guards!"

She moves to press something under her desk, and when I shift closer, I see that it's a tiny red button, a panic button.

I catch her hand and squeeze.

"Press that button," I tell her, "and I will make sure it's the last thing you touch."

She puts her hand carefully in her lap.

"How can I help you, Mr. Soros?" she asks, and she's definitely thinking about all the ways she's going to fuck up my life before the day is over.

She gives me a tight-lipped smile, which I return. I spot the liquid spilled across her chair and the floor in front of her desk and still splattered across her leather shoes. It makes me itch to set her on fire.

She cuts her eyes to Avery. "Would you like to join Ms. Bardot on a trip to the hole?"

"You aren't going to let Butcher anywhere near her," I say.

She laughs like I must be joking. I'm not.

I grab her by the throat and snatch a wad of papers from the top of her desk before cramming them into her mouth and gagging her. She screams, but it's muffled.

I pull out my lighter, flipping it across my knuckles, and her eyes go wide. I flip the lid and ignite the flame, and they go even wider.

She tries to wriggle away from me, but I'm holding her to the chair, and she isn't going anywhere, not without tearing a few layers of flesh off first.

I bring the flame to her flesh, and she cries into the gag. I lean in close to her ear.

"How does it feel?" I ask her. "Being in the other seat, your cries ignored just like you ignored Avery's?"

I cock my head at her.

"You filled her mouth until she couldn't breathe. Now I'm going to light yours up until you can't breathe either."

She yells into the gag as I bring the flame to the paper crammed between her teeth.

I let her think I care for a moment before I ignite the flame and watch it pop and take over, spreading across the paper. She's hyperventilating now, and I bet it burns on the way down as the fire spreads, licking against her lips and dipping farther into her mouth.

It's mesmerizing, the flames laving away at her mouth, cleaning away the nasty shit she wants to say.

"Grab some books," I tell Avery behind me. "Bring them to me."

"What?" she asks.

"Grab some books." With some effort, I look behind me to her. "I'm going to burn this bitch back to hell."

"No." Avery shakes her head. "No, please don't do that, Gabe."

"No?" I scoff.

"No," she repeats. "I don't want that. Don't ask me to do that."

"Why?"

What the fuck is she going on about?

"She hurt you, Firefly," I add.

Headmistress convulses in the chair, screaming, and with some effort, I let her go, watching as she spits the pieces of burnt paper onto the floor. Her mouth is charred, and her teeth black as she coughs onto the desk.

"She needs to be punished," I tell Avery. "Let me do this for you."

"You'll get sent to the hole with me," she says, "or to jail, probably. I can't let you do that to yourself."

I blink at her. She's putting me first.

No one ever puts me first, not when they can get what they so desperately want instead.

I look at the cunt still coughing on the floor. She vomits, spewing black-speckled shit across the rug.

I yank her up and slam her back into the chair. She's still coughing as I take out my phone.

"You're going to admit to everything you've done to her," I say, pointing at Avery. "All of it, every last bit, and I'm going to record it. Then today, you're going to tender your resignation and leave. If you aren't gone by this evening, I will make sure that video gets blasted everywhere. It'll be so big you won't be able to buy silence this time. Do you fucking understand me?"

She coughs again and nods.

"W . . . what happens if James—Dr. Boucher, I mean—won't accept my resignation?" she asks.

I lean in close so I can make sure she gets a good look at me. "Then you will make sure he does. I don't care what you tell him as long as it isn't about Avery or me. Tell him you have a family emergency. Tell him Hell called, and they need their best gal back. I don't give a shit."

"B . . . but . . ." she begins.

I'm starting to lose my patience. If she keeps pushing me, I'm going to light her up.

"But what?" I snap.

"Boucher will want to see her." Her gaze slides to Avery. "She cost the Academy a lot of money and almost got the police involved too."

"Look," I tell her, "I don't give a fuck what you tell Boucher, but if she ends up in the hole, I'll blame you. Tell him her parents forbid it, that they threatened to sue for every dime they've already given you. I really don't care as long as it keeps her out of solitary. Is that clear enough for you?"

She nods.

"Good." I hit the record button. "Begin."

"I, um," she says.

"State your name," I command.

"I am Blair Delores Graves," she says, with a little cough while looking at the camera. She pauses.

"I've made some mistakes in my career as Headmistress of Chryseum Academy," she continues.

"Specify it!" I snarl.

"I've . . ." she looks toward Avery and swallows loudly. "I've forced students in our eating disorder rehabilitation program to eat and drink. I've called them names and held them down when they refused to cooperate. I'm not proud of it."

"Continue," I say.

She looks at the camera again, her stare locking into place.

"I've tied them up in my office and held them against their will while I forced them to swallow. I've lied to parents about progress, and then had their child sent to our isolation unit to be force-fed when that child didn't make weigh-in. I, um, sincerely regret . . ."

"What did you do to her?" I point at Avery. "Tell them!"

"I zip-tied a student to a chair in my office and poured soda down her throat while holding her head back. I wanted it to feel like she couldn't breathe. I've oinked at her and made disparaging remarks."

She swallows again, crocodile tears coming to her eyes.

"I cannot put into words how sorry . . ."

"Then don't," I say, cutting her off as I stop the video. A minute later, I have my phone hooked up to her computer. I demand her login information.

"What are you doing?" she asks me.

"I'm making sure you can't take my phone and delete the video as soon as I step out of this room," I tell her as I find her username and password on a piece of paper taped to the bottom of her keyboard.

I login and upload the video to her desktop. Then I start to send it out. I forward it to my personal e-mail account. I upload it as a draft to my TikTok. I ask Avery for her e-mail and text Saint and Kill for theirs as well, and then I send it to all of them. I send it everywhere I can think of, and only when I have sent over a dozen copies do I start to comb through her desk.

"What are you doing?" Headmistress asks me, her voice hoarse as black saliva drips from her mouth down her chin.

I find her purse in the bottom drawer of the desk and remove her wallet from the leather bag, opening it up to grab her driver's license.

"In case you start getting second thoughts," I tell her. Then I read her driver's license aloud to her and take a picture of that too, sending it out as well before I log out of everything and turn off her computer.

"Why?" she asks with a hard swallow. If she needs me to confirm it, fine.

"Because *Blair* of 266 Feronia Drive, I want you to know exactly what will happen to you if you go back on your word." I smile at her. "There won't be a place on this Earth you can hide. I will find you, and I won't stop next time. I'll burn you to a crisp and laugh while I listen to you snap, crackle, and fucking pop."

She gasps, and it makes her cough.

"Tell me," I demand, "what are you going to do?"

"Resign."

"When?"

"Immediately."

"Good." I look at Avery. She's still bleary-eyed, like she can't believe she's in here again, and she's staring at the puddle of spit and soda on the floor from where Headmistress fucked with her. I need her right now, but more than that, I need to make today into something else.

"On your knees," I tell her.

"What?" she looks up from the floor to me and blinks.

"On your knees, baby girl."

"Gabe . . ." Her gaze slips to Headmistress, her brow furrowing.

Surely, she doesn't think one onlooker is going to stop me? I can still burn Graves, though, if she wants me to.

"She doesn't care," I tell her. I look at Headmistress. "Do you?"

She doesn't answer and looks a pretty shade of green like she's going to throw up again.

"I need you," I tell Avery, and something crosses over her face. There's hesitation, but I spot the moment she blows it to smithereens.

She takes three steps toward me, and I move around the desk and face her. As she sinks to her knees, dirty and disgusting, covered in filth from the basement and sticky soda, I undo my belt and free my cock. I fist it and stroke it slowly, from root to tip. I've never had a thing for voyeurism before, but the way she's looking at me right now like I'm the good guy, it does everything for me.

Even a villain likes to be appreciated every now and again.

"This is sick," the bitch in the chair says, coughing a little and looking away, about breaking her neck to avoid watching us.

"You made us into monsters," I say. "Don't be surprised when we act like them."

I peer down at my Firefly. Diamonds in the colors of the rainbow fall from the stained-glass window and speckle her strawberry-blonde hair.

Avery leans forward, wraps her mouth around my cock, and starts to suck. I thought her pussy was prime real estate, but this, hell, this might be even better. Maybe she forgets Headmistress is there. Maybe she doesn't care or maybe it turns her on, I don't know, but in a few minutes, she's hoovering my dick like she's trying to vacuum my soul out of it.

"That's it, baby girl," I tell her, my fingers hooking in her hair.

"Choke on my cock. Suck it like you need to breathe, baby, because you ain't coming up for air until you're finished."

She goes even harder, opening her throat and taking me all the way to the back until she gags. Then she does it again, and fuck, I feel my balls start to tighten.

I hold her head and pull her onto me even faster.

"Fuck yes," I growl, and this is the moment I want her to remember from today, when I face-fucked her in the bitch's office.

Not the torment she endured before.

Not the oinking or the waterboarding.

None of that.

I want her to think of today and remember how good it felt to make me come undone.

With Avery's hot mouth around my dick, I rock my hips, her forehead hitting low on my abdomen with every thrust. Then I slam into her one last time and to the stench of charred paper, I spill my cum down her throat.

27

AVERY

Gabe and I stand in a classroom at the front of the Academy, looking out past the curve of a turret that runs alongside the northwest corner of the classroom. Snow sticks to the ground, coating everything in white. The dead lawn, the shrubs, the sidewalks, and the driveway all sit cloaked in snow.

A black Cadillac circles the roundabout at the front of the building and parks. We've been waiting here for at least an hour, maybe more, and shouldn't Headmistress have tendered her resignation by now? What is taking her so long?

"What if she goes back on her word?" I ask Gabe before chewing my bottom lip.

We watch as staff scrape the asphalt and pour bags of road salt across the driveway. For a long moment, we stand there, watching as they work, and he doesn't say anything. Then he takes two fingers to the side of my cheek and turns my head to the right to make me look over my shoulder at him.

His breath smells like chocolate-coated mint as he peers down at me beneath hooded eyes. Dark strands of hair fall into his eyes, but it doesn't seem to bother him as he stares down at me and doesn't blink.

"She will listen," he tells me, his words soft yet confident. "She knows I'll kill her for it if she goes back on her word."

He utters the threat so calmly—like it's a normal thing to discuss taking the life of another human being—but then again, I think, maybe to Gabe it is. Look at where he's been raised. The walls of the Asylum are as cold and unforgiving as the souls that own them. There's no compassion here at Chryseum, despite what my father may think. This land is ruled by an iron fist and a crush of pharmaceuticals. Death is as natural to this place as the fringe mental illness treatments Dr. Boucher and his staff like to inflict.

"What will happen to us?" I ask him, my gaze dipping to his lips with the words.

I want him to kiss me. I need him to kiss me and make it all better. I need him to swear it.

"We will serve our time," he tells me. "We'll graduate in the spring, and then we're free, baby girl. I'll take you anywhere in the world, just name the place."

He winks at me, and I laugh. Surely, he's joking. It's ridiculous.

"With what money are we going to travel the continents, your majesty?" I ask him as my laughter dies.

"I have enough," he answers, his tone completely serious. "I have enough saved for the both of us, for a little while at least. My mother likes to buy my forgiveness, baby girl, and I like to let her do it."

Did he just promise to take me anywhere in the world? My heart ricochets against my ribs, and I don't think I'm ready to consider what his words truly mean yet.

"You never talk about her," I murmur, looking back out the window and the staff scraping the snow with big shiny shovels.

"I never talk about her because there's nothing to talk about," he says. "Your father chose your mother over you, and my mother chose my father over me. It's too late for either of them to make it better, but at least my mother's making reparations for it, I guess."

I swallow the knot tangling at the back of my throat at his words and the pain that's buried there, pain he will never claim as his own.

"I never want to be like my parents," I murmur.

"Then don't," he replies, and I'm not looking at him anymore, but I still know his face when he says it. An insouciant expression and half a grin, like his word is God's and his commandments are the easiest thing in the world to obey.

"I think about it sometimes," I continue, running my fingers through his hair again. "How I'd probably mess up my kids, too, if I had any."

He murmurs against my cheek, his late afternoon stubble prickling my skin.

"Are you trying to tell me something, Firefly?" he asks on what I swear is a purr.

"What?" I manage a moment later.

My brain moves at the pace of an ant attempting to push a brick.

Oh.

Oh no.

Ohhhhhh.

"I'm not pregnant, creep," I blurt with a laugh. "I have an IUD, but thank you for your concern."

"I wasn't concerned," he tells me, and I look over my shoulder to find him smirking at me. "I was excited."

He was *what?*

"We, me, *you* . . ." I pause, blinking at him, but there's his robot face again, and he's doing the stare-down challenge.

"We're too young to have a baby. I'm *not* having your baby, Gabriel."

"Yet." His smirk stretches even further.

What . . .

"No," I tell him firmly. "I don't even know if I want kids."

Well, no, that's not quite true. I do know what I want, and I don't want kids if it means that I turn into the two assholes who raised me.

"Yes," he says, the word slithering across his teeth and landing like a snake squeezing my heart. He says it so calmly like the matter's already gone to deliberations and just came back with a guilty verdict.

There's just one problem. I didn't get to vote.

"Noooooo." I shake my head at him.

"Mmmm," he snuggles closer. "You're so cute when you're scared."

I blink rapidly, trying to clear my head. He smells like he always does, campfires and burning embers, and it makes me want to snuggle into him and feel his warmth.

"I'm not scared," I manage. "I just don't want kids. There's a difference."

He scoffs. "You sound scared."

"I'm not," I protest.

"Good," he says with a shrug.

"Good?"

"Good." He leans in closer, sending his breath tumbling down the side of my face. "Because one of these days I'm going to tie you up and fill your tight pussy so full of my cum, you won't be able to breathe without it leaking out of you, baby girl. Then you're going to stay there until I know for sure you're fucking pregnant."

I feel like I'm too young to have this conversation.

"W . . . what?" I cough on something. It's probably my IUD

hearing his words and spontaneously combusting.

"You heard me, Firefly," he says, his hand sliding around my middle and down across my belly button to between my legs as we stand together and look out the window.

He dips his fingers beneath the waistband of my skirt, pulling my underwear away with it, and I can't breathe. My heart hammers in an offbeat rhythm, its waves breaking faster and faster against the shoreline. His forearm presses across my side and down my belly to where his magical fingertips set me on fire. I hold my breath as he dips his hand even lower and the pad of his index finger grazes my clit.

He groans and erases the distance between us until I can feel all of him, the solid plank of his chest, the hard line of his abdominals, and his rock-hard cock pressed against my back.

His fingers dip again, and he grazes my clit once more.

"G . . . Gabe," I begin.

"Yes, my Firefly," he murmurs.

"We should . . . We should . . ."

What was I saying?

He thrusts inside of me, two fingers down to the final knuckle, and I nearly come on the spot.

"What . . ." I catch my breath when he starts to move. "What are you doing?"

"Taking care of you," he murmurs, licking the shell of my ear and murmuring intelligible words that get lost in the torrent churning inside of me.

He pumps faster, and the room smells like sex and campfires.

Heat rises in my belly, climbing higher inside of me, inciner-ating my air, and setting fire to my pounding heart. I can't breathe. I can't see or taste or do anything except be.

"G . . . Gabe." I barely get his name out on a stuttered breath.

"Yeah, baby girl?" he whispers into my hair.

"I'm . . ." I never finish my sentence.

Rays of pure sunshine explode from within me in blinding white heat that curls my toes and sends my head knocking back against Gabe's shoulder blade.

He chuckles against my ear, guttural and choppy, and removes his hand. I hear him suck his fingers clean with a *pop*, and I nearly combust again.

When my eyes finally open, I look out the snow-frosted window to find Headmistress, well ex-Headmistress I guess, walking to the car, a cardboard box in her hands and more following her, carried by a couple of staff members.

"We can still burn her," he offers as we watch the former headmistress carry her belongings out the front door.

"I don't want that," I tell him.

"You sure?" He looks disappointed.

"I'm sure."

"Too bad. Let's trade. I'll brand you instead."

"Excuse me?"

"You heard me."

I laugh, and it's very high-pitched and very unlike me.

"No." I shake my head.

"Shame," he says with a tight-lipped smile.

I look at him like he's being crazy because he is if he actually thinks I'm going to let him brand me like I'm his damn cow.

"What?" he gives me a grin and shrugs. "It is."

He wraps an arm around my shoulders and squeezes tight.

"One day after I brand you," he whispers against the curve of my ear, "you're going to look like a queen, baby girl, *my queen.*"

Then he steps in front of me, facing me, and flattens his lips to mine.

EPILOGUE

GABE — FOUR WEEKS LATER

K ill leans against the stone wall behind him and stares at me, his golden hair colored orange and yellow by the flames.

"This is fucked," he says as Saint slips an arm around Willow's chest, pulling his girlfriend back against him before he dips his chin to press a kiss to the crown of her head.

It's definitely fucked up, but it's no more fucked up than the shit either one of these assholes has done. I defend my honor. Well, really, I defended Avery's honor because there's a decent chance that I'm going to have to wrestle her like a greased pig to get this done, and I don't need my stupid friends making it even harder.

I point two fingers at Kill as I fiddle with the iron bar, kneeling to roll it in the flames.

"Stop being all holier than thou, you damn deviant," I tell him. "Everyone knows what you get up to inside the mausoleum. If you took a black light in there, the fucking thing would glow like Chernobyl."

Saint barks with laughter while his girlfriend makes a

wheezing noise that tells me she did *not* know about Kill's extracurriculars.

Whatever.

Saint can explain that to her later.

Speaking of Saint, I set him in my sights next, moving my two fingers so they point at him.

"Stop laughing, you dick," I tell him. "You make your girl wear a collar like a dog, and we all know you two played hide the sausage all over Cross's body after you knifed him."

How the fuck else did they both get covered in that much blood? I thought Kill was going to cream himself when they climbed through the window that day.

It's Avery's turn to gasp now, and when I look back at her, she's paler than usual.

Oh shit. Guess she didn't know that. I add it to the list of stuff to talk to her about when she's returned to a normal color.

Saint lights up, bringing his cigarette to his lips before he turns his head and blows the smoke away from his girl's face. His blue eyes look almost clear beneath the flames as I reach down and roll the poker into the fire again.

"Bro, if you mention fucking in front of my girl one more time," Saint tells me, fire playing hide-and-seek across his inky hair, "then I'm going to know what it's like to fuck in your blood too."

I ignore his pussy threat and roll the poker once more, the flames heating my face as I do.

It's beautiful, the way they dance for me, sending their golden shadows stretching across the floor. I feel it tug at the back of my brain and whisper at me to come closer.

Fucking gorgeous.

It takes me a long moment before I tear my gaze away and give him a look that says, come at me, bro. I might bleed, but you'll *burn*. My attention returns to my Firefly, and if she was any paler at the moment, she'd need a transfusion.

Shit. Is she still hung up on the blood play?

"Cross deserved it," I tell Avery by way of explanation with a wink.

Well . . . by the looks of it, I can schedule that transfusion now. Which one of these bastards is a universal donor?

Willow nods, backing me up as Saint plays with her hair, twirling it around his finger.

"He was a bad man," she tells Avery. "He assaulted a lot of girls, me included."

Avery sucks in a breath. "I'm so sorry," she breathes.

Saint makes a sound like he's going to explode, probably because he's actually about to explode.

"Are we going to do this, or are we going to just stand here holding each other's dicks?" Kill quips.

"No one invited you, motherfucker," I snap.

"Moral support," he mutters with a shrug.

I roll my eyes. "Like you have morals."

Technically, I didn't invite any of them.

Willow's here for Avery since, apparently, they're friends now or something.

Saint's here for his girl.

And Kill tagged along because, as he put it, he wanted to see what's up.

I should tell them to all fuck off, but at this rate, Avery is never going to let me brand her, and it's all I can think about.

Day and night, in my dreams and wide awake, when I'm igniting the lighter and when I want to ignite even more, I imagine it.

Pink, sizzling flesh.

The stench of seared meat and smoke.

Her branded for me.

Mine.

I've already tried to convince her twice. The first time, she laughed until she nearly pissed herself. Then when she realized I was serious, she sank to her knees and begged for the flash paper instead. The second time, she told me she needed time to think about it and that she wasn't sure.

Pfft. She's had more than enough time to consider it.

It's a miracle worthy of notification to the fucking Vatican that I haven't tied her up and just gotten it over with already. It's no fun, though, if she doesn't enjoy it with me. So if my girl needs Willow here as moral support and these two idiots have to tag along, so be it. I'll kick them out when it's over, and then it will just be me and her and the proof that she's mine etched into her skin.

I kneel, rolling the poker in the flames again. It's thin and tapered at the tip. This time when I grab it, I can barely hold the thing. The end glows orange, matching the burning embers.

Aisling died in this very spot.

Avery will be marked here as mine.

And every time she looks down at her forearm, she'll know I am hers as well.

I look up at her, grabbing the cloth and wrapping it around the end of the poker, making it so I can hold onto it long enough for the brand.

"You ready, baby girl?" I ask her. She looks down at me, her blue eyes bright beneath the flames, and nods. She looks at Willow and then back to me as I stand, rolling up my sleeve.

"What are you doing?" she blurts, staring at me.

"Me first."

"What?" she squeaks.

I reach down, pick up the iron, and carefully hand the wrapped end to her.

"X marks the spot, baby girl," I tell her.

She's shaking and shivering, her gaze darting between the glowing end of the poker and my forearm.

Poker. Arm.

Poker. Arm.

And back again.

"Are you sure?" she asks me.

"Positive," I tell her, pointing to the spot on my forearm.

"I don't know if I can do it," she says.

I grab the end of the poker with her, covering her hand with mine.

"Do it with me," I tell her, and she nods.

I bring the iron down to my flesh, and white-hot pain shoots through me as my skin pops and crackles beneath the heat. I lift it away as an ugly pink-and-black welt forms on my skin. I turn it around, lining it up the other way, and mark the X.

It hurts even worse the second time, but I can't stop looking at it. It's beautiful.

I pull it away.

"Your turn," I tell her, and my arm is on fire as she lifts her forearm.

"Does it hurt?" she asks me.

Of course it fucking hurts, but I don't tell her that.

She offers me her pale perfect arm, and I hold it steady in one hand as I bring the poker down to her flesh. She screams when it sizzles, but I'm fast, moving it around, branding the mark, and when I drop the poker and it clatters to the floor, I can't look away. There on her forearm, my mark is forever emblazoned.

I grab her, reel her in close, lick away her tears, and whisper my next words just for her.

"For as long as we are," I tell her, "you are mine, and I am yours." I press our wounds together, entwining our fingers, and she winces. My entire arm burns at the contact as the brands press together. "You are worthy of life, baby girl. You're worthy of fucking everything."

Tears draw tiny runnels across her blotchy cheeks as I yank her even closer with my free hand, my fingers catching in her silky hair. Our foreheads collide, and I breathe in sugared strawberries and seared flesh before I kiss her.

There's no noise.

No outside world.

No anything except me and her and the pain pulsing through our brands, binding us together until we turn to dust beneath the stars.

ABOUT JORDAN

Jordan Grant loves all things romance! She likes to write about edgy bad boys and romances that delve into the blur between love and hate. She is an avid fan of all things sweet including red wine and cupcakes (red velvet, please!).

Want free romance books? Check out freebies by Jordan on her website, www.authorjordangrant.com.

Printed in Great Britain
by Amazon

29831051R00172